The Billionaire's Proposal

Love and Money Series Book 1

Natalie Dunbar

Dana Lorayne Publishing

Cover design by: Coverfresh Designs

Printed in the United States of America.

ISBN: 978-0-9913908-3-0

DEDICATION

This book is dedicated to those who have dreams they have put on hold to help and support others. Your time is coming. Your time is now. There are rainbows on your horizon if you will only reach for them.

ACKNOWLEDGMENTS

I want to acknowledge and thank my loving husband, Chet, and the rest of my family for all the support they've given me with my writing. I'd also like to thank my critique group members, Karen White-Owens and Tana Jenkins for their help in making the manuscript the best it could be. Special thanks to Stefanie Worth, who was also part of the process.

CHAPTER ONE

"None of my calls have gone through at his office and he's not answering his cell."

Hunched over her desk in Wickerfield Associates' Chicago division, Aubrey Merrill clutched her phone and listened intently as she bit at lips that had long since lost their coating of lipstick. Although her friend and client, Mira Zayne, was considered one of the most beautiful women in the world, she too was being humbled by heartbreak that was all too common.

"He could be working on something important and simply forgot the time," Aubrey said, offering an excuse she didn't believe.

"Aubrey, it's been a week. I can't hold my head in the sand any longer."

"You could go down to his office and demand to see him," Aubrey said.

"I tried that. I didn't get any further than the front lobby. His personal assistant came down and told me that he'd asked her to inform me that he was busy, couldn't be disturbed, and would call me."

Twirling one of her twists, Aubrey sucked in her breath. "And he didn't call you?"

"No! And that was five days ago. I refuse to sit outside his office and wait for him to come out."

"What about his family?"

"They're not answering my calls either. You know they don't like me! I'm wife number three and they think I'm like the rest of those money-grubbing bimbos. Aubrey, I really love Ben, and I thought he loved me too. I'd love him even if he weren't worth billions!"

"Don't do anything stupid," Aubrey offered quickly.

Mira's tone turned feisty. "Like what? Get a boyfriend on the side? Give an interview to one of those magazines that are always making stuff up about us anyway?"

Alone in her office, Aubrey shrugged, "I don't know... Like something permanent? Something that can't be fixed or forgiven?"

"Like what he's doing to me now?" Mira asked sharply, then ended her sentence with a string of rapid-fire Spanish. Mira had always been very emotional, so the new issue with her husband was more than enough to set her off. "This isn't something you do when you love someone."

Detecting movement in her peripheral vision, Aubrey glanced towards the door and saw her associate, Owen Connors, waving and indicating that he needed to talk to her. Nodding, she mouthed the words, *fifteen minutes*. Flashing the okay sign with his fingers, Owen backed into the hallway and disappeared.

Aubrey went back to her phone call with Mira. "Did something bad happen on that trip to the private island near Fiji?" Aubrey asked, wracking her brain for reasons.

"No! He's never been more loving. It was beautiful and we were alone most of the time!" Mira ended on a high poignant sigh.

Aubrey was sure her friend was crying, and it hurt her heart. Her eyes stung with the threat of tears, mostly for Mira, but some for herself in memory of the fiancé who had walked away from her and never looked back. "What can I do to help?"

"Come down, spend a week or two with me at the house in the Hamptons. I really need a friend right now and I need something else to think about. Please, Aubrey, I'll pay all your expenses."

Wanting to help her friend, Aubrey swallowed hard. Unlike Mira, she hadn't been blessed with dazzling beauty, but she had plenty of brains that she used as an investment advisor. She was well paid, but never seemed to get ahead of the debt associated with her little brother, Wyatt's cancer treatments and care. "Mira, I'm booked solid for the next week and a half except for Sunday. I'd come if I could. You know I need this job..."

"I know you have to worry about Wyatt's expenses... I wouldn't want you to lose your job, but Ben's probably going to dump me!" Mira sobbed.

"Let me see what I can do. I'll talk to my boss and get back to you," Aubrey promised.

Once she'd hung up, Aubrey ran her fingers through her twists. She really wanted to help her friend. Since Wyatt was out of the hospital and looking forward to going back to school, the only problem she had was her workload.

Opening her calendar on the laptop, she counted five appointments and they weren't the firm's major bread and butter accounts. A few could be rescheduled. There was work to be done, but she had analysts and advisors on her staff who could do it. Hadn't she seen something about her company and an event in the Hamptons? Curious, she did a search on her email and found the announcement.

This month Wickerfield Associates will be holding a series of investment seminars on the stock market, turning millions into billions, types of investments, and recommended investments for our special clients in the Hamptons. Private sessions with our preferred customers and private sessions with potential new customers will be available. Owen Connors will be heading the effort.

Shaking her head, Aubrey rubbed the sides of her neck. Owen Connors was at the same level in Wickerfield Associates that she was, so why hadn't she been offered the chance to do the sessions in the Hamptons?

Aubrey stood and took the much-needed walk down the hall to her boss's office. Chase Everett was studying a prospectus, but he glanced up when Aubrey reached his door. "Problem?" he asked, gleaning something negative from her facial expression.

She told him about the series of client events in the Hamptons and asked how the staff had been selected.

Leaning back in his chair, he told Aubrey to take the seat across from him. "Your name came up, but I didn't want to put you under any stress. You haven't travelled since Wyatt started the latest round of chemo." His expression sobered. "How's he doing?"

Aubrey smiled. "Good. He's in remission and I think he's going to be okay."

He pumped his fist in the air. "Thank God! That boy has been through more than his share of trouble. You want the assignment, you've got it. Owen's son has a play at school that he doesn't want to miss."

"I want it," Aubrey said, guessing that Owen had stopped by her office to discuss her handling the seminars in the Hamptons. She didn't just need the trip for Mira, who was going through a rough time, Aubrey needed to get away and think about a possible life beyond the right now since the chances of her precious little brother growing up had dramatically increased.

"Good. I'm glad things worked out for you and Owen. You need to be on a Sunday flight to the Hamptons, earlier if you can make it." Her boss smiled.

"I'll see what I can do." Aubrey's mind was already racing ahead to calling Wyatt and her mother with the news that she would be traveling. Afterward she would call the company travel office, book her flight, and decide what to pack. She hadn't traveled in more than a year.

On Friday, Aubrey boarded a plane for East Hampton Airport feeling hopeful for the future.

When Aubrey stepped through the arrival gate at MacArthur Airport, she was surprised to find Mira waiting for her. Flanked by two dangerous looking bodyguards in expensive suits, Mira looked gorgeous, this time in a black designer jumpsuit that barely restrained her famous breasts. Her thick, blond streaked hair was up in an artfully messy do. Gliding forward gracefully on a ridiculously high pair of Manolos, she was drawing a crowd of admirers, but there were shadows of sadness in her exotically made-up eyes.

Mira hugged her and managed a smile. "I know you have to work those seminars and stay at the hotel most of the week, but thanks for coming! I didn't want you to have to drive the fifty miles to East Hampton alone or use the car service," she explained. "You can rent a car in town or borrow one of ours."

Aubrey nodded. "You look great."

Mira shook her head. "No, Lady Zayne Cosmetics are just that good! You should have seen me before I put on this makeup!" She paused to sigh in frustration. "I sound like one of those damned commercials, don't I?"

Aubrey had to agree.

"You look good too, Aubrey," Mira said, giving a once over, "I like what you did with your hair and that dress!" She scanned the dress once more. "Good Christmas gift, huh?"

Aubrey smiled. "You have good taste."

Cameras flashed in the background. As a supermodel, especially one married to a billionaire and the face for Lady Zayne Cosmetics, Mira was news, wherever she went. Aubrey was glad she'd taken the time to get her hair done and opted to travel in the casually chic designer dress Mira had given her for Christmas.

Mira sent an assistant to collect Aubrey's bag and they headed to her car. She and Aubrey climbed into the private area in the back of Mira's limo. The two bodyguards got in the front with the driver and they took off.

As soon as the door closed, Mira's head dipped and Aubrey saw that she was crying.

"You found out something new?" Aubrey asked, handing her a tissue.

Mira nodded. "We're just a couple of months away from our fifth anniversary.

"That's not news, is it?" Aubrey gave her a blank look.

"No, but my publicist went online and did a little research. Ben dumped both of his ex-wives before they reached five years. So I checked the stupid prenup he made me sign and I get millions less if he dumps me now!"

"You think he's getting ready to dump you to save money?"

Aubrey asked incredulously. She'd seen Ben and Mira together and they were the epitome of the words, "hot couple."

"I love him, but maybe he doesn't love me anymore, and he's cutting his losses."

Aubrey gave her friend a hug. "Mira, you have to talk to him. Otherwise, you're just driving yourself crazy."

"And if I can't make him talk to me?"

"You can make him talk to you," Aubrey assured her, "You know how to make him crazy. You know his secrets. What can you do to make him come to you?"

"Something crazy!" Mira dabbed at her eyes and blew her nose. "We'll brainstorm while you're here and come up with something."

"Yeah," Aubrey assured her, "We will. For starters, what if he thought you were dead, kidnapped, or pregnant?"

"As opposed to cheating?" Leaning back against the seat Mira's dark eyes flashed. "It depends on how he really feels about me."

"We're going to make a couple of lists," Aubrey said, opening her tablet. She was worried and desperately hoping that all the things she ever thought about Bennet Zayne were true. He'd played the part of a man desperately in love with his gorgeous wife to perfection, so why was he neglecting her now?

***

Strategically located behind a column in the luxury hotel's dining room, Aubrey lingered over her coffee and lost herself in the play of sunlight on some of the tables. She'd enjoyed a light breakfast and had already gone over her notes. *I'll go to the conference room and get things ready in ten minutes*, she promised herself.

It had been a rough weekend. After arriving in the Hamptons on Friday, Aubrey had spent most of the time consoling her dear friend and client, Mira Zayne, and trying to support her hope that Mira would not be losing her husband. There'd been bright spots to the weekend, like when they'd gone to dinner and then when they'd seen a Broadway show, but things did not look good for Mira and her husband. This bothered Aubrey because Mira and Bennett Zayne were the most loving and romantic couple she knew.

People came and went in the dining room, enjoying their meals in relative peace. Aubrey loved the intimate, peaceful atmosphere of understated elegance. Tasteful art hung on the walls and the tables were not so close as to render a private conversation impossible.

The background buzz of conversation in the restaurant abruptly changed. Aubrey snapped out of her daydream and checked her surroundings. Dressed in casual Polo brand clothing, a tall, good-looking guy with dark hair and a golden tan strode confidently into the restaurant and started looking around.

She tried to quantify exactly what drew her attention to him. Sexy, fit, cool, and confident, this man did not need a business suit to command authority, attention, and respect. He was someone important, someone she should recognize. Something quickened within Aubrey as she stared, fascinated.

She watched as his searching gaze landed on the occupants of several different tables and moved on. Aubrey wondered who he was and who he was looking for. He walked further into the restaurant with a smooth, confident gait.

The column blocked her view for a moment, then unexpectedly, the Polo guy rounded the column to focus his dark-blue gaze on Aubrey. Was that recognition in his eyes? The ground shifted beneath her feet and something curled deep within her core. She gasped softly. The impact of all that male attractiveness right in her face made her mouth go dry. *Mmmph, mmmph, mmmph!*

Aubrey gawked, but tried to keep her cool. This man could give the dark haired, blue eyed Polo model a run for his money. Aubrey enjoyed the view and the unexpected attention. The good-looking guys usually walked right by her, in their pursuit of women like her gorgeous model friend, Mira. This man was homing in on her.

He smiled, with a flash of perfect-looking white teeth and a lively sparkle in his dark blue eyes. "Good morning," he said in a deep welcoming tone.

Aubrey smiled back, returning the greeting.

"I'm Carson McDonald," he continued, extending his hand for her to shake.

Nice name, Aubrey mused inwardly. For the first time since her fiancé abandoned her, she saw a man who interested her. Carson McDonald. The name was familiar, but she was a little too fascinated to recall where. She wrenched her thoughts away from all the energy that strummed through her body at his touch. "Aubrey Merrill." She said, shaking his hand firmly. "Good to meet you."

"May I join you?" he asked.

Aubrey saw the attraction she felt mirrored in his dark eyes. This would happen when I've got a seminar to do in twenty minutes, she thought. "I've got to go in the next ten minutes or so," she said out loud.

"Yes, I know. You're doing the investment seminar for Wickerfield Associates," he said helpfully.

That explained the look of recognition. He'd obviously been looking for her. Stiffening in surprise, Aubrey swallowed back a thread of disappointment and tapped down on her raging hormones. This interaction had to be about business.

"Are you interested in attending the seminar?" she said, mustering up her professionalism.

"Actually, no," he said with a rueful smile, "I wanted to talk to you. I'd like to discuss a business opportunity."

"For me?" Aubrey's brows went up.

"For both of us." He drew out the chair directly in front of her. "Mind if I sit down?"

"No, help yourself," she said, trying to wrap her brain around what he could be about.

He placed a leather folder on the table, dropped down into the chair, and scooted close.

"I don't compete with Wickerfield Associates," she said. It was a non-negotiable fact.

"Yet you do have a few private clients," he said, intriguing her.

"A few. Most are people who don't meet the company's account requirements," she acknowledged. Aubrey swallowed carefully. Carson MacDonald had done his homework. She knew that all the company literature referred to her by name and deed, no pictures, no indication that she was a woman. "What sort of business opportunity would you like to discuss?"

"A big part of my success comes from liking what I do and surrounding myself with the best. The person I'm looking for must have impeccable leadership skills, business savvy, wealth development and management skills and experience. You, Ms. Merrill, are at the top of my list for the job. I thought we might talk about the opportunity over lunch since the morning seminar ends at eleven."

Flattered and intrigued, Aubrey hesitated. What could he possibly have in mind? She didn't want to do anything to jeopardize her job. On the other hand, outside of her job, people did not approach her with business opportunities every day. Behind Carson, she saw one of the marketing people trying to get her attention. She held up five fingers to signal that she would be along in five minutes.

Carson MacDonald threw her a sharp look. "Ms. Merrill? May I call you Aubrey? You should at least hear what I have to say."

He was right, she acknowledged inwardly. In addition, she was very curious. She tilted her head. "I've heard your name before, but you're not a Wickerfield client."

"No." Carson inclined his head relaxed back into his chair, "Not to brag, but you probably recognize my name because I've done well with real estate. I started flipping modest houses before I graduated from high school. Things escalated from there to better houses and on to hotels and prime properties in New York and California. Then I got a windfall blessing when oil was discovered on a large parcel of land I bought for a subdivision."

"Those were a lot of blessings," Aubrey murmured, beginning to wonder just how well Carson MacDonald had done. Now she was certain she should know who he was. He apparently didn't consider himself too successful to make a business proposition to her.

Carson grinned. "I could say the same about you. You've accomplished a lot."

Aubrey's thoughts touched on the nice money she made for doing what she loved. It had paid for several experimental medical treatments her little brother Wyatt needed to beat cancer and she could afford to live in a nice neighborhood. "Yes, I've been blessed, too."

"So, we'll discuss that business opportunity over lunch?"

"Yes," she said, finally deciding to meet with him. Getting a firm grip on her imagination, she guessed that he probably wanted her to handle his funds.

"Good. I'll wait for you outside the conference room. We can pick a place or have lunch in the executive dining room."

Aubrey glanced at her watch and began to gather her things. She needed to get going or she would be late. "I've got to run!"

"So do I." Carson MacDonald signaled two rough looking men in designer suits and headed towards them. Meeting him halfway, they flanked him on each side.

Is there a louder way to scream bodyguards? Aubrey wondered. Okay, if this guy needs bodyguards, he's into the big money or the illegal stuff! She hurried to the conference room as fast she could while maintaining her dignity. Just outside the door, she handed her purse and briefcase to one of the company assistants and paused to catch her breath and gather her inner strength.

Inside, the room was nearly two-thirds full. Gathering herself, Aubrey took a deep breath and let it out. Then she stepped into the room. As always, when she started the investment seminars, there was the initial shocked silence among the clients who had never met her. She felt the temperature in the room drop.

The combination of her MBA from MIT and her undeniable success in the investment field meant that most people were surprised to discover that she was a black woman. Not traveling for years had also kept her out of the limelight. However, when it came to making money, most eventually realized that nothing mattered but how well Aubrey did her job.

CHAPTER TWO

Aubrey walked confidently to the podium at the front of the room, returning the greetings and hails from the few clients who had met her previously. It brought more warmth to the enclosed area.

"Good morning." Aubrey stopped and smiled at her audience. "I'm Aubrey Merrill and I'm going to share some basic information about today's markets for investments and what they mean for the wealthy. As most of you know, Wickerfield Associates is well known in the industry and has enjoyed several mutually beneficial years advising the wealthy and investing their funds. I will highlight some of those successes, then answer any questions you might have and then I will discuss new markets and opportunities we're planning for this year."

Pausing, she scanned the room. Most of the occupants had gotten over their initial surprise at seeing a black woman instead of a British male as her name might imply, leading a company seminar on wealth management. Settled down with their premium coffee and gourmet pastries, they looked alert and interested. Satisfied, she launched into her presentation on the subject she dearly loved.

Afterward, she answered questions and directed those who needed or wanted to talk to her in private to make an appointment with the marketing people at the back of the room. She knew some appointments had already been scheduled and that the staff would send her an update by the end of the day.

Aubrey checked her watch as she accepted her briefcase and her purse from the company assistant. It was after eleven o'clock. She needed to get going if she was going to the business lunch with Carson MacDonald. She didn't exactly know what he would propose, but the combination of her curiosity and his handsome features and deep masculine attraction put butterflies in her stomach. She didn't think she was his type, but there was nothing preventing her from enjoying the view and entertaining a fantasy or two.

Aubrey went out the door and found a spot to stand that didn't interfere with the customers exiting the room. She looked around, but Carson was nowhere to be seen. Aubrey ignored the small stab of disappointment. After all, she'd just met Carson MacDonald.

Performing a quick search on her cell, she discovered that Carson MacDonald was a billionaire real estate mogul. A billionaire? Aubrey felt the heat of embarrassment deepen the color in her face. How had she missed that? He had mentioned oil. The bodyguards and the familiar sound of his name should have been a big clue. What sort of business opportunity could a billionaire have for her? The hand holding the phone trembled.

Aubrey slipped the phone into her bag and took a few deep, calming breaths. Scanning the hall, she spotted Carson MacDonald in a nearby alcove, his bodyguards close enough to protect but far enough away to grant him the illusion of relative privacy.

A sexy redhead in a light, breezy dress that revealed more than it concealed had draped herself on his lean, lanky frame. Carson was speaking to the woman in a tone so private that no words reached Aubrey. He looked serious, as if he were carefully trying to explain something.

Another stab of disappointment pricked Aubrey. He hadn't

seemed like the stereotypical rich guy, taking advantage of all the perks that came with his status. Unable to look away, she watched the redhead lift toned and tan arms with a flash of perfectly manicured nails to frame his face with her fingers. Aubrey felt a little envious as the woman drew Carson's head down for a kiss so carnal that Aubrey felt herself blushing. *Somebody needs to get a room! Or did they just come out of one of the luxury hotel bedroom suites?*

Carson seemed to enjoy the kiss, participating with the laid-back sort of enthusiasm of a man used to receiving that sort of attention. Capturing the redhead's hands, he gently extricated himself, an affable smile on his handsome face...

As she turned away and gave the two some privacy, Aubrey heard Carson utter the words business and meeting. Determined to get her mind off the couple, she opened her briefcase. In the inner pocket, she found the hotel listing of restaurants and menu descriptions. Opening it, she scanned the offerings.

Near her, people continued to exit the conference room, many taking their leave and murmuring their appreciation as they passed her. As she ended her goodbyes to another client and glanced back at the hotel brochure, she heard Carson's voice.

"Aubrey, I apologize for keeping you waiting." Sincerity filled the simple words, almost instantly soothing Aubrey's nerves.

She looked up from the menu descriptions to gaze into Carson's eyes. Unlike the Polo model he resembled, his were a dark blue color that drew your attention and made it hard to look away. She liked the fact that he didn't bother making up a lie about why he was late. Honesty was very important to her. "No problem, I wasn't standing here long," she answered. "Where are we going to meet?"

"Well, I was thinking we'd go to Pierre's, which is on Main Street, but on second thought, it's more of a place to see and be seen. I don't think we'd get much business done."

Gorgeous billionaire or not, Aubrey wasn't quite ready to go anywhere less public with him. She reached for her official reason for being in the area for an excuse. "I have a client appointment scheduled for one-thirty, so I'll need to get back early enough to do a quick review of my notes on their portfolio." She stopped talking, suddenly aware that Carson was avidly staring at her.

"I am in awe your investing skills," he said. "I've studied your list of accomplishments and you are too good to be stuck in a back room at Wickerfield."

Aubrey smiled, though she felt a little uncomfortable. The compliment meant a lot, coming from a self-made billionaire. "Thanks. I admire the success you've made of yourself."

"Thank you." Carson checked his watch. "We've lost some time. Would you mind the hotel's private dining room? I reserved it this morning as a backup. They've assured me that the full main restaurant menu will be available. I've eaten there many times and found the food to be excellent."

"It sounds fine," Aubrey admitted. "It'll make it easier for me to make my appointment too."

"So, it suits us both." he declared. "Let's go."

***

The private dining room was adjacent to the main dining room but held only four white linen covered tables. Vibrant blue rugs accented the hardwood floor and vintage blue and white wallpaper enhanced with artwork depicting local scenes covered the walls. Aubrey recognized the Queen Anne chairs she'd seen in an antiques magazine.

Except for the pleasant hostess and Carson's bodyguards, who sat at another table, Aubrey and Carson were the only occupants. The hostess showed them to a table near the window with a view of the water and handed them fancy menus. Aubrey put her things on one of the extra chairs. As they sat down and studied the menus, a perky young waiter appeared and introduced himself. Then he left to give them time to decide on lunch. Minutes later, he came back.

Aubrey, who hadn't had to worry about her weight since she broke up with her fiancé and lost a good thirty pounds three years ago, ordered seafood pasta, a side salad, and clam chowder. She passed on the glass of wine.

As soon as Carson ordered the New York strip steak with garlic mashed potatoes, asparagus, and a double shot of scotch, the waiter headed off.

"Have you ever thought of going into business for yourself?"

Carson leveled his gaze at Aubrey.

Aubrey swallowed hard. Carson wasn't making her uncomfortable, but his question reminded her of all the things she'd strived for that had fallen by the wayside. "Yes, I've thought of having my own business. When I got into college, all through college, and when I graduated. I had all kinds of plans."

Propping his elbow on the table and placing his chin on the open palm, Carson gave her an expectant look. "What happened?"

"Life." Aubrey met his gaze head-on.

He arched an eyebrow. "That's pretty vague. We all deal with the curveballs life throws at us," Carson observed. "Which one got you?"

"I needed to work for one of the big companies to build my credibility and I needed money to establish myself. I interned one summer with Morgan Stanley and another with Capstone."

Dropping his hand from his chin, he let his hand rest on the table. Carson nodded approvingly, silently urging her on.

Aubrey cupped her hands around the cool, damp water glass. "My first job was with Castle Wealth Management and it was wonderful. Shortly afterward, my brother came down with cancer and he's been battling it until recently. I couldn't do the required travel and hours, so I got a job at Wickerfield and they've been more flexible."

Aubrey was still celebrating Wyatt's recovery and the prospect of the new life just starting for him, herself, and her hardworking mother.

"You took care of him? What about your father?" Carson nudged, listening in a calm, open, non-judgmental manner.

"He died in a car accident when I was sixteen."

Leaning towards her, Carson released a sympathetic sigh. "And your mother?"

"My mother is a cancer survivor. She put herself through college after Dad died and she works from home mostly as a software developer. She's had to be available to take Wyatt for tests and treatments and help him maintain some semblance of normalcy."

Aubrey grew silent. She swallowed hard, struggling with herself on giving voice to the fear that gnawed at her sense of peace. "At times, I thought I would lose them both."

Carson's big hand reached across the table to briefly touch hers. "You've been through a lot."

Jolted by his touch, Aubrey struggled with her reaction. The man was a study in contradictions. They even extended to his hands, clean and well-manicured, but calloused like a working man's and warm as a small heater. The gesture, the kindness in his voice and his warmth surprised her, but she found them comforting.

Aubrey blinked and caught herself. Carson MacDonald was a stranger, and a potential employer. Why was she giving in to her emotions in the middle of what amounted to a job interview? *Pull yourself together!*

Her gaze fell to their hands on the table, his golden tanned, hers nut brown. She drew a breath, let it out slowly, and straightened. "Sorry."

Carson's dark blue gaze was sympathetic. His voice rang with sincerity. "There's nothing to be sorry for. Thank God we're all human. Sometimes we just realize that we've been bottling things inside us for so long that we must get them out, give them voice, before we come apart."

Aubrey nodded. She liked the words he'd used to explain what had happened. Wyatt and her mother didn't usually come up in her conversation because their struggles always made her emotional. Aubrey had never voiced her fear, but it was always at the back of her thoughts.

He waited a beat as Aubrey took a sip of water. "You good?"

"Yes." She was glad when the waiter appeared to set down her glass of iced tea and Carson's drink. "One last comment about my family," she said as the waiter disappeared, "I love my family. I'm blessed enough to have been able to help, financially, physically, and emotionally."

"I appreciate you being so transparent with me about your family and how it has shaped your career and decisions. Family is important. It's the glue that keeps us together."

Nodding in agreement and trying to keep his understanding blue gaze from distracting her, Aubrey felt certain she'd shared more than enough. *What's done is done.*

"Up to now, your family has figured into most of your career decisions," Carson acknowledged. He took a sip of his Scotch and set it down. "Your brother's good diagnosis is a Godsend, and the timing is almost perfect."

"Mmm-hmmm." Aubrey listened, wanting to believe that her family had finally made it out of the dark.

Carson fixed her with an intense look. "There are rainbows on your horizon, Aubrey, and you need to start reaching for them. It's time for you to make a new start."

Aubrey swallowed tea. "What are you proposing?"

Carson's eyes lit up. "I'll start with my vision. I recently bought out Crutchfield and Donner and I'm looking for you to run with it."

Crutchfield and Donner! That got Aubrey's blood to pumping. She knew that Crutchfield and Donner had been one of the big names in wealth management until Crutchfield passed away and Donner went through a messy divorce. Between Crutchfield's heirs and Donner's ex-wife, there'd been no choice but to sell the company. "I haven't seen the sale of Crutchfield and Donner published anywhere."

"You wouldn't." Carson looked pleased with himself. "I bought it through one of my holding companies to keep the price competitive. I want to see the company back to its former profitability and status and beyond. This is a prime opportunity for me to recoup my investment and knock the rate of return out of the ballpark."

Aubrey found her voice. "So where would I come in?"

Carson smiled. "Real estate investing is my specialty and I would be the last word on all real estate related issues. I want the company to be more diversified. I want you to take that ball and run with it."

Aubrey leaned forward, excitement building inside her. She was good at what she did, but opportunities like this almost never came along. "You want me to run Crutchfield and Donner?"

"Yes, as CEO and partner."

"Partner!" Aubrey couldn't control the eagerness in her voice.

"You're phenomenal at what you do, and I believe in motivating people to exceed all expectations," he explained. "What better motivation is there than working for yourself?"

Exhilaration fluttering through her, Aubrey sucked in a breath. "I can't think of any! What percentage a partner would I be? Would I get some sort of compensation in addition to the partnership, at least to start?"

Carson nodded slowly. "Of course, you would get monetary compensation, but I want you to understand that we wouldn't be equal partners."

"I-I wouldn't really expect that at this point," she admitted.

Carson held her gaze. "I'm thinking something like a third of the company, tied in with your making it a success."

Aubrey's brows lifted despite her attempted bland expression. The job would be difficult, but a one third partnership at Crutchfield and Donner was a generous offer for someone coming in the door.

"You would run the company since I have several other interests, but I would participate and have the last word for anything relating to real estate."

Brain buzzing with excitement, Aubrey nodded in agreement. "If I bring the company back to its former glory and beyond, I'll probably want more."

"And I'd be more than happy to give it to you. It's all about success." Carson grinned. "So, I take it you're interested?"

Aubrey found it hard to sit still and maintain her businesslike manner. "Yes, yes I am. I'll need to see the fine print and have a lawyer look at it, but I'm definitely interested."

"Good."

The waiter arrived with their food. Aubrey was so excited she found it hard to finish her meal. The prospect of running Carson's wealth management and investment firm was the kind of thing she'd hoped for and dreamed of for years. She could barely believe that she wasn't dreaming. In her excitement, she ignored the negative voice in her innermost thoughts that asked, *Do you really think you can do this? Can you keep your mind on work with a man like Carson around?*

With her thoughts accelerating into what might be required, she realized that she might have to move to New York. That's where the Crutchfield and Donner offices were located. It meant that she wouldn't be close to Wyatt and her mother unless they agreed to move too.

After years of taking them into consideration in her assignments and place of work decisions, this thought gave her fits. What if Wyatt's cancer returned? What if her family needed her? She glanced up to find Carson studying her.

"Don't ever play poker," he said. "You have a very expressive face. Everything you think and feel is there for the world to see."

Lowering her lids, Aubrey focused on presenting a neutral expression. He'd just met her. He shouldn't be able to pick up on her thoughts and feelings so easily! Aubrey decided then and there that she'd have to work on her poker face.

"You have an issue or problem with the offer?" he asked, calmly cutting into his steak.

"Yes." At the risk of sounding like a naïve amateur she asked, "Would I have to move to New York?"

Caron MacDonald chewed and swallowed. "You'd have to be there to help set up the office, meet with clients in the beginning, talk to the press once marketing gets going on this, and interview the current staff, help decide who we keep. You know the drill."

"Yes, I do." Aubrey had performed many of the same tasks at Wickerfield Associates for people who had stood in the limelight and taken the credit. She knew that the job would require that she spend several months in New York at a minimum. It would realistically take a year if she wanted it to be a success and poured her heart and soul into it.

"But once you get it going," he added, "you could go back and forth between New York and Chicago."

I could, but that's not how I want to spend my life, Aubrey thought. This was a problem, however, that could be solved, especially if she were a partner.

Finished with his meal, Carson pushed back his chair to sip Scotch. When he set the glass down, he asked, "How soon could you leave Wickerfield Associates?"

Aubrey swallowed a mouthful of seafood pasta with difficulty. She felt sort of loopy. Her throat was so dry she eased it with a few sips of tea. "I don't know. They've been a very good place for me to learn and grow, so I don't want to leave them high and dry. They also made many accommodations for my family situation."

"I'm sure I could be just as accommodating and more," Carson declared resolutely. His blue eyes sparkled invitingly. "I'm prepared to woo you."

Something in the comment and his tone sent Aubrey's thoughts into a totally different direction. Unobtrusively eyeing his lean, athletic body in the custom suit, she wondered just how accommodating Carson McDonald could be and she wasn't thinking about investments. She felt drawn to him. Aubrey checked her watch.

It was getting late, and she had to go over her company client's account to prepare for her meeting. Aubrey reached for her purse.

"Do you have to go?"

The need to get on with her business weighed on her. She didn't want to go. Despite her difficulty in catching her breath, she found Carson MacDonald more than mesmerizing and his business offer was one she'd dreamed of receiving. Aubrey pushed back her chair and stood on shaky legs. "Yes, I have to go! It's one o'clock."

"I knew you had a one-thirty appointment and we started late," he reassured her. "Let's review where we stand. I've extended an offer to you and you've indicated that you're interested. It'll take a few days for my staff to get the paperwork together and then we'll have the lawyers look at it. You should have all the written details in the offer by Friday. Will that work for you?"

"Yes." Aubrey reached out and shook his hand. "I'm excited at the prospect of working with you, being a partner, and bringing Crutchfield and Donner back from the ashes."

"I'm excited too," he said, giving her hand an extra shake. "I'm also looking forward to your answer to our partnership on Friday. I don't think I could find a more suitable candidate."

"Thank you!" Clutching her things, Aubrey said her goodbye, and for the second time in one day, fled Carson MacDonald's presence to attend to Wickerfield Associates business.

Once she'd gone, Carson ate more of his food and finished his Scotch. Wickerfield was a prime training ground for wealth management and investing. He had ordered full reports on Aubrey and her associate, Owen Connors, in the hope that one of them would agree to run his company. He'd also reviewed the readily available information on both their records of success from Wickerfield Associates and though he'd leaned toward Aubrey, convinced himself that either would be fine for his new project.

Carson knew he was a good judge of people, their character and personality. Would he have clicked as well with Aubrey's associate, Owen Connors, if he'd shown up to do the seminars? Carson doubted it. He honestly liked the refreshingly unexpected Aubrey Merrill and admired the sacrifices she'd made for her family, but would she accept his proposal?

CHAPTER THREE

In her excitement over the forthcoming offer from Carson MacDonald, Aubrey extensively researched him and the company he'd purchased, Crutchfield and Donner. She found that through his real estate successes, he was often brash, forthright, and imaginative, but always personally involved. No surprise there, she mused.

His list of successes seemed endless, and he owned some of the most desirable properties in places she'd only dreamed of visiting. Carson MacDonald was also the force behind a new chain of technology centered hotels spreading across the country. A common theme in the articles was his connection to people.

Apparently, Carson wasn't the sort of man to get his successes from climbing up on the backs of others. He'd shared his successes with others involved in his real estate buying, selling, and development processes. People liked working and dealing with him. On paper, he sounded like a good partner.

Personally, she liked his vibe. He'd connected with her on a personal and professional basis. If his offer turned out to be everything he'd promised, her only issues would be moving to New York for at least a year, being away from her family, and stepping away from Wickerfield Associates, where she'd been nurtured, sheltered, and protected for years.

From the financial reports, Aubrey gathered that several of the Crutchfield and Donner big accounts had been taken by competitors, but a few were holding to see how things would develop. If she got to run the company as Carson had promised, she would find a way to bring it back.

After the morning seminar the next day, Aubrey's afternoon appointments ended early, so she and Mira decided to spend the gloriously warm day at the beach.

Carrying their beach bags, snacks and drinks, Aubrey and Mira strolled across the warm sand of Montauk Beach. One of Mira's bodyguards walked close to her, securing the area. Aubrey didn't turn to look, but she knew that another of Mira's bodyguards followed at a safe distance. Aubrey was trying to ignore them, the way Mira and Carson MacDonald seemed to do, and finding it difficult. The water positively sparkled in the afternoon sun and the beach was dotted with patrons enjoying the sun, sights, and sounds.

Certain that her billionaire husband was headed to divorce court, Mira had been cranky and a little depressed. Being out on the beach in her gold La Perla bikini seemed to cheer her up. Squishing her bare toes in the sand as she walked, Aubrey listened as Mira talked about bathing suits and body types. Mira had helped Aubrey select the deep plum colored one piece she wore. It flattered her athletic figure and stood out against her deep caramel-colored skin.

With a glance to her right, Mira stopped talking and did a doubletake. "Oh, that's-that's Vivi! I haven't seen her in years!"

"Who's Vivi?" Aubrey asked, following the direction of Mira's stare. Aubrey's gaze slowed and stopped at the sight of a familiar redhead reclining in a beach chair in a black bikini that barely covered the essentials. It was the woman who had been kissing Carson McDonald in the hotel. Could Carson MacDonald be far away?

"I'm going over to speak to my friend, are you coming?" Mira called as she headed towards a beautiful blond on the beach further to their right.

Before Aubrey could take another step or look further, she heard Carson say in a slightly amused tone, "Aubrey Merrill, wealth advisor extraordinaire, fancy meeting you on the beach!"

Following the provocative sound of Carson's voice, Aubrey spotted him coming from one of the vendors with a drink in each hand. His tan stood out against the snowy white T-shirt and blue swim trunks that accented his lanky athletic form. "Investment advisors need fun and sun too," she quipped.

His blue eyes inspected her frankly, from her bare toes to her one-piece swimsuit and the hair Mira had pinned up in a messy topknot. It was a natural thing to do and he did nothing inappropriate, but Aubrey's body tingled in response. Holding herself in check, Aubrey resisted the urge to do the same.

He stopped in front of her. "Good to see you getting around town. Are you having fun?"

"Mostly," she admitted, sparing a quick glance for Mira, who was talking animatedly to her friend. "My friend is going through a tough time and I've been trying to cheer her up."

Carson turned to look at Aubrey's friend. "Your friend is Mira Zayne?"

"Yes, she is," Aubrey confirmed, "Her husband Bennett's family is also a Wickerfield client."

"Beautiful woman, and she's done a lot for Lady Zayne Cosmetics," he added, surprising Aubrey.

Thankful he didn't mention any of the fairytales and dire predictions currently being printed by the gossip magazines, Aubrey tilted her head, squinting in the sun. "You pay attention to the cosmetics industry?"

"I pay attention to all the methods people use to make and expand their wealth," he said, "I may specialize in real estate, but I'm always looking for new ideas."

Aubrey nodded, "So am I."

Carson shifted on his feet. "I have my yacht here. We were going for a cruise in a bit. Would you like to come along? A change of scenery might be good for you and your friend. At the very least, it would cool you off."

Still trying to flush out her sense of who Carson was as a person and determine what it might be like to be partners with him, she thanked him for the offer and said, "I'd like that. Let me talk to Mira."

Carson turned to look at the redhead. "I'll be over there with my girlfriend, Giselle. Come on over and I'll introduce you. You'll enjoy yourself. I promise."

"I'm sure I will," Aubrey said as she headed towards Mira. Mira stopped talking when Aubrey closed the distance between them and introduced Aubrey to her modeling friend. Then Mira used the opportunity to end her conversation and move on with Aubrey.

"I saw you talking to a good-looking guy. Who was that?" Mira asked as they moved down the beach enough to have some privacy.

Aubrey quickly filled her in on Carson and his offer of a cruise on his yacht. Then she reminded Mira about his partnership offer.

"Dios, as if I could forget!" Mira said, "We're going, right? Maybe this time the paparazzi will end up helping me for a change! It could happen."

"It could happen," Aubrey said, echoing her phrase. She

desperately wanted Mira to get some good news.

Mira stopped walking. "Are you sure you don't have any qualms about working for a guy who looks that good, likes you, and is worth more than a billion?"

"What makes you think he likes me?" Aubrey asked, favoring the thought, but not ready to own it.

Mira gave her a *you're hopeless* look. "Observation. It might have looked like I was all into the conversation with Vivi, but I was also watching you and the real estate baron. And what about that partnership offer? Billionaires don't offer partnerships to just anyone!"

"That's different," Aubrey said, trying to explain, "I make money for my clients all the time. You know I'm good at what I do."

"And so is he," Mira added, tilting her head, and raising her brows.

Aubrey decided to change the subject. "If we're going, he wants us to meet his girlfriend," she said.

"Competition?" Mira asked softly.

Aubrey slanted her a glance. "It's not like that!"

"Isn't it?" Mira laughed softly. Aubrey enjoyed the sound. It hurt to see Mira crying over Ben.

Mira and Aubrey grew silent as they made the trek across the sand to Carson and his girlfriend. He stood up as they approached and started making the introductions. Giselle smiled politely, but when Carson told her that Aubrey would be his new partner in a company he bought, once she signed the paperwork, Giselle flashed Aubrey an unfriendly look.

"I'm a wealth management advisor and director at Wickerfield

Associates," Aubrey explained.

"I know who you are," Giselle said, cutting her off in a nasty tone.

Turning his head, Carson eyed his girlfriend quizzically.

Aubrey recoiled mentally, trying but failing to understand the emotion or thought process behind the woman's attitude. Aubrey liked Carson and knew he was quite a catch, but it wasn't as if she were a threat to Giselle's position as Carson's girlfriend. He'd approached Aubrey for business reasons.

She saw Mira narrow her eyes at the woman.

"You're Mira Zayne," Giselle said, offering Mira a phony but pleasant smile, "the face of Lady Zayne Cosmetics."

"Yes, I am," Mira said cautiously. "I'm married to Bennett Zayne."

"Giselle is an actress," Carson told them. "You may have seen her in *The Lessinger Project*."

Aubrey and Mira looked at each other, shaking their heads. "No, we haven't," Aubrey said.

"She's done some work in television commercials too," Carson added helpfully.

"I may have seen one your commercials," Mira said, giving Giselle a critical look. "Carolina Coffee?"

"Yes!" Giselle said, with a smile that lasted all of three seconds. Lowering her lids, she slanted a snarky glance at Aubrey.

At a loss for words, Aubrey resisted a shrug and kept her mouth shut. What was she supposed to say? She hadn't seen any of Giselle's work and that was the truth.

Seemingly oblivious to the somewhat unfriendly interplay and conversation between the women, Carson offered to get Mira and Aubrey a drink. At their polite refusal, he finished his drink and began gathering his things. On an unspoken cue, Giselle did the same.

The group, both sets of bodyguards and all, accompanied Carson to an area where they were picked up, taken to the marina, and deposited near Carson's yacht. It was long, sleek, and modern looking. Along the side, Aubrey read the words Carson's Mistress in large black letters. She smiled.

Noting her reaction, Carson declared, "Any man who has a boat or yacht has a mistress who is as demanding of his time and money as any woman!"

"How big is your yacht?" Mira asked Carson as a member of the yacht's crew helped each of them board safely.

"Sixty feet," Carson responded. "I have a larger boat, but this is the one I like to run around in. It has an enclosed bridge. Would you like a tour?"

"Absolutely!" Aubrey and Mira said, taking in the luxurious surroundings.

"I'd be happy to show them around, sir," one of the crew members stated.

"Good," Carson replied. "Aubrey, Mira, please go with him, Giselle and I will be out on the sun deck getting ready to take off when you're done."

"This is a Viking yacht," the crewman began. "There are four staterooms below, crew's quarters, and the engine room. Let's start there."

Though she worked for the wealthy through Wickerfield Associates, Aubrey hadn't been on many yachts. Because of her family situation, she spent most of her time in the office. She liked what she saw but noticed that the master bedroom and VIP guest rooms didn't look as if they had been used very much. Apparently, Carson didn't spend much time with his mistress.

When they arrived on the sun deck after the tour, the engines were running. Giselle was already artfully arranged on a deck lounger. Sunglasses covering her eyes, she appeared to be asleep. Seated nearby, Carson was pouring liquid from a drink pitcher into a bunch of glasses.

"Ladies, did you enjoy your tour?" he asked.

They assured him that they had.

He pointed to the loungers and chairs scattering the wide deck. "Please make yourselves comfortable. For the safety note, I've placed an inflatable life vest for each of you on the bar, so try them on and keep them close. I haven't lost a guest yet. On a hospitality note, I have homemade margaritas and as captain, I insist we drink to take off."

Removing her flowered print cover-up, Aubrey cinched a black inflatable life vest over her swimsuit. It fit comfortably, so she put it on the chair next to her. She saw that Mira also elected to leave her life jacket on a nearby deck lounger, making it easy for her flattering gold bikini to be appreciated.

Aubrey went over to the counter for her drink. Accepting the drink, she took a sip. "Good job! It's delicious!"

"Personal recipe," he shot back. "Glad you like it."

The ship's horn sounded loudly, startling her.

"We're taking off," Carson explained.

Apparently asleep, Giselle remained on the lounger while Aubrey, Carson, and Mira went to the rail and watched the boat pull away from the dock.

"You're not going to pilot the boat yourself?" Aubrey asked, teasing a little as they passed other boats.

"I could, but I'm drinking today," he said lightly. "I've designated another captain to pilot this cruise."

Standing at the railing and sipping her drink, Aubrey watched the other boats and the shoreline until they were out of sight. Then she closed her eyes and let the warm wind caress her face and mediate the heat of the day. This trip was exceeding all her expectations.

A gracious host, Carson pointed out various landmarks and some of the navigational aids as they passed them. He talked about life on the water and how he'd learned to sail while crewing for others, then graduated to power boats as he'd started to make his fortune. Slipping away from them, Mira stretched out on a lounger with her drink and dozed in the sun.

"As a partner in Crutchfield and Donner, this lifestyle and any other lifestyle you might desire would be within your reach," Carson said, standing close enough for Aubrey to hear him above the wind.

"With my brother's cancer in remission, it would be like a new start for me," Aubrey said, "Sometimes you get used to things, good or bad, and it's hard to let go."

"You'll make the right decision," he assured her. "Have you discussed the offer with Wickerfield?"

Turning, Aubrey placed her empty glass in a strategically located cup holder. "No, my boss was out of the office. I'm waiting for him to call me back."

"They have to know they can't keep you forever," Carson said, "You're too good."

Aubrey loved her work and it showed with all she'd been able to accomplish. Still, it felt good to have Carson standing close and acknowledging her efforts. Being so close to him and basking in his attention added to Aubrey feeling of flying high.

A chair scraped noisily against the deck, startling them. They jumped, moving further apart.

"You two look cozy," Giselle remarked, getting up from the lounger.

Beneath her critical gaze, Aubrey felt as if she'd been caught doing something inappropriate. She had merely been talking to Carson. Women like Giselle didn't usually feel threatened by her when it came to their men.

Carson said nothing, but there was a challenge in his eyes when he looked at Giselle.

Apparently aware that she'd gone a little too far, Giselle managed a slinky walk across the deck. Winding her well-toned arms around his neck, she pressed her scantily clad body against his, drawing his head down for a sensual kiss.

Aubrey had seen enough. She didn't need to witness a repeat of the couple's kiss in the hotel, so she moved away. She heard Giselle say in low sultry voice, "I'm sorry, baby! You know I'm crazy about you and that means that I see any woman as a potential threat."

"No need to protect your interests here. We're talking business. Maybe you should go below and take a nap," he suggested.

"Will you come with me?" she asked, almost begging.

"We have guests," he reminded her.

A helicopter sounded somewhere above them.

"It's the damned paparazzi again!" Giselle said, a hand going to her mussed hair. "I think I *will* go below and take a little nap."

Taking the seat next to Mira, Aubrey saw that she was awake. They scanned the sky, spotting the helicopter overhead, closing in on the yacht.

Giselle went past them on her way below deck.

"If you don't want your picture on the news or in one of those gossip magazines, you should go inside or below," Carson said.

Mira and Aubrey shared a look.

"I believe I'll sit front and center for this one,' Mira said, rearranging herself on the lounger.

Aubrey shrugged. "I don't think anyone will know or care who I am and why I'm on your boat."

"You'd be surprised," Carson assured her.

The helicopter hovered for several moments, adding to the wind and noise. Then, when Carson was almost totally annoyed, it went away. The rest of their cruise was uneventful.

"I hope you enjoyed yourselves,' Carson said as Aubrey and Mira thanked him for the trip and his hospitality. They assured him that they had. "I'll be in touch," he added for Aubrey's ears alone.

As they went down the gangplank and strolled the dock, Mira asked, "Do you think anything will come of the helicopter's pictures?"

Aubrey shrugged, then shook her head. "I could be wrong, since they've been making up stories about you and Bennett, but I wouldn't count on it."

In between bites of an everything omelet a couple of days later, Aubrey gazed dreamily at the ocean view showcased through floor to ceiling windows at Mira's South Hampton home. The horizon extended as far as the eye could see. The stretch of tree-dotted white sandy beach looked like something off a postcard.

Sipping her coffee, Mira went through a stack of daily and weekly papers and magazines. She stopped to stare at one and gasped. "We made it into the papers!" She held up a color insert from the gossip section of a newspaper showing both with Carson on his boat.

Aubrey scanned the picture. Mira was stretched out on the lounger in one of her signature poses, the gold bikini looking decadent, her hair artfully mussed. "You look great!" Aubrey exclaimed. She studied Carson in the picture. Who would ever expect a self-made billionaire to look so good? The picture didn't do him justice. Studying her own picture, Aubrey saw that her suit flattered her figure, but seemed a little old fashioned. She looked okay, attractive, but not glamorous like Mira. She shrugged it off, telling herself that she couldn't have taken a better shot.

Mira caught her reaction. "It's a decent shot of you, Aubrey. You know you're not into glamor."

"True," Aubrey admitted, "but sometimes I wonder if I should try to get into it."

"For Carson?" Mira asked, raising a brow.

Aubrey hesitated. "For *me*, if I decide to do it." She knew herself, what made her comfortable. Did a woman exist who didn't want to be wanted for herself?

"For the record, he sought you out for your investing abilities and the way you think," Mira reminded her, punctuating her words with a string of Spanish.

"Phew!" Aubrey forced out a breath. "Let's stop talking about Carson MacDonald."

"Okay," Mira said between sips of coffee, "but he's still on your mind."

"His proposal is on my mind," Aubrey corrected her. "Running something like Crutchfield and Donner is what I've always wanted to do."

Mira looked puzzled. "Is there any reason why you can't accept his proposal?"

Mira's phone rang, startling both women. Mira glanced down at her phone. "It—it's Ben!" she exclaimed. She let it cycle through another ring.

Aubrey scanned the pictures from the boat and then let her gaze come back to rest on Mira. Watching her friend close her eyes and take a deep breath before switching on the phone, she genuinely hoped that Bennett Zayne still loved his beautiful wife.

Mira spoke into the receiver, only a slight tremor in her voice. "Ben? What's going on? I didn't think you wanted to talk. I can't forget the things you said at the office. I was afraid that. . . ."

Aubrey got up from the table. She could hear the unaccustomed vulnerability in Mira's voice. It was so poignant that Aubrey's eyes stung in sympathy. She'd been hurt in the past, especially when the man she'd loved had chosen to walk away, but she'd never experienced the intense pain Mira was living through.

Determined to give Mira and Ben some privacy, Aubrey moved to the window. One more glance at the picture postcard view, and she was heading outside for the private beach.

On the beach, Aubrey found a spot on the powdered sand beneath a tree. Leaning against the trunk, she stared out across the rolling waves. She had been focusing on the breathtaking opportunity Carson proposed, though the man himself presented as potent an attraction as a beacon in the dark.

With the decision she faced, it felt as if she were standing on the edge of a cliff. What if Wyatt's cancer came out of remission? The thought of being hundreds of miles away, burdened with obligations when her family needed her was scary.

Working in the background at Wickerfield had provided her with a somewhat protected environment. With all her accomplishments, she might be great at wealth management, but she'd never been a CEO, and she'd never been out front in the limelight. Then there was the fact that Carson MacDonald physically and emotionally attracted her. If he stayed attached to his girlfriend, she could appreciate him from afar and keep her heart and her career safe. But some men changed girlfriends like they changed their shirts. Was Carson one of them? He seemed so. . . accessible.

Did her new career opportunity come attached to the man who could break her heart?

CHAPTER FOUR

Aubrey's hands shook as she dialed her boss at Wickerfield Associates, Chase Everett. There'd been no details in the message she'd left previously, so he would get a surprise. She hoped he'd take it well. Now she would be meeting Carson at the conference hotel in a few days to look over the agreement and most likely sign her way to a new future.

"You've been enjoying yourself," Everett teased, when he answered. "I saw a picture on you on that billionaire's boat. Is Mira trying to match you up with a billionaire?"

"Actually, no." Aubrey hesitated, then decided that this was the time to get it all out. "Carson MacDonald sought me out at the conference hotel. It turns out he bought Crutchfield and Donner and he wants me to run it. He's offered to make me a partner."

Her boss's stunned silence seemed to go on forever. "I knew something like this was going to happen sooner or later," he admitted finally. "Congratulations, Aubrey! You deserve this!"

"I haven't actually accepted yet," she quickly explained.

"Why the hell not?"

"I thought I should at least talk to you first, have a lawyer look at the agreement, see how long it would take hand over my accounts. . ."

"Are you scared?"

Aubrey nibbled on her bottom lip. "Yes, this is big, in more ways than you can imagine."

"It's going to be fine. Carson MacDonald is a top-of-the-line guy. He's got a sterling business reputation."

"I know. I did look that up," Aubrey admitted. "I've been doing the background work for so long that I'm just not sure I'm ready for the change..."

Her boss chuckled. "Tell that to someone who believes it. Aubrey, this is the perfect opportunity and exactly what you would be doing if life hadn't gotten in the way. It's time for you to fly, little bird."

Aubrey had to laugh. "What about my clients?

"Owen can handle most of them. I can give the rest to a couple of the newbies. Some clients may follow you to your new job. All we ask is that you don't actively recruit clients away from us."

"That's covered in the employment agreement I signed," she reminded him.

"Exactly." He cleared his throat. "I also have the signed resignation letter you wrote when you started. I can put the appropriate date on it once you sign his agreement."

"Thank you." Aubrey felt the threat of tears once more.

"I'm urging you to get started right away," he said, emphasizing his point. "I'm going to text you the name of an excellent lawyer and I'll tell him to expect your call."

"Thank you," she repeated.

"Aubrey, if you want to come back to Wickerfield Associates, you can, no matter what, but as your mentor, I'm advising you go with your gut."

"I'd already decided to go with my gut," she admitted, "but it didn't feel right to do it without first talking to you and Momma."

Chase Everett's voice picked up. "Have you talked to her?"

"Not yet. I've been holding off because it feels like I'm deserting her and Wyatt. . . ." Aubrey stopped speaking, aware for the first time of what she'd just said and that it was true.

"Call your mother," he advised from the other end of the line, "I think she'll surprise you."

Aubrey dialed her mother next, but this was one of the rare times her mother did not answer her phone. A little disappointed, Aubrey made her way back inside. It took a while for her to find Mira in the maze of her luxurious mansion. Her friend had already changed clothes and was doing her makeup at the vanity in her powder room.

"I-I'm going to lunch with Ben," Mira said, with a brittle smile that managed to convey both hope and dread. "I'd invite you along, but we need to talk."

"Of course, you two need to talk in private!" Aubrey said quickly. "I hope you can kiss and make up."

Mira's eyes glittered. "I couldn't bring myself to tell you before, but after he avoided me all that time, I went by his office and it wasn't good," she admitted. "I'm almost afraid there's nothing more to say," Mira added.

"Oh Mira," Aubrey said putting a comforting arm around her friend, "You can work this out."

Mira delicately dabbed at her eyes with a tissue. "You and I can go to dinner later."

Aubrey shook her head. "No. I'm going back to the hotel for an afternoon appointment and dinner at Pierre's. I'll spend the night at the hotel. I don't want to be in the middle of you guys working things out."

Mira nodded. "I'll call you."

Aubrey hugged her and headed for the door. "Good luck."

"Ben wasn't one of your Wickerfield client appointments, was he?" Mira called out.

Aubrey stopped and turned around to face her friend. "No, not this time. I would have told you."

Mira nodded. "I had to ask. I reread my prenup. If he dumps me before we've been married five years, he'll save several million."

"You don't think he's meeting you to...?"

"That's exactly what I think!" Mira snapped with a string of Spanish.

"Then flip the script," Aubrey advised her. "He never could resist you before."

Mira sighed, tears sparkling in her beautiful dark eyes. "The man I love would never think of dumping me. If Ben wants to dump me, I'm not sure I want to fight it." Mira shook her head, as if to discard the thought. "But this is war, isn't it?" She gave her dress a critical look. "I should change dresses. I could at least show him what he would be missing."

Aubrey smiled, glad she'd been able to help Mira change her focus. By the time Aubrey reached the door, Mira was already at her closet with the closet rod remote, watching the designer dresses go by.

On the way back to the hotel in one of Mira's cars, Aubrey tried her mother again. It was very unusual for her mother to be unavailable. Because Aubrey knew that Wyatt was fine, she tried not to worry. Being off the grid had to be an unaccustomed pleasure for her mother.

In the afternoon Aubrey met with the last scheduled appointment for Wickerfield Associates. Because of her client's questions, it took a good hour, but it ended well.

Once the client left, Aubrey gathered her papers and notes. She took extra time to make sure the files were complete with the notes attached. Bright sunlight still filtered in from the window as she stood and stretched.

She felt a little light-headed as she checked her watch. Carson had asked her to meet him in the private dining room after her client appointment. Aubrey wet her lips nervously. She couldn't imagine Carson making an offer that she shouldn't accept, but what if he did? Was she strong enough to resist? Was she strong enough to hold on for the right offer? And most of all, was she strong enough to resist falling for the man?

You're being silly! It wasn't as if she'd never been attracted to a man. She'd just quit looking after her fiancé made other plans. Dry mouthed, she lifted her glass of water from the table and drank it all. Then she walked to the door and opened it.

She came face to face with Carson, who stood just outside the door. Startled, Aubrey shrank back with a squeak.

"I didn't mean to startle you," Carson said, his handsome face full of concern. "I just got the paperwork from my lawyer and was thinking I'd bring it up here so you could review it before our meeting."

Aubrey gazed at him with a bit of wonder. Did he have to look like a male model? Did he have to be so personable? "You're not like any billionaire I've ever met. I've yet to meet your assistant."

"Assistants," he corrected her with a slight smile, "and you haven't met any of them because I'm excited about this project. That means that you get my *personal* attention. You need to know that you can work with me. How do you think I got to be where I am anyway? It wasn't just real estate, oil, and luck, and it wasn't by having other people do all the important things. I like connecting with people."

Quit drooling, girl! Aubrey blinked, forcing herself to break the link with his hypnotic eyes. "I've finished with my client. I was on my way down to see you," she admitted.

"Looks like I saved you a walk." He offered Aubrey a book like folder with her name embossed across the top in gold letters.

She accepted the folder, a thread of sensual awareness shooting up her arm to spread throughout her body when his fingers grazed hers. Aubrey shivered. She glanced up to find Carson studying her.

"You've been working hard," he observed.

"Yes, I have, but I like my work."

Carson gave her a thoughtful look. "I'm betting that you'll like the work at Crutchfield and Donner even more."

Aubrey wet her dry lips. Was she picking up even more intensity from Carson? She glanced down at the folder.

"I'll give you some time to review the offer," he said. "We should at least discuss your initial thoughts and impressions."

Aubrey's head came up. She knew it was time to hold her ground. "I'll review it, but I won't sign until my lawyer says it's ok."

Carson looked amused. "I wouldn't ask you to. I have too much respect for your skill and talent to try to railroad you into anything. This will be a monumental opportunity for both of us. If things work the way I've planned, this is only the beginning."

Aubrey felt like a bunny hill novice at the top of a gigantic mountain. *Is he trying to scare me? Not gonna happen.* Aubrey raised her brows and gave him a steely gaze. Then she found her voice. "I think I'll stay here and review your offer. I'll meet you in the private dining room in a couple of hours to discuss my initial impressions."

He nodded. "It sounds good. See you then."

As he left, Aubrey made her way back to the table with her heart pounding her chest. Her knees were like jelly and her hands were shaking. Except for the tragedies she'd lived through, this was the biggest thing that had ever happened to her. She hoped she didn't give herself a heart attack.

Settling back into the chair, she opened the folder. The inside pages were embossed with her name in gold and the CEO title above Crutchfield and Donner. She stared at the words, excitement making it impossible to read further. Gradually, she calmed down enough to read the offer Carson had drawn up.

Aubrey paused on her second read through the offer. It had been written in plain English, so she understood every word. It contained the stuff her dreams were made of. He was offering her a partnership and the CEO position at Crutchfield and Donner, with the power to make all the decisions except those related to real estate investments, Carson's area of expertise.

A life changer, the employment contract was more complete than she could have imagined. It laid out her role as CEO and final authority on almost everything except the real estate related decisions and Carson's areas of the partnership. Wickerfield Associates paid her a generous salary for her hard work, but Carson's offer nearly doubled it. The company would also be providing bodyguards for her and a place to live in New York until she found her own. The agreement included four company financed trips home to Chicago for the next year. Aubrey took a few minutes to digest those facts.

Rereading the contract one last time, Aubrey stopped at the part about the bodyguards. She'd been snickering behind the backs of those who found it necessary to travel with bodyguards. Now she might be one of them.

Living in New York instead of Chicago, being on her own, and partnering with a real estate billionaire to run a company were all big steps. Was she crazy to consider doing them all at once?

CHAPTER FIVE

Aubrey found Carson in the hotel's private dining room studying the screen on his iPad. The two bodyguards nodded as she virtually danced by on her way to Carson's table. He glanced up as she reached the linen-covered table, an energetic look in his dark blue eyes. "Well?"

Aubrey couldn't contain her smile. The higher-pitched voice coming out of her mouth didn't sound like hers. "It's good! Everything you promised! But I still want my lawyer to look at it, and I'm not actually going to sign until he says it's okay, but it looks like we're going to be partners," she gushed.

"Your lawyer's not going to find anything wrong with that contract." An infectious grin lit Carson's face, transforming it as he got to his feet. "Welcome to Crutchfield and Donner, partner," he said, offering his hand.

Aubrey took it. She startled at the electric shock that sparked and then tried hard to ignore it. The grasp of his big, long-fingered hand sent a thrill of primal excitement through her body. *Oh yeah!*

It's just a handshake! Aubrey reminded herself internally. She shook hands with people all the time. She'd experienced everything from the light, two fingered not-serious shake, to ones where you wondered if the other person was trying to break the bones in your hand. This was different. It felt as if the temperature in the room suddenly shot up several degrees. Did Carson feel that spark too? Her eyes widened as she admired his handsome features and met his magnetic gaze. He looked. . . excited. She'd never experienced such an intense physical reaction to any man's handshake.

His grip was firm and businesslike, but warm. He held on for several precious seconds longer than what would be considered polite. Finally, he gazed down at their clasped hands. The contrast in their coloring and the relative sizes of their fingers stood out in the lighted room.

A look of surprise skittered across his face as he seemed to realize that he was still holding her hand. He released it. "We're going to bring this company back and make a killing in the markets!"

"We are!" Aubrey agreed resolutely.

"This calls for a celebration!" he declared.

"Ahh…" Aubrey shifted on her heels and gave her purple power suit a critical look. It was an expensive designer suit, but obviously meant for use in the business world. Here, in a town where the rich and famous styled and profiled in public she didn't want to look drab.

"You look fine!" he assured her. "Besides, I'm just talking dinner with champagne."

"Where'd you want to go?" she asked. She'd been in town all week, but had spent most of her time giving seminars, meeting with clients, and supporting Mira.

"We never made it to Pierre's," he reminded her, "This would be a good time to go."

"I could go to my room and change. It wouldn't take long," Aubrey said, thinking of being in a crowd of rich people in evening wear while she still wore her business clothes.

"This is not a date," Carson declared in a matter-of-fact tone. "This is a celebration of the start of a successful business partnership."

Aubrey's gaze flew to his face. He looked calm and unaffected by the sensual heat she'd felt at his touch. Though he wasn't proposing a date, she felt a strange mixture of nervousness and excitement at the prospect of being at dinner and having champagne with the billionaire whose face and antics graced the pages of the business and gossip magazines and newspapers.

"How do people dress at Pierre's in the evening?" she asked.

Carson flashed her a cocky grin. "Any damned way they want to. One thing I've learned as a billionaire is that money covers a multitude of eccentricities."

Realizing that she was going to have to deal with the situation, whatever it was, Aubrey turned to Carson and said, "Lead on, partner!"

Later, as Carson pulled up to valet parking at the restaurant in his Maserati, Aubrey studied the tasteful sign with the restaurant's name in script. The white brick building sported plenty of glass and looked like a trendy place to eat. The large patio surrounding the building was filled with dining patrons. Through the open window of the car, she could hear a small band playing pop music.

Aubrey cast a wary eye at the line of people waiting outside for a table.

"The line is not a problem," Carson declared, obviously noting the direction of her gaze. "I have a standing table reservation here."

The valet appeared at Carson's door, greeting him by name. As Carson turned to chat briefly with the valet and get out of the car, Aubrey studied the crowd. Although a few of the men wore suits, the variety of clothing ran the range from casual to designer club wear. Maybe she would blend in after all.

While another valet helped her out of the car, she saw a news van for one of the local stations at the nearby corner. Watching the crew survey the crowd and scan every car that came up the street, she guessed that they were lurking in the hopes of catching one of the stars known to frequent the restaurant.

Carson led her past a line of people waiting to get into Pierre's. One of the news crew approached with a cameraman close behind. "Mr. Macdonald? Sir, I'm Jim Neulander, WVTH, Hamptons, Channel 51. Can we have a quick word with you and your guest?"

Carson shot Aubrey a questioning look. She shrugged, inwardly gathering herself at the prospect of speaking to the press on such short notice. Doing investment work in the background for Wickerfield Associates, she'd never had to speak to the press. Working as Carson's partner and the CEO for Crutchfield and Donner, she'd have to accept the challenge.

She wondered what the press wanted to discuss with her. After all, no one familiar with Carson Macdonald and his taste in women would ever think he was taking her on a date. They were celebrating a possible new agreement, but she hadn't officially signed or notified anyone.

"Sure, what did you want to discuss?" Carson said, stepping to an adjacent area on the edge of the patio. Aubrey followed, maintaining her place at his side as the cameraman switched on the camera.

"Are you celebrating tonight?" Neulander asked, his gaze swinging between Carson and Aubrey. The reporter obviously knew something.

Carson shot Aubrey another questioning glance. "Yes, but what we're celebrating is not really official yet, so. . . ."

"Sir, a Channel 51 news source has stated that you've purchased Crutchfield and Donner. Is that true?"

Aubrey's spirits sank like a stone. *They're going to ask about me.* . .. Standing at Carson's side, she wished she had comic book character invisibility. If she had to speak in public, she wanted to be prepared. She wasn't ready for the limelight.

How could she talk about working for Carson when she hadn't even signed the agreement? Furthermore, Aubrey didn't want her family to hear about her new job on the news before she'd discussed it with them. And had the conversation earlier today with her boss given him enough time to date her resignation and inform the company? And what about the legal review? If the lawyer found unresolvable issues with the employment offer and contract, she couldn't work for Carson.

"Yes, it's true that I've purchased Crutchfield and Donner," Carson confirmed, "It's been confidential company information, but our clients were notified. I've already started restructuring the company and will be providing my expertise in real estate investing."

The reporter pivoted to face Aubrey. "And what about you Ms. Merrill? We know that you have extensive expertise and experience in wealth management and investments. Our source has informed us that you're going to be running the company as CEO. Is this true?"

They knew her name and all the details of her job offer? Aubrey's temper shot up as she struggled to control her facial expression and form a reply. Somehow, she had been set up for this ambush and Carson seemed like the most likely culprit. Abruptly, she remembered that the reporter was waiting for her to speak. She faced the camera and said the only thing she could, "No comment."

Behind the reporter, she saw Carson watching her intently. His eyes narrowed. If she were to successfully run the company, she had to be able to deal with the press. *But I'm not the CEO yet!* she reminded herself.

"So, you being the CEO for Crutchfield and Donner is still in question?"

"No comment," Aubrey repeated, willing herself to project calm.

Carson maneuvered his way back to the camera and the

microphone to speak confidently. "Ms. Merrill has personally reviewed the offer with positive results. The legal review is just a necessary formality. Ms. Merrill *will* be the next CEO for Crutchfield and Donner. You have my word on that!"

Carson's saying the words in front of a cameraman and a reporter for the local news had more impact than when he'd said them at the hotel. Aubrey felt as if she'd been prematurely thrust in the limelight and like a newborn, she wasn't prepared.

The reporter thrust the microphone back at Aubrey. "When my current status changes, I'll be happy to speak to the press," she said. "Thank you." Damned if she was going to say anything more. She bit the insides of her cheeks as she turned away.

"Congratulations on your new job, Ms. Merrill!"

Aubrey acted as if she hadn't heard the reporter.

Turning to face the camera in a close up the reporter added, "Only on WTVH! You heard it here folks. Billionaire real estate Czar, Carson MacDonald has purchased Crutchfield and Donner and appointed Aubrey Merrill, formerly of Wickerfield Associates, to run it. As he noted just seconds ago, Mr. MacDonald will be running the real estate portion of the company. This is Jim Neulander, reporting for WVTH Channel 51."

As the reporter finished his story, Carson urged Aubrey towards the restaurant entrance. She didn't like surprises and felt as if she'd been manipulated into this one. Her ears were ringing. "Did you know they'd be here?" she asked, so filled with the need to vent that it was hard to form the polite words.

Suppressed agitation showed in the depths of Carson's blue eyes. "No, I like to call my own press conferences and have everyone prepared in advance. I also like the people in my organization to sing the same song to the media. Couldn't you have said that you'd tentatively accepted my offer?"

Aubrey faced him, knowing he was not happy with her. "No, I couldn't." She wasn't happy with him either. She knew that people were going to believe the billionaire, and hear that she was the new CEO, not the no-name investment advisor waiting for her lawyer's approval on the deal.

Carson studied her face. "I've got a leak in my organization or someone *you* talked to spilled the beans."

"Normally that might be true, but I didn't know we would be coming here tonight," she reminded him. He wasn't going to shift the blame for this fiasco to her.

"True, that narrows the list to people on my end. My apologies for that. I'm going to find out who and it won't be pretty." He stopped and gave her a sharp look. "You're pissed."

"Annoyed," she confirmed, wishing hard she could chew somebody out, "I haven't discussed this with my family, and I don't want them to find out on the news. I just barely discussed it with my old boss. This could have me looking bad to my company and our clients."

Carson's gaze sharpened. "Hold on. That contract and the job offer is damned generous. If your lawyer's any good at all, this is a done deal. Bottom line, you'll be working for me, we're still part of the show and we're here to celebrate. Unless you're going to do a happy dance right now, you need to get a hold of yourself. Bringing Crutchfield and Donner back will be hard enough without us having a lot of negative press at the start."

"It would be easier if I'd already accepted your offer and we'd prepared for the press," Aubrey shot back.

"True, and I think I've already acknowledged just that. We don't always get what we want," Carson countered. "I wasn't about to let anyone think the job was still open or that you were less than *thrilled* at the prospect of being the CEO."

Aubrey forced herself to swallow. Something in Carson's words and tone had the effect of a mental shake. Her future was at stake in more ways than she dared to contemplate. *This isn't the time to have a hissy fit. I'm going to have to suck it up!* Her thoughts turned to success with Carson, doing what she loved. "I am thrilled."

Carson studied her for a couple of beats. "Good! That's my new CEO!" He flashed her a delighted grin, but his eyes still managed to convey some threads of sympathy for her. As they passed the man at the door and entered the restaurant portion of the place, he beckoned to the host.

"How soon do you think his report will hit the air?" she asked.

"We're news, but not red-hot news," Carson informed her in a low voice, "You've probably got an hour, tops."

The host hustled over to personally greet Carson and introduce himself to Aubrey. As they followed him to a table located in a prime spot, Aubrey checked her watch. The interview hadn't been more than five minutes ago. "I've got to call my family. . . ."

Carson's words reached her in a confidential tone as the maître d drew out a chair for Aubrey. "As soon as we're seated and put in our order, there's always the ladies room."

Aubrey nodded gratefully and thanked the maître d as she settled in her chair.

Minutes later, she made it to the Ladies Lounge and used her cell phone to call her mother.

"Aubrey!" Her mother's voice cracked with emotion. "I was going to call you! Just know that this has been a hell of a day. Wyatt has been exceptionally tired and a little weak for the past few days, so I took him in for tests."

"Is Wyatt okay?" Aubrey asked, unable to keep the wobble out of her voice.

"They didn't find anything, so they gave him a vitamin shot. But we won't have all the test results for a few days."

Aubrey gasped. It felt like the black cloud was hovering over Wyatt's head all over again. In all the other times, Wyatt's cancer had reappeared. "Do you and Wyatt need me to come home right now?" she asked, torn, but knowing she could never forgive herself if she stayed away while her family went through more trauma.

"Aubrey, no! There's no reason to drop everything you're doing. We've got to stop the waiting around and get on with living our lives as best we can."

Unshed tears stung Aubrey's eyes. "I'm not sure I know how to do that."

"Then try harder, sweetheart. Wyatt's been worrying about all the school he's missed while he's been sick, so he applied to Grayland Academy. Honey, your brother tested so well they're giving him a scholarship!"

"Momma!" Aubrey exclaimed. She closed her eyes and murmured a quick prayer of thanks. "It's wonderful news!"

"Isn't it?" Her mother replied, her voice clogged with tears. "We're touring the campus and checking out the room he'll stay in tomorrow if he's feeling better. Is it any wonder that I forgot to charge my cell phone and it died on me? I was going to call you in a few minutes. How are things, honey?"

Aubrey told her mother about Carson's job offer.

"Thank you, Jesus! Now I've got to sit down!" Anitra Merrill declared. "Did we just slip into *The Twilight Zone*? Except for Wyatt's being under the weather, it seems like things are finally turning around for us. You did accept the man's offer?"

"Yes, pending my lawyer's okay."

The pitch of her mother's voice went up. "What lawyer? When did you get a lawyer?"

"Actually, Chase Everett recommended one and he's reviewing the offer and the employment contract."

"Now Chase is one good man and he's always been firmly in your corner."

"Best boss ever," Aubrey agreed. "Momma, you don't mind about me having to be away from you and Wyatt and live in New York for a while?"

Her mother gasped. "Aubrey Ann Merrill, I always knew you would grow up one day and pursue your own dreams! We all got stuck for a while when we lost Dad and had to fight for Wyatt. Aubrey, you're my star and the sky is the limit, baby. Words can't express how proud I am!"

Aubrey blinked back tears. "Thank you, Momma. I love you."

"Love you too, sweetcakes. I'm here for you, Aubrey, whenever you need me. Wyatt's going to be busy with his new school and new friends, but we can visit on the weekends and holidays. And you can always come home."

"And you know I will," Aubrey said. It struck her that her mother was suddenly facing solitude for the first time in years. "What are you going to do, Momma?"

Her mother sighed. "A lot still depends on Wyatt, but I'm working it out. I'm praying that this time will be different."

"Me too," Aubrey said.

Let me get Wyatt," her mother chuckled. "If you tried his phone, it was dead too. Not because he forgot to charge it, but because he was busy playing video games and watching a movie…"

     ***

Carson MacDonald sat at his private table nibbling on sushi and calamari. A bottle of expensive champagne chilled in a silver bucket set close to the table. The empty gold rimmed champagne glass at Aubrey's place setting and the rapidly cooling calamari seemed to emphasize the fact that she had been gone for at least fifteen minutes. Where the hell was she? Yes, she had to call her mother to head off the news report, but how long did that take? He resisted the urge to glance in the direction of the ladies' room. Aubrey was a big girl, and she knew what the stakes were.

Although they hadn't called for a press conference to promote their new venture, they'd gotten one just the same. If she were the smart and savvy woman he believed she was, she'd make the most of this opportunity.

A woman strolled towards him confidently, drawing his attention and that of several others. It wasn't the phony, model's walk his girlfriend, Giselle used. That walk always made him feel like he was part of a commercial. This woman's walk oozed confidence, power, and enough feminine intrigue to make him lean forward.

As the woman neared, he recognized Aubrey. She'd taken off her suit jacket and jazzed up her hair and makeup. Carson stared, unable to look away. Something about Aubrey Merrill fascinated him and brainy women did not usually interest him. With his need for her skills to run his newly acquired company, he'd chalked the attraction up to her brains and the intelligence that had increased many a fortune. Now Carson wondered if there was more to pull he felt whenever Aubrey was around.

CHAPTER SIX

Two days later Aubrey was seated in the back of a limousine with Crutchfield and Donner emblazoned on the side in discreet gold lettering. As they drove through the streets of New York City, Aubrey stared out, fascinated by everything. Her lawyer had reviewed, and approved Carson's job offer and partnership agreement in a couple of days. Caught up in the whirlwind of Carson's goal to get her onboard as quickly as possible and her need to make a success of her new position, she'd signed the paperwork and started the preparations to stay in New York City. She was living her dream, but she hadn't gotten to the good part yet.

Now she was headed to the corporate apartment she'd be using until she found her own. She didn't need a welcome sign to know she was in New York City. The streets and houses had a distinctiveness all their own. This area that Carson had called the West Village was particularly interesting.

The car turned down Cornelia Street, an intimate, tree-lined street, and stopped in front of an attractive building with alternating patterns of brown and tan checkerboard squares and brown stripes. Assessing the surroundings, Aubrey assured herself that she would get used to the seeming overabundance of gray cement sidewalk. She was used to seeing lots of trees, flowers, and plants. Here, the only dirt with things growing in it, was in the little boxes around the trees lining the street. She saw no flowers or shrubbery.

Bruno, the bodyguard Carson had insisted on, surveyed the area, before they exited the car. Inside the building, the lobby was a study in understated elegance with crystal chandeliers, hardwood floors, and polished brass. The doorman introduced himself and gave

Aubrey the key and directions to the unit owned by Carson's real estate conglomerate. He told them he'd send the manager up to speak with them.

Aubrey used her key with some trepidation. She didn't know what was good by New York standards and if she could afford it. The outside of the building was attractive, but it hadn't impressed her. Despite that, she knew that anything Carson purchased was either worth a lot or had the potential to generate a lot of money. That meant that if she didn't like this place, she definitely couldn't afford anything better.

As the door opened on the condo, her first impression was of a place filled with light. Several large windows provided wonderful views of the city. When Aubrey crossed the hardwood floor of the great room to look out, she saw a landscape filled with buildings of various sizes and shapes, accented with rooftop patios and lots of greenery.

"That's the Freedom Building," Bruno pointed out helpfully, indicating a tall, modern looking structure.

"You mean the Freedom Tower?" she asked, thinking of the World Trade Center.

"Yeah," he confirmed. "And you can see the Empire State Building from the master bedroom.

Trying to imagine herself living in the space, Aubrey walked around the furnished apartment. There was even a small, attached suite complete with kitchenette, bathroom, and separate entrance for the bodyguard. "This add on suite was easier, and Mr. MacDonald didn't want to pay for another apartment for me," Bruno explained.

Although she wouldn't have had the time, expertise, or money to select most of the expensive modern furnishings she saw, Aubrey liked them. No time like the present to begin living her dreams. She stood in the middle of the apartment and did a slow, three-hundred-

and-sixty-degree turn. Yes!

Apparently, the building manager had arrived. A thin, energetic-looking man with large black eyeglasses taking up most of his face was now hovering in the doorway under Bruno's watchful eyes. He introduced himself.

Aubrey greeted him and introduced herself. He responded with a nod and barely audible grunt.

"Does the furniture come with this place?" she asked.

"Everything here belongs to Mr. MacDonald's company," Bruno answered quickly.

"Mr. MacDonald employs an interior design and staging firm for all his properties," the manager replied. "If the style is not to your liking, I can call the company for you. They're pretty responsive. They remodeled this place in a matter of days."

"I like the furniture," she assured him after peeping into the mauve and gray master bedroom and finding a king-sized sleigh bed.

"Good." He stepped forward, entering the condo to hand her a black leather book. "This book has a list of all the people you need to contact for issues related to this condo, its furnishings, and appliances. If all else fails, feel free to contact me."

Aubrey scanned the book filled with names, hours, and phone numbers. If she was supposed to use the book, what did the manager do? "Is there an issue with me contacting you first?"

"No, no," he replied quickly, "but there may be times when I'm occupied with other tenants' issues and I may not respond as fast as you might like."

What a cop out! And in advance! Resisting the urge to roll her eyes, Aubrey decided that if she had a problem with the apartment, she would take her chances and call the manager first.

Thanking the manager, she took his card and slipped it into the back of the book. Her cell phone rang. She checked the display and saw that it was Carson. She switched on the phone. "Good morning, Mr. MacDonald."

"I thought we were past that," he grumbled on the other end of the line.

"Okay, partner," she amended, half kidding, but also a little at a loss as to how to comfortably address her new boss and partner.

Carson failed to respond. His silence had more impact than anything he could have said.

"Carson," she corrected, brightly. She was just going to have to get used to calling her billionaire boss by his first name.

"That's better. How do you like the place?"

"I like it! It's a little sterile looking on the street outside the building. . . ."

"That's a prime area! You'll be surprised to discover some of the VIPs you have for neighbors and it's close to everything," he assured her. "I've stayed there myself."

"Really?" Gazing around the master bedroom, she decided that it did have a masculine edge. "When?"

"I moved to the Upper East Side last month."

Aubrey's gaze swept the apartment with a different focus. She saw clean lines and comfortable, but trendy furnishings.

"You'll have to see my new place sometime," Carson said.

"Yes, I will." Aubrey checked her watch. "We'll be heading to the office in a few minutes."

"Good, but you still have time to unpack your bags! My assistant showed me the interview schedule for this afternoon," he said.

Finishing her call, Aubrey confirmed her bedroom choice and unpacked her bags. Seated on the bed, she appreciated the room that had been decorated in mauve and gray. Her feet rested on a gray checked rug with hints of mauve. It matched the bed covering. The walls were mauve with little dots of gray with a few pictures of New York scattered between shots of people with interesting faces. Gray checked vertical blinds matching the rug and bedspread graced the windows. The long rectangular dresser and tall chest of drawers stood out against the beautiful hardwood floor and would hold all the things she liked to keep in her bedroom. *Yes,* she sighed inwardly, *this place suits me very well.*

Aubrey was grateful that her mother had met the moving company Carson sent to her Chicago apartment and supervised the packing of Aubrey's things. The truck was scheduled to arrive sometime in the evening. Tired of the sparse clothing she'd packed for her Wickerfield meetings, Aubrey eagerly anticipated its arrival.

Quickly freshening up, Aubrey locked the apartment and headed back to the limo with the bodyguard. She felt anxious and excited to get to the office. Until she arrived and officially started work, nothing seemed quite real. Suddenly starving and knowing nothing about the area, she listened to the bodyguard when he suggested a deli where they could pick up a carryout on the way to the office.

Aubrey arrived at the Crutchfield and Donner offices in Manhattan clutching her bag full of corned-beef sandwiches, pickles, potato chips and pop. Her nostrils filled with the fragrant scent of the food, her stomach growling, as she stood on the sidewalk and looked up at the tall building. Several people passed as she counted the windows up the side of the building to the 23rd floor, where the company offices were located.

"Mr. MacDonald's buying the building," the bodyguard told her. He'd been giving her little tidbits of information on the surroundings and answering Aubrey's questions.

Excitement mounting, Aubrey entered the building with the bodyguard, heels tapping against the floor as they strode past the security guards, the information desk, and several people in the cavernous lobby to the bank of elevators. The doors opened on one of them opened with a chime. They got on and Aubrey pressed the button for the 23rd floor.

The elevator doors opened right in front of sparkling glass doors and windows with the Crutchfield and Donner name printed in gold and black letters. A receptionist and a couple of people Aubrey guessed were clerks or secretaries sat at desks in front of a reception area filled with couches, tables, and chairs.

Stepping off the elevator, Aubrey took a few steps and walked into the offices of Crutchfield and Donner at last. Standing in the reception area, she tried to get a feel for the company she would be running. Hunger and exhilaration overwhelmed her, overloading her senses.

Several of the staff members took one look at her and got up to greet her warmly and introduce themselves. Identifying herself as one of Aubrey's executive assistants, a staff member showed Aubrey to her corner office, explaining that it was considered the best available, but there were several others she could choose.

Privacy film-coated floor to ceiling glass windows covered two massive walls in the room. Crossing the ceramic tiled floor, Aubrey took in parts of the New York skyline that she'd only seen in pictures. The furniture was modern, but comfortable looking. As Aubrey settled into her desk chair, the assistant gave her a copy of her schedule for the afternoon, informed her that Carson was working in his office, then left

Aubrey to enjoy her lunch.

Aubrey called her back momentarily to take the extra sandwich, drink, and sides to Carson's office. She didn't know what he liked, but it felt rude to bring food into the office and not consider anyone else.

Using the desk cleaning spray she found in a drawer, Aubrey wiped down the glass top on her desk. The phone on her desk rang seconds later. Lifting the receiver, she spoke into the phone.

Carson's warm voice filled her ear. "Hey Aubrey, thanks for bringing one of my favorite lunches!"

"You're welcome. I didn't think I would be the only starving person in the office."

"Sometimes we order carryout as a group, sometimes people do their own thing, it varies," he explained, "I'd say why don't you join me in the conference room for lunch now, but I need to get through the files one more time before our meeting at two."

Meeting at two? Aubrey scanned her the list of her scheduled appointments for the afternoon. She found the two o'clock meeting with Carson. "Shouldn't I have a copy of those files?" she asked.

"I had Lee place them on the right corner of your desk. It's a blue folder."

Aubrey found the blue folder filled with papers. A little sticky note on the top of files read, Read Me ASAP. "Found it!", she announced brightly, "Since I've got work to do, I'll see you at two."

They ended the call. Aubrey took a precious minute to scan the first few pages in the file. Then hunger took over and she demolished half of the large, corned beef and Swiss cheese sandwich along with a pickle and chips. Coming up for air, she made notes, quickly scanned through the next couple of files and scribbled more notes.

Ten minutes before the scheduled meeting, Aubrey's executive assistant arrived to show her to the conference room. At the two o'clock meeting, Aubrey sat across the conference table from Carson studying her notes on the current employees. Some would be kept, and others would have to find new jobs. She felt a little frazzled, but triumphant. It had taken a good hour and a half to eat her lunch and go through the files for the meeting. She'd have loved more time to review the files but had learned that first impressions were often the right ones.

Aubrey didn't need to look at Carson to feel the impact of his presence in the room. He was a dynamic man and the air seemed to vibrate all around him, as if all the cells in his body were jumping up and down. It took conscious effort to keep herself from staring at him.

Carson told her that he had spoken to a few of the top employee candidates before he'd offered her the CEO position. She knew from personal experience that Carson was very good at figuring people out and recruiting them for his team, but a few of his choices caused concern. One, a very successful market analyst and broker, had come out of a messy divorce and landed in drug rehab.

"Why'd you circle Henry LaRosa's name on the list?" Carson asked, almost as if he'd somehow gleaned the direction of her thoughts.

Aubrey glanced up to meet his dark blue eyes. "Because I thought we should talk about him."

"Because of my notes about his personal situation?"

"Yes." Responding to what seemed like a challenge, Aubrey set her pen down.

"If you fire everyone who has or has had a problem, you wouldn't have very many people working for you. I believe in second chances, especially for top performers," Carson said.

Aubrey smiled. "So do I, but I also believe in limiting my risks."

"Always," Carson countered. "How do you want to apply it here?"

"I want the legal department to put together an agreement that ties his performance and ability to remain drug free to his future with the company. It should be company policy, if not already."

Carson threw her a stubborn look. "I did promise him a job in our company."

"And he'll have one as long as he can continue to perform and stay away from drugs," she said firmly. The she leaned forward, trying to decode the look she saw in Carson's eyes. "You didn't already sign an agreement with him, did you?"

"No. Would it be a problem if I did?"

"No," Aubrey replied smoothly. "Any agreements are subject to company policy, unless written otherwise, right?"

"All right, Ms. CEO." Carson's voice held a trace of humor.

"No issues?" she asked, just to be sure.

"No issues," he assured her, "but I may insist on some changes to company policy when it comes to the real estate investment division."

"I think it would be better if we just came to an agreement on company policy," Aubrey said, determined to keep her voice and tone even.

Carson's brows went up. "Why? I've given you everything to manage except for the real estate division."

Aubrey spoke carefully, trying to be reasonable. "But we're partners and still part of the same organization. Doesn't it make sense to treat everyone the same, subject to the same rules?"

"It does until I need to handle an employee or procedure in a way you don't agree with." Carson tapped a finger on the conference table, subtly indicating that he'd had enough of this conversation.

Deciding to move on, Aubrey suppressed a smile. *Did the man always get his way? Probably.* She found herself wondering how much he'd interfere with her running the company. *Had she been naïve when she believed his promises that she would have full control other than the running of the real estate related work?*

Aubrey checked Henry LaRosa's company performance stats again. He had been very successful until his problems surfaced. When they interviewed him, he was calm, direct, and professional. As soon as Aubrey brought up his past, he took responsibility and promised that it would not happen again. Once she confirmed Carson's previous offer of employment, Aubrey informed Henry that his continued employment would be tied to performance and his ability to stay away from drugs.

After Henry exited the room, Carson's Apple watch started chiming. He stood up. "I've got to go. It's been a long day."

Aubrey checked her list. "We've got two more interviews."

He tugged at his tie, loosening its hold on his neck with a finality that wouldn't be denied. "If you need me to be involved, you'll have to reschedule."

Aubrey read their names out loud. "Any agreements or issues with these two that I should know about?"

"No, and they don't work real estate. See you in the morning." He headed for the door. In the act of opening it, he turned and reminded her that she would be addressing their clients at a dinner meeting in two days.

Excited at the prospect, Aubrey told him that she would be

ready. She'd already started writing her speech. And what about a press conference as the new CEO? The words had barely formed in her mind when realized that Carson had already gone. He'd virtually ran out the door. *Someone's got a hot date!*

Before Aubrey could start her next meeting, the moving company called to say they were an hour away from delivering the things they'd packed at her condo in Chicago. Excited, she called Mira, who had insisted on coming to help her unpack, and arranged for Mira to meet the moving truck and get into Aubrey's new place.

It was getting late. Some of the office staff had already started leaving for the day. Determined not to watch the clock, Aubrey focused on the needs of their new company and proceeded to interview the last two people on the day's list.

Surprisingly, one of them was a writer who had been working in the marketing department. Aubrey quickly reassigned her to writing the speech she would give to their clients as the new CEO.

CHAPTER SEVEN

Going back to the condo in the limousine that evening was an exercise in patience. Gridlocked traffic surrounded them everywhere and people filled the sidewalks. At times, Aubrey felt certain that she could have walked and gotten home much faster. Reclining against the cushy seat, she tried to catch her breath.

More than once, the thought of reviewing some of the work in her briefcase came to mind, but it had been a long day. Dealing with the mountain of boxes most likely filling her front room would take energy she didn't have.

Finally, the car turned down Aubrey's new street and excitement lifted her spirits once more. *New job, new home, new life, I can do this!*

The bodyguard checked things out, then told Aubrey he would be in the studio attached to the condo if she needed him. As Aubrey entered her condo, she spotted Mira in a tank top and designer jeans, with her hair tied up in a bright scarf. Sitting in the front room emptying an open box of books, Mira was directing traffic. She greeted Aubrey with a cheery grin.

Scanning the room quickly, Aubrey saw several boxes, but not floor to ceiling, as she'd imagined. The moving company was gone. A stack of already emptied boxes dominated one corner of the room. A middle-aged woman with dark hair was busy emptying a box of glasses into one of the cabinets. A young man was busy placing one of Aubrey lamps on a table.

"I brought some of our cleaning and maintenance staff," Mira explained, introducing Aubrey to both staff members. "I know you'll want to arrange things your way but figured that getting everything out of the boxes and put away was better than having to deal with it for weeks on end."

"Oh yeah!" Aubrey exclaimed, "I really appreciate your coming to help me like this."

"No problem," Mira assured her. "I want to help you and I need to keep busy. Besides, things get done so much faster when you have help."

"I can pay for their time," Aubrey offered, looking around.

"Don't even try it!" Mira said with a dramatic toss of her head, "I already owe you big time for coming down to help me." She blinked, her eyes misting a bit.

"It's going to be all right," Aubrey assured her.

"No, it's not." Mira shivered and shook her head. "We can talk later, over dinner."

"Okay," Aubrey agreed, still studying her friend. She knew that Mira had gone to meet her estranged husband last weekend at his request. Hearing nothing further, Aubrey had assumed things went well. Then she'd gotten busy with signing the contract and moving to New York and starting her new job.

"I'm thinking that you want these reference books in your office," Mira said, looking down and quickly changing the subject. When Aubrey agreed, Mira directed the young man to place them in the office bookshelves.

Aubrey went into the kitchen and answered the other aide's questions on where she wanted the contents of several boxes to be placed. Then she went to her bedroom and began to unpack her most personal items. It was work, but she was so much further along with Mira and the help she'd brought.

Later that evening Aubrey and Mira sat around the kitchen table with cartons of Chinese takeout food. They'd already sent the aides home and since Mira planned to spend the night, the guards had also retired for the evening.

"What happened when you met Ben?" Mira asked, finally feeling as if they could talk without anyone overhearing them.

"Nothing. He didn't show."

"He didn't show?" Aubrey said, repeating the words she'd heard.

"No." Mira's answered was clipped.

"Did you call him?" Aubrey balanced food on her chopsticks and placed it in her mouth.

"No!" Mira grasped a large section of her hair in her hands and tugged in the gesture she often did when she was nervous or upset. "The last time I saw him he said terrible things. When he called, I was hoping he'd changed his mind, but when he didn't even bother to show up..."

"Something could have happened. He could have been in an accident..."

"No, more likely, he's playing games!" Mira said, lapsing into angry Spanish.

"But if you didn't call..."

"You don't understand," Mira said in an emotion filled voice, "I just couldn't bring myself to tell you everything before, but when I went by the office and finally got to see him, he told me that he didn't love me and never has. It was humiliating and he hurt me more than I can say."

Aubrey dropped her chopsticks. "I don't believe it. Ben loves you." Aubrey would have bet her life on that fact.

Mira shook her head. "That's what I always believed, but Ben's different now. He's cold, and hard. He says it's over." Mira wiped a tear with the back of her hand.

Aubrey found the box of tissues and gave her a wad. Rubbing her friend's shoulder, she asked, "Is there anything I can do?"

Mira shook her head and answered in a tear-choked voice, "Just keep on being my friend."

"Of course," Aubrey said, then added, "Did you get a lawyer?"

Mira sniffled and blew her nose. "I've got it covered. Let's change the subject. What about that hot-looking boss of yours?"

"What about him?" Aubrey went back to her chair and sat down.

"Has he put the moves on you?"

Aubrey went back to eating her pepper steak and rice. "He can't, and it wouldn't be very professional of him if he did."

"But there's a spark between the two of you," Mira insisted.

Aubrey threw her friend a challenging look. "Just because there's a spark doesn't mean there'll be a fire."

"But it's been so long since you even had a spark," Mira insisted, hanging onto the idea.

Aubrey chewed a swallowed a mouthful of food. "To be honest, I don't think I'm his type. You're more his type than I am."

"He's not admiring my brain and singing my praises," Mira reminded her.

"But you saw his girlfriend," Aubrey said sharply.

"Who's on her way out of the picture," Mira shot back.

Surprised, Aubrey looked up from her food. "How can you say that?"

Mira shrugged. "Wasn't it obvious? He wasn't that interested in her. She was window dressing."

"I can't believe you said that." Aubrey set down her chopsticks and closed her food container.

"Sometimes that's all there is in a relationship," Mira insisted.

"You're not comparing you and Ben to Carson and his girlfriend..."

"No! I don't know them." Mira closed her carryout container and looked down at the mostly uneaten food on her plate. "It's become obvious that even though I love Ben, I don't know him either."

Searching for something to say, Aubrey wanted to comfort her friend. She remembered how devasted she'd been when her fiancé ultimately decided to walk away. At the time, there was nothing anyone could say to comfort her. "What are you trying to say?" Aubrey asked, finally.

"I'm saying that when you feel that spark, that connection with someone you like, you should pay attention and check it out, because it can grow into something real and true. Your fiancé didn't deserve you, Aubrey. He's just cleared the way for you to find someone better suited to you."

Thanking her, Aubrey put the leftover food in the fridge. Then she took the plates of the table and got them ready for the dishwasher. "I really appreciate everything you've done today."

"De Nada! You are so welcome!" Mira assured her, "I like to keep busy."

"So where do you want to sleep? There's an extra bedroom down the hall from mine, but it's kind of bare right now. You could also sleep in my office."

Mira chose the bedroom down the hall and both women retired for the evening.

***

Excited about his new pet project with Aubrey at Crutchfield and Donner, Carson spent three or four days a week at that office. He still managed to spend one or two days a week at the offices of his conglomerate, C.M. MacDonald Enterprises. The luxurious offices were at the top of a Manhattan skyscraper several blocks from Crutchfield and Donner.

Arriving early at the offices of his conglomerate, Carson settled in his custom desk chair to peruse the multimillion-dollar agreement scheduled to be finalized and signed today. It involved several business properties and a key parcel of land that would be the centerpiece of a multi-million-dollar development that he'd personally planned.

Opening the security-sealed personal file on his laptop, Carson stared at the planned development. On a lake with a golf course, various income levels of premier housing, retail stores, and restaurants, this project would be one of his greatest accomplishments when complete. Most of the required planning was still in the initial stages, but quite doable. Some permits had already been pulled and contracts signed under a few of his smaller companies.

Tilting his reclining desk chair back, Carson gazed out at the gorgeous Manhattan skyline. Despite the thick privacy glass, morning sun from the window warmed his skin. The day looked sunny and bright. A satisfied smile spread across his face.

This was the kind of deal-making he loved to do. It didn't hurt that he'd moved quickly and quietly to purchase most of the surrounding land. He was paying a fair price for the prime piece included in today's deal, but if they knew of his plans, they'd demand much more.

Carson's stomached rumbled nosily. He'd been too excited to eat before he left his condo. Using the phone on his desk, he ordered a light meal from one of the restaurants on the lower level. Then he scanned the paperwork and went over it in a short meeting with his staff of lawyers, realtors, and executive assistants. Finally satisfied that the paperwork and any potential questions had already been addressed by his staff, he was able to eat the steak and egg breakfast that he'd ordered.

The other team arrived around nine-thirty and began setting up in the larger conference room. Carson joined them at ten. A person who studied people, he picked up on a different vibe from Jerry, the young man who was selling a lot of the property his grandmother had left him.

Instead of being outgoing, friendly, and talkative as he'd been in the previous meetings, Jerry seemed quiet and more introspective. Carson could have taken this as a bit of Jerry's regret at not doing what his grandmother would have wanted with the properties, but Jerry had a hard time meeting his gaze.

"Everything good with you this morning, Jerry?" Carson shook his hand.

"Yeah." Making very brief eye contact, Jerry participated in the handshake, applying minimum pressure, then quickly moved along to the seat he'd taken.

In contrast, Jerry's lawyer and his realtor were more animated than usual. It could be nothing, Carson mused inwardly, but he'd learned to trust his gut.

The meeting began with each group addressing lingering questions. That went smoothly. When Carson's team prepared to print the final documents for the required signatures, Jerry spoke up. "I hate to do this, but we need to renegotiate the price on this deal."

"On the basis of what?" Carson asked.

Jerry nailed him with a hard look. "On the basis of the fact that you're doing a big development in the area and some of the properties we're selling are prime components of that development."

"What C. M. MacDonald Enterprises does with the property after the sale has not been a concern or part of these negotiations," Carson's lawyer stated.

"That's my point," Jerry said, "A new development and my properties being a key part means they're more valuable."

Someone has tipped my hand. Anger caused Carson's temper to skyrocket. Barring the emotion from his expression he asked in an even tone, "Where did you get this information?"

"It doesn't matter," Jerry said, breezing by the question, "Is it true?"

It mattered to Carson. He obviously had a leak in his organization, and he was going to find it and eliminate it. Carson ignored Jerry's question. It wasn't anyone's business what he planned to do with properties he purchased. "Do you have another buyer?" he asked.

Almost smiling, Jerry caught himself. "We've gotten another offer for some of the properties."

"Which ones?" Carson asked.

Jerry named the property at the center of Carson's deal and one adjacent to it.

"What do you want for it?" Carson asked, getting to the point.

Jerry named a figure that was several thousand dollars more than they agreed on.

Carson felt like he was the bull and someone had waved a red flag in his face. He wanted to charge, to roar with rage. He knew that he'd probably turned red. "I'll need to discuss this with my staff," he said, getting to his feet. "Let's take a twenty-minute break. My staff, meet me in the executive conference room in two minutes."

Minutes later, Carson and his staff talked about the agreement changes. "I don't have to tell you all how angry I am," he said. "We have a leak in this organization and I'm going to find it. Confidentiality is a requirement for employment here and this fiasco is cutting into company profits. I want the names of everyone who's worked on this project."

One of the executive assistants nodded and started tapping away on her laptop.

"Can you do the development without the property in question?" his lawyer asked.

Carson tapped the table with the ball of his hand. "Yes, but it will lose some of its appeal and who knows what someone might build next to it and bring down the value."

"So, we're going to agree to paying more?" his realtor interjected.

"Yes." Carson nodded. "They've got us on this one. If I have to, I'll give them a little more, but they must sign the contracts today. I don't let crap like this go on for extended periods."

Shortly afterward both groups reconvened, and Carson offered a small increment on the figure Jerry had named for the properties provided that the contracts were signed immediately. When Jerry hesitated, Carson informed him that if the contracts were not signed today, all deals were off the table.

Jerry signed the contracts reluctantly. Both groups shook hands on the deal then dispersed.

Later, Carson sat at his desk stewing over what had happened. Someone had it in for him. They'd used his business information to increase the cost of his project. They'd even made a counteroffer on properties he's personally scouted. Either his old adversaries were trying new methods, or he had managed to make a new one. Either way, he had a traitor in his camp.

This incident was bigger than someone leaking the news that he'd bought Crutchfield and Donner and was signing Aubrey to run it as CEO, but it was along the same lines. Someone that he thought was in his corner was in fact actively working against him. He thought of several other questionable instances and decided that he might need internal and external help on this one. Opening a desk drawer, he searched for the card of the private detective a friend had recommended.

***

It was another day and early in the morning. Aubrey had an assistant, but she liked the ritual of getting her own coffee. She was in the breakroom, fixing her coffee when Carson came to get coffee.

"Any coffee left?" he asked, sounding more than a little tired.

Aubrey realized that she was blocking his view of the coffee pot. "There's plenty!" She shifted sideways to clear the pathway. Apparently,

Carson wasn't moving very fast this morning. She miscalculated on the timing it would take for him to pass and bumped into him. It was like hitting a solid wall of hot male. Seeing that the man was in great shape was an entirely different experience compared to colliding with the indisputable evidence. *So, this is what they mean when they go on and on about beefcake!* "Excuse me!" Aubrey exclaimed.

Carson threw her a look of mild annoyance. Then he nodded. His navy-blue eyes were as gorgeous as ever, but there were threads of red in the whites of his eyes. Studying him discreetly, Aubrey decided that he was most likely hungover from the night before.

"Are you always this cheerful and bubbly in the morning?" He growled then winced.

She couldn't resist a smile. "Actually, yes. Especially when I've got the dream job!"

"Then have a little consideration for the rest of us and keep the volume down," he grumbled as he lifted the pot and poured himself a cup.

"Hard night?" she asked, surprising herself with the familiarity of her statement. She hadn't meant to imply anything by the statement, but it hung on the air, conjuring all kinds of visions in her mind.

"Actually, yes," he said.

Stirring cream and sugar into her coffee, Aubrey bit back a smart remark. She could just imagine his "hard night." She knew it was wrong, but her eyes zeroed in on his fine rear, nicely displayed in his custom suit, then traveled upward to his handsome head bent over his coffee cup. His body displayed the results of a man who spent time exercising.

Carson McDonald was seriously sexy! His midnight blend of waves and curls had just the right amount of disarray. She wondered what it would feel like to touch his hair, wished she could. Though a lot of people paid good money to look like he did, many of them didn't make it!

He must have sensed her scrutiny or felt the weight of her gaze, because he glanced up and caught her staring. "Something tells me that you have a wonderful imagination."

"And that something would be right," she quipped, "But don't worry, I'll keep my imagination to myself."

"I had a charity event and a real estate closing," he explained, "and then the. . .uh usual Wednesday night date."

The usual? Aubrey wanted to pull her brows down because she was sure they gone up. So, Wednesday was hump day for Carson? Had Giselle worn him out? "A little hungover?" Aubrey muttered, under her breath.

"It's that obvious?" Carson met her gaze.

"Yes, it is," she answered, lowering her tone.

"I'll take something for it," he said, his voice resolute.

Aubrey flashed him a sympathetic smile. "I won't ask you for much today," she promised softly as she turned and headed back to her office.

"I don't need you to go easy on me, I'm here to work!" Carson called after her.

Safely back inside her office, Aubrey yielded to a bout of silly giggles. She liked Carson. He just added that extra bit of fun to an office. And he was smart too! What more could a girl want?

Hours later, Aubrey started her shutdown process for the day a little early. Although New York was known as one of the top places for a shopping trip, she hadn't ventured out. Most of her time in her new city had been spent getting the office and her new condo set up.

At one point she contemplated asking Mira for help, but her friend was moody and absorbed with the loss of her husband. Aubrey tried to help, but sometimes dealing with Mira was too mentally exhausting. In the effort to find a solution, Aubrey had asked the company staff and obtained a list of stores and boutiques where she might find a suitable outfit for her dinner meeting with the clients their office managed.

Staring at the stores and shops on the list, Aubrey recognized several of the designer names and specialty stores. She wondered if she could afford anything they might have. Yes, Carson paid her a wonderful salary and had slathered on many juicy benefits, but sooner or later, she'd have to pay for a place to stay and give up the limo ride to and from work each day. New York was a high rent district.

Someone knocked on her office door. Surprised, Aubrey stared at it for a moment. She wasn't expecting anyone and the last time she'd seen Carson, he'd been in his office negotiating a big real estate deal. It was probably the bodyguard, she decided since he would have to accompany her on her shopping trip. "Door's open, come in," she called out.

The door opened, and Carson leaned in. "Did you get something to wear to the dinner meeting tomorrow?" he asked.

"I was planning on leaving early to go shopping," she admitted.

Carson looked amused. "No pressure, but I have someone I'd like you to meet."

"Now?"

"Yes, now. It will help with your present situation."

Deciding to play along, she asked, "Your office or mine?"

A hint of a smile played on his lips. "How about the executive conference room? There'll be room to spread out there."

Spread out? Aubrey followed Carson to the executive conference room. A tall, slender woman dressed to the nines in a dark red designer suit and matching heels that looked like they cost a week's salary, stood near the conference room window. Her sandy brown hair was almost light enough to be called dark blonde and was cut and shaped in a sophisticated pixie style. Dark, doe-like eyes regarded Aubrey with admiration as the woman introduced herself as Sasha Garren.

"Sasha's brother is my tailor and one of my favorite designers." Carson explained, "Sasha designs sportswear at one of the local design houses but hasn't been able to get an audience for her personal designs."

"You have such presence and style. I saw you on the news with Carson, trying not to talk about being the new CEO and I imagined what you would wear to your meeting with the clients. This is what I came up with." Sasha opened the portfolio on the conference table to remove a sketch and offer it to Aubrey.

Accepting the sketch, Aubrey stared at it. The model even looked like her. The outfit was a very sassy version of the body hugging little black dress and ended just above the model's knees. Rhinestone grommets accented the shoulders and ran down to the waist, giving the impression of a jacket that culminated in a peplum ruffle at the waist. The peplum had been designed in such a way that it did not interfere with the frontal silhouette of her curves. The added material did stand out from the dress, adding to the overall hint of a jacket.

Carson leaned closer to get a look over Aubrey's shoulder and said, "Sasha, this is one of your best."

Beaming with pride, Sasha thanked him and turned her attention back to Aubrey. "It's silk jersey. I guessed your size. Do you like it?"

"Yes, it's gorgeous!" Excited, Aubrey couldn't take her eyes off the design. It was what she had been hoping to find. It wasn't a dinner suit, but close enough. It didn't look slutty or have that closed-down, covered-up look that many evening suits projected. It would make her look like a smart businesswoman, but also glamorous and sexy.

"You would wear your hair up, like in the picture and your shoes. . . ."

Aubrey stared at the high-heeled evening sandals in the sketch. "Are those Manuelos?"

The woman smiled. "No, but they look like it, don't they?"

Carson cleared his throat and stood. "Aubrey, Sasha has a proposal for you. She would like to design clothes for your major meetings and media events."

Aubrey turned to look at Sasha. "Can I even afford you?"

"I'm sure I have some things you can afford," Sasha said quickly. "I've going to give you a big discount on that dress. You can wear most of the clothes I'll design and have them cleaned and returned after the event. I ask that you tell others how much you like my designs, keep some of my cards, and give them to others when asked."

"So, my wearing the clothes..."

"It would be an advertisement, and you would look like you spent a million bucks on your clothes. Yet you'd still have most of your money in your pocket," Carson explained.

Aubrey glanced back at the sketch. "It sounds like a deal!"

Carson nodded. "It is. I've got to go now, but I think you two need to talk specifics."

Both women agreed. As Sasha removed another sketch from her portfolio, Carson hurried out.

Aubrey did her best at pretending not to notice Carson running off for another hot date. If wasn't as if he were her boyfriend leaving her to work while he went on a date. Still, it affected her and took a lot of the energy from the room.

"Did you need him for something?" Sasha asked astutely. "He's usually very good about taking care of business."

Aubrey met Sasha's curious gaze, determined to act professionally. "No, I don't need him to do anything. He's taken care of all his office business for the day."

She studied the sketch of the dream dress once more. "Is it possible for me to get this dress for my dinner meeting tomorrow?"

"Of course. I actually had it made and brought it for you to try, just in case I needed to make a few alterations." Sasha pointed to a stack of boxes on the conference table.

"Oh snap!" Aubrey stood and began to delve into the boxes. "I hope it fits," she muttered, opening the biggest box, and drawing the silk knit cocktail dress from the tissue paper.

Sasha eyed Aubrey's form critically. "I think it's going to fit."

Moments later, Aubrey tried on the dress in the private bathroom adjacent to her office. It fit like a glove. The shoes Sasha provided fit too. There was even a matching clutch.

Aubrey felt like Cinderella except that she wouldn't have a prince for this "ball". Hurt when her fiancé deserted her, dating became almost nonexistent. She couldn't even think of borrowing Carson because his girlfriend Giselle, was sure to come.

Inwardly, Aubrey chastised herself. She didn't need a man to appreciate her. Then of course, there would probably be no dancing. Unlike Cinderella, who had only herself to think about while she attended the ball, Aubrey needed to make the clients feel comfortable about her being CEO and running the company. Carson had booked a top restaurant for several hours and was treating their clients to dinner.

"I love this dress!" Doing her imitation of the model presentation spin on the high heels for Sasha, Aubrey touched her ears. "No earrings?"

Sasha assessed her look. "Something big that sits on the ear. I didn't see anything I liked for you. Do you have pair that might work?"

Aubrey shook her head. "No, I tend to go too conservative when it comes to jewelry because I haven't gotten out much in the past few years." Realizing that she'd given away a little too much information, she added, "I think it should be something that stands out without being gaudy."

Still assessing, Sasha inclined her head. "I agree. Let's both look for something unique. Your ears are pierced. I have a few possibilities that would work if all else fails." She handed Aubrey a little card compact. "Here are my cards. Call me if you find something. I'll do the same."

Then Sasha explained how she would work with Aubrey and meet with her to plan outfits in advance of her events, then schedule for the fitting, and help her perfect her look on the special days. "You're going to get tired of me!" she joked.

"I don't think so," Aubrey said, "I like nice clothes, but I don't have the glam gene. I haven't had the time to devote to looking my best in quite a while. Do you have my address?"

Sasha smiled. "Yes, Carson stayed there for a couple of years. We've known Carson since he hung out with my brother in college."

"Okay." Aubrey wanted to say more, wanted to ask about Carson and his past, but she kept the questions and comments to herself. Hopefully, she would be around to get to know Carson. She especially hoped there would be a future that included a personal relationship.

When Aubrey left the office for the evening, she had a smile on her face, extra pep in her step, and a second draft of her speech. The empty-handed bodyguard led the way to the waiting limousine, citing his need to keep his hands free in the interest of protecting Aubrey. One of Aubrey's assistants carried several boxes from Sasha.

***

Aubrey knew from experience that hard work more than anything else ensured success. Home in her condo apartment at last, hours later, she practiced the speech she would give to the clients several times. One of her staff members had done an excellent job of shaping Aubrey's ideas and the points she wanted to make into a coherent and impressive speech. When Aubrey felt confident in her delivery, she began recording her run through and then modifying it based on her impressions and thoughts of what she heard. She was about ready to throw in the towel when her phone rang.

Aubrey startled, her heart pounding as fear rose. *Wyatt!* Concerned for her brother who was still not feeling as well as he should, she grabbed her cell phone and checked the display. It was Carson! When she answered the phone, his warm, rich voice brought the usual excitement. There was a slight difference in the strength of his tone, as if he might be lying down.

"Hey, with the big day tomorrow, I figured you wouldn't be asleep. How's it going?"

"Everything's good."

"You don't sound good. What's wrong?"

Aubrey let her breath out slowly. "When the phone rang, I thought you were my mother, calling about Wyatt. He hasn't been feeling well and they haven't been able to find anything wrong."

"Sorry I scared you."

"I've already recovered, and I'm all set for tomorrow except for a few minor things I need for my outfit."

As usual, Carson zeroed in on the most important thing. "Are you happy with your spiel? Is it ready?"

"Yes. I've been practicing."

"Are you nervous?"

"Yes, because this is so important. I've got to nail it."

"You will. I picked you. You're not a failure. I don't make that kind of mistakes," he asserted confidently. "If it would help, you could pitch it to me."

"Tonight?" Aubrey checked the kitchen clock. It was ten-thirty.

"No, next week!" Carson joked.

"It would make me feel better," she admitted, "but it's kind of late."

"Wake up the bodyguard and meet me at the coffee shop around the corner," he said, insistence in his tone.

"Let's just wait until morning," she suggested.

Carson grew more insistent. "If you forgot to cover something or you need to make some major changes, you're not going to have a lot of time to take care of it tomorrow," he reminded her. "And did you forget we have some potential client meetings scheduled?"

Aubrey sighed. She didn't feel like going out. She was tired and knew that if she met Carson and drank coffee she might never get to sleep. "Just come on over."

"You sure?" Carson's voice held a hint of surprise.

"Yeah, we can have a meeting at the kitchen table."

"There is a well-equipped office on the other side of the kitchen," he noted.

"Just come on over." Aubrey repeated. "We can have a meeting at the kitchen table."

"Give me fifteen minutes." Carson ended the call.

Fifteen minutes! Aubrey assessed her outfit. She needed to change clothes. As much as she liked Carson and found herself starting to use him to fuel a few fantasies, it would hardly be professional to meet him in her nightgown. Sure, she wore a robe too, but it was much too provocative for a business meeting. Aubrey hurried to change.

***

Carson felt restless. Usually, a short weeknight out followed by energetic sex with Giselle mellowed him. But lately, it hadn't been working. He chalked his restlessness up to his new venture with Aubrey. Together, they were an unstoppable brain trust in the world of real estate and financial investments. The future stretched before them, filled with tempting possibilities that occupied his mind.

Not up to sitting in the back of the limo, Carson drove his Maserati, leaving one of his bodyguards to follow in a separate car. He knew that his insistence on hearing in advance the speech Aubrey would give to their clients amounted to hand-holding that she probably didn't need. But she hadn't asked, he'd offered. He was invested in her success and dammit, he wanted everyone to know how good she was.

He turned down Aubrey's street and parked in his old spot. Although he still liked the area, coming back to his old condo felt weird. The doorman greeted him and his bodyguards by name. By the time they stepped into the elevator, he was slipping into old habits. He hit the button for Aubrey's floor.

The door opened, and the scent of coffee, vanilla, and jasmine filled his nostrils. With her hair down around her shoulders, Aubrey stood in the doorway in a pair of black jeans and a jewel encrusted black tank top. He had only seen her in business clothing, covered up. Carson stared, unable to take his eyes off the rich brown skin the top revealed. Her skin reminded him of buttered toffee. His mouth watered.

"Hi. Come on in," Aubrey said, opening the door wider to let them in. "You know where the kitchen is."

Closing and locking the door, she followed them on bare feet. Carson studied those too, noting the deep purple polish on her pretty toes. *Somebody has a thing for purple.*

"Coffee?" Aubrey asked, "Its decaf, but I can make some regular if it won't keep you up.

"Decaf is fine," Carson answered. Then he noticed that she'd also made coffee for the guards, sliced some fruit, and put it out along with some nuts, chips, and cookies. "What's this? Southern hospitality?"

Aubrey smiled. "My momma hails from Georgia, but I was born in Detroit, Michigan. Anyway, she taught me that you should always have something to offer guests."

"When I was a kid, my momma always said that the apples don't fall far from the tree," Carson mused, pouring himself a cup of coffee, and adding the cream and sugar.

Aubrey nodded. "I'll take that as a compliment."

"As it was meant," Carson assured her. He prompted his bodyguards to help themselves to food and then join Aubrey's bodyguard in giving them some privacy.

"Other than Mira's coming to help me get things in order, you're the first to visit me here," Aubrey said, when they were alone.

Carson quickly squelched any rising feelings of guilt. This was about business. He'd handed Aubrey a great opportunity. Furthermore, she was a big girl, capable of making her own decisions and bearing the consequences. "I'm not surprised. I know your friend, Mira, lives relatively close. How is she?"

Looking a little troubled beneath her professional demeanor, Aubrey shook her head. "Things aren't good between her and Ben. She's thrown herself into her work to take her mind off the problems."

"That's too bad."

"To the first of many visitations," he said tapping his cup of decaf against hers in a toast.

"I hope so," she confided. "I spend most of my time working, so it's not usually a big issue. But here at the condo, I miss Momma and Wyatt."

"There's nothing keeping you from taking a flight back to Chicago this weekend to visit. Just so you're back before Monday," he added. "Maybe they'd like to visit you. You could show them New York."

Aubrey looked a little uncomfortable. "I don't know much about New York, yet."

"Then you need to learn, especially since our home office is here. You could book a private tour."

"I-I'll think about it." Aubrey grabbed her folder and stood. "If we keep chatting like this, you'll be here all night," she remarked.

The words bounced around in Carson's head, stirring his imagination. *Him? All night at Aubrey's place? And what would they get into?* His imagination ventured into dangerous territory and lingered. Except for some friendly banter, he'd kept things strictly professional between them.

He wasn't usually attracted to brainy women, but something about Aubrey drew him, and made him want to be around her. She wasn't gorgeous in the supermodel sense of the word, but her soft, full lips looked like they were made for kissing, and her big brown eyes made him think of melted chocolate. The jeans and tank top revealed the lush curves she'd been hiding beneath her power suits.

Aubrey caught him staring. She met his gaze and smiled. Was there just a little bit of naughtiness in that smile? He considered the thought that he might be projecting on her, seeing what he wanted to see. Carson found himself wondering if a brainy woman could be better at being naughty.

Behind a makeshift podium consisting of a vegetable bin placed on the kitchen table, she began her speech. "Good evening, I'm Aubrey Merrill, the new CEO for Crutchfield and Donner. I have an MBA from MIT and I have an extensive background in wealth management and portfolio growth. There's a copy of my resume in the company folder at each of your place settings. I'm proud and honored to have been selected for this position, and excited to stand before you and talk about our very profitable future."

Carson's thoughts moved past her appearance to focus on her words. *She was good, damned good.* By the time she'd finished her speech, he was on his feet and clapping. "Fantastic! I don't see how you could make it any better! It's got the right amount of humility, strength, and savvy to knock their socks off!"

Aubrey smiled with a flash of teeth. "Thanks!"

"I didn't need to come tonight. I think I've wasted your time and mine," Carson mused, half to himself.

She placed a hand on his arm. "You helped, a lot. I appreciate it. Thanks for making sure the speech was all it needed to be. I know you have an interest in what I do because you have invested heavily in me and this company. I want you to know that I will not let you down."

Carson inclined his head in agreement. "No, you won't. Now I'm leaving so you can get some sleep."

CHAPTER EIGHT

During the pre-dinner cocktail hour at a fabulous New York restaurant the next day, Carson, Aubrey, and the restaurant's host formed a casual reception line and greeted each client as they entered and introduced themselves. Dressed in suits and evening wear, many seemed pleased with the choice of establishment, which rotated on top of a popular New York skyscraper. Pleasantly surprised as the cocktail hour advanced, Carson noted that at least ninety-five percent of those invited had arrived.

Making the rounds to chat with their clients and make them feel welcome and appreciated, Carson and Aubrey worked together for a time, then they split over to cover more of their guests. Because this evening was so important, Carson wanted to stay mentally sharp. He limited himself to one drink. He knew that Aubrey was making do with a cola.

Interacting with people and getting them to trust and like him was one of Carson's gifts. He knew that Aubrey's gifts were more cerebral since she'd spent most of her professional life behind the scenes, but it wasn't evident as she confidently worked the room, smiling, laughing, chatting with their clients.

Clothed in the black, rhinestone enhanced dress Sasha had

designed with a flap just below the waist, Aubrey almost appeared to be wearing an evening suit. She'd pinned her hair up, and diamond crusted disks sparkled in her ears. The overall effect was that Aubrey looked beautiful and fully capable of running a multimillion-dollar wealth management company. So far, she done nothing but add to the mounting evidence that he'd made a phenomenal choice for CEO of Crutchfield and Donner.

"It's very progressive of you to select a black female CEO," one of the clients said, eyes brimming with curiosity.

"It's not about being progressive," Carson answered, "I had specific requirements and she was the best person for the job. You'll get to see that for yourself," he added confidently. He'd expected a few comments from the clients but nothing he and Aubrey couldn't handle because the CEOs of most of the major companies were white males, and Aubrey was black and female. As he worked the room, he kept track of Aubrey, the clients, and the fancy crystal clock on the wall.

A little later, Carson conversed with another client, his gaze sweeping the room for early signs of issues or problems that might need to be addressed. Aubrey was usually included in his checks because she was new, exciting, and he liked to see how she worked her magic.

Facing Carson, Aubrey was talking with an older woman on the other side of the restaurant. Abruptly, he saw Aubrey's smile freeze, then fade to be replaced by a determinedly polite and professional expression. The gray-haired, heavyset woman chatting with Aubrey wore a navy satin evening dress with impressive looking diamonds sparkling at her throat, ears, wrists, and fingers. Carson had quietly purchased the business and met only a few of the clients, so he found himself wondering, who was that woman and what had the woman said to Aubrey?

The client with Carson turned her head to follow the direction of his attention. She studied Aubrey and the other client for a moment, then her nose wrinkled. "That's Auxsana Paxley, of the Paxley Department Stores," his client said, answering part of Carson's unasked question. "That woman never has a kind word for anyone."

Had his client answered the other part of his question too? As he'd learned the hard way, people would always do and say whatever they wanted, especially when they were spending their money. It wasn't as if he could protect Aubrey from nasty clients and comments. Carson knew that Aubrey had been in business long enough to grow a hard shell and was more than capable of taking care of herself.

He quickly decided that the best thing he could do was not comment. Returning his attention to the client at his side, he said, "Forgive me for being a little distracted. I'm so glad I got the chance to speak with you. Do you have any questions or issues we need to focus on?"

"No, I don't have any questions or issues," his client replied, taking Carson's hand and patting it gently amid a flash of diamonds. "I do have a comment though." Leaning forward with a big smile she said, "Good job on your new CEO! I did my research. The woman's a genius and worth every penny we're paying. Probably more."

Suppressing a laugh, Carson allowed his lips to curve upward. "I'm glad you approve of my choice."

The client nodded and added, "I know that ultimately, we're not all here and letting your company manage our wealth because we like or dislike anyone. We want good results. We want to see our money grow."

"And it will," Carson assured her. As he moved on to continue circulating, he saw that Aubrey was already talking to someone else. The dinner chimes began to ring. Everyone headed for their assigned tables.

Carson sat at the head table with Aubrey and their clients with the largest holdings invested with Crutchfield and Donner. Not surprisingly, both Auxsana Paxley and the client who had complimented Carson earlier on his choice of CEO were seated with them. Conversation flowed agreeably as they dined on a sumptuous meal of New York Strip Steaks, Chilean Sea Bass, salad, garlic whipped potatoes, and grilled Italian vegetables.

After dinner, Carson gave a few remarks then talked about his thoughts and goals when he purchased the company and selected a CEO to run it. Afterward, he presented Aubrey to their clients.

As he'd predicted, Aubrey's get-acquainted-talk with the clients as the new CEO of the company went very well. She looked stunning as she spoke to a rapt audience at the dinner meeting, and the planned question and answer period went over by more than an hour. They loved her!

Carson cruised through the rest of the meeting on the buoyant cloud of success. When the last client departed, Carson took Aubrey's hand and shook it enthusiastically as the restaurant staff hurriedly worked at returning the restaurant to normal. "Great job! I knew you could do it! I knew they would love you."

Aubrey smiled, returning his handshake. Her fingers felt warm against his. "I did my best." She sighed. "I'm glad that's over!"

"Me too, partner," Carson said. "Toast?"

At Aubrey's nod, Carson signaled one of the waiters, who brought a bottle of champagne and a couple of glasses. When the waiter finished filling the glasses, Carson took one and gave the other to Aubrey. "To Crutchfield and Donner."

Touching her glass to his, Aubrey repeated the toast. She took a couple of sips and set the glass down. "Wonderful champagne."

Carson nodded, taking the time to finish his. He felt like talking and enjoying the success they'd just experienced. "Any issues or concerns?" he asked.

Aubrey finished her champagne, looking content. "No, everything went pretty much as planned."

"More champagne?" Carson asked, when the waiter returned to refill their glasses.

"No, I'm saving myself for work tomorrow," Aubrey said regretfully.

"I saw you talking to Auxsana Paxley," Carson remarked, watching Aubrey's soft lips tighten. He wondered what she would say.

Aubrey met his inquisitive gaze. "And?"

Carson shrugged. "Nothing, I guess. I noticed that something she said changed your demeanor."

Aubrey sighed softly. "I've got to work on that."

"What did she say?" Carson prodded curiously.

"I wasn't going to bring this up," Aubrey said, pausing as if to choose her words carefully. "She questioned whether I, as a person of color, would be able to handle the job of CEO and insure the growth of client holdings."

"Wow!" Carson's brows went up. He hadn't expected anyone to get quite that nasty. "What did you say?"

"The same thing I'd say to anyone who was concerned about how their money would be handled," Aubrey replied calmly. "I have exceeded the amount of education required to do the job, and my record in the field of wealth management speaks for itself."

Well, she handled that! As a person who had started out in real estate development and sales while he was still in high school, Carson knew how it felt to be counted out because of appearances. Inwardly, he acknowledged that his experience wasn't the same as being thought less of because of his skin color, but youth was another delimiter people used to deny opportunity to others. "Well said," Carson said.

Aubrey nodded. "I'm glad you think so."

"I happy with everything that's gone down since you signed that contract," Carson said, with a bit of a grin, "It just makes me anticipate the future that much more."

Aubrey's responding soft musical laughter drew his attention. He listened, lost in the unique sound.

"It's getting late," she said, eyeing the clock on the one of the walls. "I've got to get home."

"Okay." Carson noticed that the restaurant staff had almost returned the restaurant to its normal state.

Aubrey gathered her belongings and signaled her bodyguard in an efficient flurry of movement. "I'm leaving now. See you in the morning."

"See you in the morning," Carson repeated. He'd barely finished his sentence when the Aubrey cleared the exit. He wasn't used to working so closely with women as brainy and business-like as she was. Yes, he had male and female assistants and associates, but Aubrey was different.

Only a few days had passed since the meeting, but the positive impact on the number of their clients was undeniable. Some who had been on the fence, decided to stay. A few clients who had moved on, decided to come back.

Determined to get out of the office but too keyed up to go home after a long day, Aubrey and Carson ended up at the coffeeshop around the corner from her condo to talk about what had happened and decompress. It was the perfect neutral spot.

Aubrey had kicked off her heels and was resting her feet on the chair beside him. When Carson glanced down, he got a partial view of shapely brown legs, and long, pretty feet with petal pink polish.

He wasn't a foot man, but the sight of them drew his attention. His hands itched to touch them, but touching was off limits when it came to employees and associates. That meant he ignored the sparks between Aubrey and himself. It also meant he ignored the fact that her feet were tired, and he knew how to give a good foot massage.

"That was some quick thinking and you executed some seriously smooth moves," Carson told Aubrey. Seated across from her at the tiny table, he slumped back in his chair and cupped his hands around a hot mug of coffee.

Aubrey smiled. "Thanks, but I couldn't let our client just walk away like that."

"But the personalized plan you had for his assets, the rates, the risks, everything... It was right on the money."

"It's what I do, and I've brought that to the team," Aubrey explained between sips of sweetened Colombian decaf, "I'm always looking for a less risky way for my clients to build their wealth."

"Some of the account work must have fallen by the wayside when the company founders' issues became too much, and things started falling apart."

"Obviously," Aubrey said, nodding in agreement. "I split all our client files among the four teams. Each team has been charged with studying their files, analyzing the current portfolio holdings considering the client goals and current wisdom. We do account reviews every Tuesday and Thursday to assess our successes and develop a plan B for each account."

Carson's gaze was filled with admiration. "So, you just happened to have finished analyzing his account?"

Aubrey nodded again. "We got lucky. That evaluation was completed a couple of days ago."

"Thank God for that!" Carson pressed his back to the hard wood behind him, "He was one of our customers with the largest holdings. I wonder what got him so riled up?"

Aubrey shrugged. "Who knows?"

Carson could tell she was tired. Her eyelids seemed heavy and most of her decaf remained in the cup.

"One of our competitors could have bent his ear," Carson suggested, "Pointing out our weaknesses..."

"We don't have any weaknesses," Aubrey said quickly.

"No, we don't," he agreed.

"And we're the best!" she added.

"Yes, ma'am." Carson gave her a mock salute.

Aubrey yawned, covering her mouth with the tips of her fingers. "If I'm to get up in the morning and do this all over again, I need to get home."

"Yes, you're right." Carson agreed reluctantly. Something about Aubrey made him want to hang around. He liked getting her opinion on some of his ideas too. "Let's head home," he said, signaling the bodyguards.

***

Carson took the time to have breakfast in his kitchen before he went into work. He'd already dismissed his chef and finished his steak and eggs and was enjoying the last few sips of gourmet coffee with the morning paper when Giselle wandered down the stairs.

She didn't live in the condo with him, but often spent the night and some weekends there. It was usually a good thing, but lately, her presence was beginning to chafe his nuts because she had become too clingy and hard to deal with. He didn't know why she'd changed on him, but he didn't like it.

He watched her glide across the ceramic tile floor, a vision of beauty in Victoria's Secret lace and mink puffed mules. "About to leave for work?" she asked as she reached the table.

Carson checked his watch. "I've got about ten minutes."

She pushed aside the newspaper and moved in to plant her shapely, silk-covered rear in his lap. He inhaled the complex blend of flowers, citrus fruit, and woody vanilla scent she wore. Today it bordered on cloying.

"Do you have time for a quickie?" she asked, rubbing herself against him.

"Not if I do it right." Carson's replied in a low voice. He met her gaze head-on, not missing the determination in the depths of her beautiful eyes.

She pulled his head down for a warm, lingering kiss, then rested her head against his chest. "I know you've been working hard with the company, your clients and your new real estate deals. I'm sorry for being so . . . bitchy lately."

Threading his fingers through her silken red hair and curving his fingers around her angular face, he tilted her chin up. "Can you explain why you've been so difficult?"

Her green eyes were luminous. "I feel you slipping away from me. You're spending less time with me and even when we're together, you're not thinking about me. What's even worse, you take me home from a date to go talk business with Aubrey."

Carson hugged her closer. "Giselle, I apologize if you feel I've neglected you, but you know my work comes first. I've invested heavily in Crutchfield and Donner and I'm doing everything in my power to ensure its success. Would you be so concerned if Aubrey were a man?"

Giselle slanted him a glance. "No, I wouldn't be concerned, because I know how much you love women!"

Startled, Carson studied Giselle's cat-like expression. She'd taken a dislike to Aubrey from the beginning.

"Why do you dislike Aubrey so much?"

Giselle stared back, hints of defiance in her green gaze, her lips pouty with a hint of anger. "I've seen you work with the other women in your offices. You don't see them. They're just people who do a job, but you look at her like she's a ten-carat diamond, or the best thing since sliced bread!"

Stunned, Carson wondered briefly, *Could Giselle's accusation be true?* He quickly dismissed the thought. "She's actually quite intelligent and something of a genius," Carson shot back before he could stop himself, "She's also not my type."

Giselle wiggled provocatively in his lap. "Maybe you're changing your taste in women?"

"No, you're still my type," he assured her, with an appreciative look. He liked looking at Giselle and spending pleasurable times with her. Aubrey intrigued him, but not in the same way, and he wasn't one to mix business and pleasure.

"We probably should have discussed this more, but I'm going to be extremely busy with the company for at least the next six months. Do we need a time out?"

"No!" she said, clinging to him, "You know I feel about you! I want to be with you!"

"But I won't have a lot of time to devote to you and when you're unpleasant, it just makes things worse."

"Then I won't be bitchy," she said brightly.

Carson eyed her skeptically. "Can you do that?"

"I can try. What more could you ask for?"

"I can ask that you be successful at it," he replied succinctly. He wished she could find a way to be more agreeable.

Giselle flashed him an angelic smile. "I love you, Carson!"

He didn't believe her and didn't know how to respond. They'd agreed to a fun and sex relationship without strings. Now she was saying she loved him. Could Giselle be trying to change the game? "Love? As in mister and misses?" he managed.

"Yes," she answered, pressing a kiss to his lips, "Are you proposing?"

"No." Carson sharpened his gaze. She was kidding, but beneath her cavalier manner, serious purpose and intent lurked. "Didn't we agree to just have fun and enjoy each other?"

"Yes, I agreed to the arrangement, but how could I know you'd be so lovable? My feelings have changed."

Carson pushed back at a rising tide of unpleasant emotion. He tried to name it. Fear? Annoyance? Guilt? Maybe a little of all three. "You are beautiful, and I like being with you. I'm just not ready to be serious with anyone right now," he said as gently as he could. "We should go back to seeing other people."

Giselle's fingers curled around the lapels of his shirt. "Don't punish me for being honest with you!"

"That's not my intent." He tried to gently nudge her off his lap. It didn't happen until he was almost standing. "I'm being honest with you. I don't want to lead you on."

A tear slipped down her flushed cheeks.

Knowing that he'd hurt her, Carson rubbed her shoulder gently and gave her a quick hug. "I've got to get to work now. We can discuss this over dinner tonight."

She nodded, stubborn hope still glittering in the depths of her eyes as he made his getaway.

Inwardly, Carson acknowledged that his relationship with Giselle had been deteriorating for some time. He needed to do something. No matter how hard he tried, he was not good at long term relationships.

***

Since she'd been working in New York, Aubrey had been losing weight. Recently, her weight had dropped below her comfort level. Last night she'd gone to dinner with Mira and noticed that she wasn't much bigger than her professionally skinny supermodel friend. It was a wakeup call. She'd been so absorbed with her work with Carson that she hadn't been eating much.

Today, she'd made a rare stop for breakfast on her way to work. Therefore, she was just arriving. As she walked through the lobby of their office building, she recognized Carson coming in from the opposite direction.

The wavy, beautiful hair that any woman would envy looked tousled and sexy. His handsome features drew lots of feminine attention as he strode to where they stood waiting for the elevator.

The elevator doors opened. Aubrey greeted him as he arrived. Everyone stepped into the elevator.

Lost in thought, he gave her an automatic response. Then, as the elevator doors closed, he actually looked, saw her, and managed a warm smile. "Good morning, Aubrey. Sorry, I was lost in thought."

"Yes, I noticed." she said, as she pressed the button for their floor, "Is something bothering you? It's not a problem with the company, is it?"

Shaking his head, he scanned the people on the elevator, no doubt noting that except for the bodyguards, they were alone. "You and I take good care of all the potential problems and issues with the company," he said.

"Trouble in paradise?" she quipped, and immediately wondered if she'd gone too far. It wasn't as if Carson MacDonald was her friend, but most of the time, it felt like it.

He flashed a half smile that quickly disappeared. "I may be losing my love for supermodels."

Supermodels? Or the supermodel who'd been parading around town on his arm? Aubrey smiled at the thought but reminded herself that it wasn't as if she would be benefitting from this possible change of heart.

"Don't laugh! Wipe that *smile* off your face!" he cracked. "There are certain images and expectations that go with achieving billionaire status."

Aubrey thought about her experiences with Carson. He was fearless in the things he did. He'd hired her and put her at the head of his company despite her young age, sex, and race, because he believed in her. And she knew that he'd never forgotten his humble beginnings. He cared about people. His charity foundation gave millions to the poor, homeless, and abused. He drove a Maserati, lived in an exclusive building, and had a supermodel girlfriend, but he'd never fit the stereotype of the insensitive billionaire playboy.

"When did you start caring about fulfilling the expectations of other people?" she asked.

Carson inclined his head at the implication of her statement and said, "All things considered, I'm still a man, and women, cars, and good Scotch are high on my list of basic necessities."

Aubrey laughed, and was surprised when he joined in. The elevator doors opened on their floor. Carson waited as Aubrey exited. She promptly caught her heel on something and stumbled.

With lightning-fast reflexes, his warm hands latched firmly onto her bare arms as he caught her before she could fall. Sensual heat, hot and provocative as a siren song on a lonely sea, shot through her and went straight to her core. Even the embarrassment of being so clumsy in front of Carson and the bodyguards was just a fleeting thought as she struggled to stand on suddenly weak knees. Was she imagining the heat Carson's hard body generated against her back? She wanted to lean back and bask in it. The man's pheromones were all but begging her to turn around and taste his sexy lips.

"You okay?" he asked, his husky voice close to her ear.

"Yes," she answered breathlessly. She swallowed. "You've got quick reflexes." Aubrey lifted the offending heel, which was thankfully undamaged, and rebalanced on more even footing. As she turned to face him, he let go of her arms. Their gazes caught. The naked desire in his eyes had Aubrey imagining herself moving naked beneath his sweaty form on a big bed. She caught her breath as the moment seemed to go on and on . . . .

The arrogant buzz of the still open elevator intruded on her daydream, startling both. Aubrey checked Carson's face once more. He looked as surprised as she that they'd been standing in the elevator entrance outside their offices drooling over each other.

Forcing herself to breathe, Aubrey shuffled closer to the glass entryway doors, while the rest of the bodyguards exited the elevator. She glanced back at Carson. This time, he'd assumed the almost bland business expression he wore unless he was negotiating a contract on the phone. Gone was the man who'd oozed enough sexual heat to singe the both of them.

"Thanks for saving me," she murmured, and made her way into the office with one of the guards close on her heels.

Forcing his tense body to relax, Carson took his time entering the office with his bodyguards. Was he crazy? What had just happened? What had Aubrey Merrill done to make him think she was hot enough for him to jump her sexy bones right there in the hall outside their offices?

He'd noticed in the past that there had been a subtle bit of sexual chemistry between Aubrey and himself but hadn't deemed it a problem since she was not his type and he had Giselle. So, what had made him so vulnerable today? He'd virtually refused a quickie with Giselle less than an hour ago. He wouldn't have been able to refuse the same offer from Aubrey.

When he'd touched her, her skin had been soft and supple. He'd wanted to lose himself in it, and in her. He'd even caught a strong, tantalizing whiff of her lavender and vanilla scent. She'd been looking exceptionally hot in a dark blue shirtdress that draped and hugged her curvy figure in all the right places and revealed enough of her shapely legs to spur his imagination onward.

"Sir?" One of his bodyguards opened the glass doors of their office.

Acknowledging the guard, Carson thanked him and entered. For him to be so vulnerable, he'd obviously stayed with Giselle too long. Reminding himself of his long-standing rule of not dating the women he worked with, he decided that he needed to distance himself from Aubrey.

It wasn't as if she'd offered herself to him, but something in Aubrey's brown eyes when she'd looked at him made him confident that the attraction was just as strong with her. With the heat he'd felt at the elevator, she was a challenge just waiting for his pursuit. He liked Aubrey and he didn't want to hurt her. Furthermore, he didn't want to contemplate the consequences of a relationship with Aubrey on Crutchfield and Donner. No, he had to keep his distance and his hands off Aubrey Merrill.

CHAPTER NINE

Carson sat with his custom-made executive chair tilted all the way back. A dreamy view of New York stretched before him, courtesy of the floor to ceiling windows that graced his office. He'd even started the heated massage cycle on his chair, and he had to say that he deserved the pampering. He'd just put the finishing touches on a multi-million-dollar hotel deal with Noblique Hotels. Crutchfield and Donner investors were in the deal for a very profitable piece of the pie, but he'd also risked a good chunk of his fortune. Closing his eyes, Carson focused on the soothing classical music coming through the speakers on his chair.

Gradually, he noticed a soft rhythmic knocking on the door to his office. His first thought was, *Why didn't I go home to celebrate?* Wait. . . he knew the answer to that. Giselle. Better not to dwell on it. His assistants knew better than to bother him when his door was closed, he fumed silently. He knew that Aubrey didn't have the patience to keep knocking on the other side of the door. She would have barged in by now.

So, who was disturbing him? Glancing at his desk, he saw that his phone light was blinking red. The person at the door was most likely his secretary. In a low growl, he granted her entry, putting both out of their misery.

"I tried to get you on the phone sir, but since I couldn't get through," she began.

"What's the problem?" he asked, impatient to handle it and get back to relaxing.

"That detective you hired is back and insisting that he has to talk to you right away."

"Send him in." Carson pushed a button and his chair shifted into an upright position. He cut the soft classical music off, but kept the massage going. He had a feeling he was going to need it even more when he heard what the detective had to say.

A bundle of disjointed energy, the detective hurried in. In his mind, Carson had named the detective Columbo Jr., after the brilliant but rumpled television detective who solved many a case on network television when Carson was a kid. This guy was younger but had a lot of the same mannerisms and an air that caused people to underestimate him.

"Mr. MacDonald, I found out who leaked the information about your new CEO to the press," the detective began as soon as the door was closed.

"Who was it?" Carson ground out as the detective took a seat across from him.

"Your girlfriend, Giselle."

Carson inclined his head, then shook it in disbelief. "You have proof?"

The detective showed him a large deposit that had been made to Giselle's bank account on the same day the press got an exclusive from him and Aubrey. Other records showed that the funds had come from a station employee. "Her contact at the station is someone who's done publicity for her modeling career and he has connections at several of the magazines that have been doing stories on you." The detective showed Carson a picture of Giselle and another man. In it, she smiled provocatively. The man's hand rested comfortably on her rear.

Carson studied the picture. "She's sleeping with the guy," Carson guessed.

"Yes, off and on for several years," the detective confirmed matter-of-factly.

Carson fought the sinking feeling in his gut. He had been played! All the evidence pointed to it. He'd given Giselle the information she'd needed before Aubrey accepted his partnership offer. She'd also had the Information about the property he wanted to purchase for his development. It was a good thing he'd been too busy working this hotel deal to give Giselle the details on that, he mused.

Carson stood, all thoughts of a chair massage falling away in the wake of the news of Giselle's deception. He'd never suspected a thing. "Good job. I like the way you work, so there'll be more work coming from me." He gathered the records and the picture. "Is there anything else I need to know?"

"Yes." The detective eyed him gravely. "She's been talking to your biggest competitor. They met this morning."

Swallowing, Carson grabbed his keys. Am I just stupid or what? He'd really liked Giselle until she became too demanding and tried to change the boundaries they'd mutually established for their relationship. In his mind, Giselle had been a beautiful woman more than willing to spend her time and his money with him in a mutually beneficial relationship. It was the type of relationship many of his wealthy friends and acquaintances enjoyed and several had been envious.

He hadn't told Giselle about his new deal, and he had locked his office. Was she desperate enough to break into it? He didn't want news of his new deal out before the ink was dry. "I've got to go. My assistant has your check. I'll have him put something extra on it."

With his mind already on the fastest way home, Carson hurried out. His bodyguards rushed to keep up with him.

    ***

"No news? Still?" Worry and frustration tinged Aubrey's voice as she sat at her desk talking to her mother on the phone. It was only two-thirty, but she timed her breaks to ensure she gave the company all the time it needed. "Momma, this waiting and worrying is driving me crazy! There's got to be a reason why Wyatt's not feeling well. Whatever it is, things could be getting worse. I think it's time to get a second opinion. Maybe another doctor or another hospital or clinic can figure out what's wrong with Wyatt."

Aubrey sighed and took a moment to glance into the outer office as her mother launched into a long, drawn out explanation of why Wyatt's doctor was the best and should be kept.

Having already seen the detective go into Carson's office, Aubrey sat up and took notice when Carson zipped past the tinted glass panel on her door with his entourage close on his heels. Carson was a man of action, but he usually kept her informed and involved when critical business meetings and incidents came up. Something was wrong.

"Momma? Momma, I've got to go," she said, breaking in on the continuing diatribe, "Something's come up. I'll call you later."

With her mother's acknowledgment, Aubrey ended the call and hurried out to Carson's secretary. "What's going on?" she asked. "I saw Carson leave in a rush."

Seemingly torn between her need to maintain Carson's privacy and the need to tell Aubrey exactly what was going on, the secretary took a minute to frame an answer. "Something came up. Mr. MacDonald had to go home. He doesn't expect to be back in the office today and said he would call you later to address any hanging issues."

Aubrey nodded. Across the room, at the desk of Carson's assistant, she saw the detective he'd hired waiting as the assistant wrote a check. She bit back a smile as all the bits of information clicked into place. Apparently, there was trouble in Carson's paradise at home.

She didn't ask herself why the prospect made her happy. She knew that Carson deserved more. Sometimes she wished he'd give her the chance to give it to him.

Carson called to check in before Aubrey went home that day but did not go into detail as to why he'd bolted from the office. Gone was the upbeat, easy to talk to partner. Instead, he seemed more introspective.

In the absence of real data about Carson's personal life, Aubrey's imagination ran free. She guessed that Giselle was gone for good. And that was good, wasn't it? Aubrey hadn't sensed deep feelings on either side when she'd been with the couple. In her heart, she felt that Carson deserved a girlfriend who really cared about him, someone he could love. Maybe someone like her.

Aubrey had been struggling with the idea of having a more personal relationship with Carson for a long time. The alarm bells that normally sounded in her head and kept her from doing something she would regret, no longer rang. Aubrey wanted to be the best CEO Crutchfield and Donner had ever had, but she also hid a growing curiosity and desire for Carson McDonald as a man who might do more than inspire her fantasies.

The next couple of weeks were hectic at Crutchfield and Donner. Aubrey, Carson, and their staff scrambled to cover new clients and stay ahead of the other wealth management firms. They were so busy that Aubrey considered hiring more people. Carson surprised Aubrey by insisting that she take Saturday off and offering to use the time to show her around New York.

It was Saturday morning. With her need to impress Carson and show him that she had more going than her financial savvy, Aubrey was nervous. She'd changed her outfit several times. In frustration, she'd even called Sasha and Mira for ideas. Now she assessed the outfits each of her friends had recommended and tried to decide.

In the end, she settled for a short blue designer jumpsuit that ended a few inches above her knees. Angled gold zipper pockets and a large gold zipper that dipped between her breasts accented the outfit. Gold gladiator sandals, gold earrings, and a gold bracelet she'd found on a shopping expedition with Mira completed her look.

Sasha and Mira had offered to come help Aubrey with her makeup, but between the two of her flashier friends, she'd learned a few techniques. She used them to make her eyes more dramatic and even her skin tone. Then she added a dark berry lipstick and gathered her shoulder length twists into a style that would allow air on her neck.

When her apartment buzzer went off, she grabbed her small cross body bag and opened the door to Carson.

He stared hard, his gaze covering her from head to foot. His eyes sparkled with obvious appreciation. "You look amazing," he said finally. "Should I go home and change?"

Aubrey eyed his khaki-colored cargo shorts and matching safari shirt and sandals. Her gaze lingered for a moment on his strong, masculine legs and the fit of his outfit. The man was an athlete who maintained his body. He looked as if he'd stepped out of the pages of GQ. "Don't be silly," she muttered. "You always look great."

"I'm glad you think so," he responded with a bit of a smile. "Let's go." He waited for her to lock the door to her condo. "I drove the Maserati today, so everyone else will be following in the SUV."

Aubrey finished locking the door, dropped the key into her purse and said, "That's good. I like your car." She also realized that it meant their time today would be more private. She treasured her time with Carson and planned to spend the time getting to know him better.

In sandals that were as close to flat as he'd ever seen on her, Aubrey virtually bounced along beside Carson as they went to the car. As soon as Carson got Aubrey settled on the blue and white leather seats of his convertible, he got in and took off.

"I want you to know that I really appreciate you taking the time to show me New York," Aubrey said as the sportscar rounded a corner.

Reaching up to fit his designer sunglasses on his face, Carson nodded. "We're both been working very hard, and I do sympathize with you being new to the city and away from your family. I don't think there's anywhere quite like New York."

Turning her head to take in some of the scenery and people flashing by Aubrey agreed. "When you started giving me suggestions on places to go check out, I thought you were going to recommend a tour company. This is much more personal."

Carson tried to focus his attention on the road ahead. Several people had suggested that he provide Aubrey with a company-funded tour guide. "I wanted to take the time to show you the things I like about the city," he explained.

The late morning heat was steadily increasing. He was grateful for the breeze that ruffled his hair and played with Aubrey's twists. He tried to ignore the decent but still distracting expanse of her legs and thighs as he drove. He could almost imagine them wrapped around his waist. Why hadn't he considered that she might wear shorts and why was he so surprised at the length and shapeliness of her legs?

It took a minute to realize that he'd never seen Aubrey in anything other than business attire except for one time at her condo and the dinner meeting with the clients. Most of the time, she covered up the physical attributes he noticed most in women. As a man who'd officially dumped the pretender who'd been masquerading as his girlfriend, he was certainly free to look and act on his impulses if the subject of his attentions were willing. But did he really want to get with Aubrey?

After a while, Aubrey turned to him and asked, "Where are we going?"

"I thought we'd start with the Empire State Building," he answered, "It's iconic for New York City and if you like art deco. . . ."

"I do," she assured him, "and I'm excited to be going."

"There's usually a lot of waiting in lines," he warned her.

Aubrey said she didn't mind, but Carson confided that he was still glad he'd bought express passes to allow them to skip the lines.

They spent the rest of the morning and early afternoon taking pictures of the lobby and the breathtaking view from the observation deck. Carson saw that Aubrey also enjoyed hearing the history of the building from their tour guide. He'd done the tour on numerous occasions, but Aubrey's bright-eyed appreciation and pleasure added to his.

Because it was a Saturday, the crowds were huge, so his express pass did not eliminate all the waiting. By the time they left the building, Carson had had enough of crowds and lines and was ready for lunch. He noticed that Aubrey was less animated.

"I'd planned to do Central Park too," he confided, "but I'm hungry."

"So am I," Aubrey commiserated. "Do we pick up something to eat at the park? Or get something at the park?"

Carson tried to gauge the expression behind her dark sunglasses. He still couldn't see her eyes. "I'd rather go for lunch at Docks. If you're up to it, it's near Grand Central Station and we can go there afterward."

Aubrey smiled and shrugged. "I'm following you, Carson. Whatever you want to do is fine."

He returned the smile. "Docks it is then."

It seemed natural for him to catch Aubrey's soft hand as they pushed through the crowds of tourists behind the perimeter of his bodyguards and headed for his car in the simmering afternoon heat. The contact strengthened his connection with her.

Back in the car, Carson kept the convertible top down, but rolled up the windows and turned on the air conditioning. It made the heat more bearable. "Are you enjoying your tour?" he asked Aubrey.

"Yes, I am!" She reached across the seat to squeeze his hand resting on the center console. "Thank you, Carson!"

He basked in the warmth of her words and her smile. He always enjoyed Aubrey's company.

Lunch at Docks was a hit. "I think I'm a little homesick," Aubrey said as she ordered lobster mac and cheese.

"I think you're just hungry," Carson shot back as he ordered the Mediterranean Sea Bass. They each had a glass of wine and a side salad. Aubrey raved about her dish and promised to put the restaurant on her list of New York favorites.

Carson placed his napkin on the table and finished his wine. He felt stuffed. Somehow the idea of trekking through Grand Central Station seemed a lot less appealing.

He studied Aubrey. She seemed more rested.

"Still up for Grand Central Station?" he asked.

She hesitated. "I could probably use the exercise," she said carefully.

"But you're really not feeling it?" he asked.

Aubrey burst into laughter. "You're too good at reading me!"

"That's because I'm not feeling it either," he admitted. "If it's okay with you, I'd like to continue your New York tour some other time."

"Whatever you say," she replied agreeably. An odd intentness in her expression emphasized her words.

Carson gave her a hard look. "You can get into trouble with statements like that."

Eyes sparkling with mischief, Aubrey laughed again. "I'm a big girl and I work hard. Sometimes I think trouble is just what I need. Are you trouble, Carson?"

"I can be." He let his tone dip a little lower. "It depends on what you want, what you need."

She looked beautiful and vulnerable and inviting to him. Her mouth was slightly open. She closed it and wet her lips as if thirsty. Was she thirsty for him?

Carson knew he was vulnerable because he hadn't replaced his girlfriend and sex was high on his list of basic human needs. In truth, he had always been a little vulnerable to Aubrey. If they hadn't been in a restaurant full of people, he would have leaned forward and kissed her.

He stared at her soft full lips. They looked ripe and exotic. He wondered what it would be like to feel them moving against his. Would he be able to stop there? "Maybe I should take you home," he suggested, testing her unspoken invitation.

"I'm good with that," she responded.

Carson tossed a wad of bills onto the table and stood, taking Aubrey's hand. Still smiling that mischievous smile, she stood, and they left the restaurant.

CHAPTER TEN

Carson held onto Aubrey's hand. Was she trembling? Or was that him? Pulsing heat surged through their joined hands, feeding the growing need in his gut.

He was in a rush to get her back to her condo so he could. . . do whatever they were going to do. He wanted to explore the mystery of Aubrey. At the very least, he would know what it was like to kiss that sexy mouth. He'd know what Aubrey tasted like. Carson wanted it bad. He wasn't going to push himself on Aubrey, but he damned sure planned to keep going until she gave him the red light. The decision excited him and made him bold.

Neither talked on the way back to her place, but each time their gazes connected, the tantalizing desire grew. Carson maintained a tenuous hold on his hormones and tried to concentrate on the road. Aubrey kept her hand on his, squeezing, stroking, never letting him forget what might await him when he got her home.

Back in the lobby of her building, they paused, waiting as a member of the security team checked in with the guard. The others were parking the cars. "We're going up," Carson announced, "I'll call you when I'm ready to leave."

The bodyguard who'd detached himself from the group to

follow his employer halted mid-step and signaled his agreement.

Carson stepped into the elevator with Aubrey. She keyed in her floor and the door slid shut. They weren't touching; he didn't dare, not with that state-of-the-art security camera recording their every move. But they were close enough for him to feel the heat coming off her body and smell her vanilla musk scent. Their gazes locked. He saw a challenge, a dare, and an element of disbelief. This was an Aubrey he'd only glimpsed. He couldn't resist her.

The elevator doors slid open with a chime. Exiting, they almost ran down the corridor to Aubrey's condo. She fumbled with the key several times, dropping it once in her excitement.

"Let me help you," Carson murmured, steadying her hand, and then accepting the key. Inserting the key into the lock, he got the door open.

Clasping his hand, Aubrey drew him into the apartment, shutting the door behind them. For a couple of beats, they just stared at each other. Aubrey struggled to breathe. She couldn't believe that she was really in this moment and Carson wanted her. His dark blue eyes seared her with the force of his passion.

"Last chance," Carson mumbled softly. "Are you sure you want this kind of trouble?"

"Oh yes." Aubrey moved closer. "I've been dreaming about it."

"Me too," Carson grunted, reaching for her.

Suddenly she was in Carson's arms and his mouth was moving on hers, kissing, tasting, and tangling his tongue with hers with a persistent passion that overwhelmed her. Threading her fingers through his dark, wavy hair, she closed her eyes and returned his kiss. He tasted like wine and felt like a dream beneath her restless fingers. As he backed her to the door, she lifted one leg, wanting to climb his lanky length.

His hands traced her body, gripping her buttocks and massaging her breasts. He swallowed her moans with fevered kisses. She struggled to touch as much of his hard body as she could. Her fingers grazed the smooth, warm skin beneath his shirt to linger on the hardened length of him. She ached for Carson.

Cool air hit Aubrey's skin as Carson slid the jumpsuit zipper down and unsnapped her bra. The front of her suit gapped as he bent and traced the opening with his tongue. He covered her bare flesh with hot kisses...

"Carson!" she gasped, standing on shaky legs.

He pulled at her jumpsuit, riding the edge of their sensual frenzy. "I need this off!"

She helped him with the shoulders, wiggling as he drew the garment down and off. He tossed her bra across the room.

"Yes! This is what I want!" he grunted, staring at her in wonder. He pressed a warm kiss to the front of her black lace panties.

Aubrey pushed at him and tugged on his shirt. She wanted him badly, but she wasn't going to give herself to Carson while he was fully clothed. "Strip!" she ordered.

Taking a step back, he stripped in record time. Aubrey stared in mute appreciation. She knew she would savor and remember this day forever. Her gaze lingered on his huge erection. She reached for him.

"Come on!" he urged, pressing their bodies together once more. His hands explored her body with an enthusiasm that stoked her urgent need. His lips covered hers in another searing kiss. She panted, rubbing herself against him.

In an unexpected move, he lifted her and carried her to the sofa. Legs splayed open, Aubrey locked gazes with him as he hooked his fingers in the sides of her panties and slid them down and off. Then he covered her body with tantalizing kisses until she couldn't take it anymore. He paused, and she helped him put on protection.

"Now!" he grunted, sliding into her, and filling her to the hilt. Aubrey locked her legs around his waist. He held onto her butt, squeezing, and gripping it. She tried to match his rhythm as he pistoned into her. Each deep stroke sent them higher and higher until they went out over the horizon and tumbled back to earth. Passion overflowed.

Afterward, Aubrey lay loose-jointed and spent in Carson's arms. Her body hummed with a satisfaction she'd never experienced before. She could still feel his heart pumping madly. "Aubrey, you are one hot lady!" he said, gently pushing sweat damp hair back from her face.

She grinned at him. "And you are amazing. I couldn't have asked for more."

"More? Would you like more?" he asked, tracing a finger down the curve of her side.

"If you're up to it," she teased, "I'd like it very much."

"Give me a few moments," he promised.

Hours later, Aubrey awakened alone in bed. She checked the clock. It was after ten o'clock. High on physical satisfaction, her body hummed like a piece of well-oiled machinery, but she was a little sore. After the initial foray on the sofa, they'd had sex in her bed and then again in her shower. Carson had been holding her when she fell asleep. Now, the door to her room was closed. She listened in the dark, somehow certain she was not alone.

Aubrey pulled on her favorite nightdress, opened the door, and padded out of her bedroom on bare feet. She didn't know what to expect. As she walked towards the kitchen, the delicious scents of food filled her nostrils. She'd never been with a man in all the passionate ways she'd been with Carson. Her ex-fiancé had never stayed after they'd made love. Had Carson cooked for her? She couldn't have imagined this.

She found him standing at the stove, naked except for the towel tucked around his waist. "Aubrey." He turned to stare hard, his dark blue eyes glittering. "French lace, black silk, spaghetti straps and a sexy split! If you're trying to tempt me back into bed, it's working."

Despite all the down and dirty things they'd done in her bed and shower Aubrey felt herself blushing. "I happen to have a weakness for sexy lingerie," she admitted.

"So do I." Carson clasped her hand, lifted it, and made her execute a full turn for his viewing pleasure. "Damned if you don't look good enough to eat. I really like what you're wearing, and I can't wait to take it off you." He drew her close to where the front of his towel was already beginning to form a tent. "I'm not usually this insatiable."

"Me either. I think it's because we're new." Aubrey kissed him. She tried to resist the rising call of desire and the urge to rub herself against his hard body and even harder erection. "Maybe we should eat first?"

"We should." Carson dropped an arm to her shoulders, turning them both to face the stove. He'd already placed one omelet on a plate. The other one was ready. "Spinach, ham, and cheese omelet? I lived off them while I was in college."

"Mmmmh, I want one. It looks and smells delicious," Aubrey said. "I have some wine and croissants that would work with it too."

"Good," Carson said, releasing her very reluctantly, "but you're going to have to sit on my lap."

Aubrey laughed. "Oh, I was planning on it."

The next morning, Carson was worn out from spending most of his evening and a good part of the night making love to Aubrey, but he wasn't cranky. He was on his way into the office and damned if he didn't have a smile on his face. Satisfaction had a way of smoothing over life's issues and problems. He couldn't remember being so excited about being with any woman.

Wonder of wonders, he met Aubrey at the elevator in the lobby of their office building. She greeted him in the warm, professional way she always did, with no sign of having spent a good part of her evening riding him into oblivion.

Keeping it together, he returned her greeting. He'd never let his private life get in the way of business and he wasn't about to start. What he and Aubrey did with their nights and evenings was no one else's business.

They climbed into the elevator with their entourage. He took in her conservative-looking black shirtdress and heels. His mind superimposed the sight of her in the sexy little slip dress she'd worn last night, and he relived highlights of the passion they'd shared in the kitchen. Carson cut the memory short of the satisfying conclusion. He needed to get a hold of himself.

The elevator chimed. When Carson finally shuffled off, Aubrey had already gone inside with half their entourage. By the time he made it to his desk she was standing in the doorway of his office with a fragrant cup of premium coffee. "I thought you might need this," she said. "Have a great day!"

Mumbling his thanks, Carson accepted the cup and took a long, grateful sip. When he glanced up, Aubrey had gone. During the rest of the day, he saw Aubrey in her office preparing with an assistant, then meeting with a couple of clients. He and Aubrey both participated in a working lunch and brainstorming session with the Crutchfield and Donner staff. Afterward, he caught a glimpse of her hard at work on her laptop.

Carson lingered at the office past his usual time. This situation with Aubrey was new for him and he wanted to maintain their privacy. Not wanting to add to workplace gossip, he left the office with Aubrey hard at work.

The urge to call Aubrey felt overwhelming. This was new for Carson. Although sex with the women he dated was always good, they were usually interested in being seen with him, getting expensive gifts, and furthering their careers. Aubrey had welcomed the job opportunity he offered, but they'd both benefitted. She was more than capable of making her own employment opportunities.

As he rode home in the limo, Carson thought about what he should do next. He didn't want Aubrey to think their time together meant nothing, but he also didn't want to pressure her. A trip to the gym took the edge off his growing concern, but afterward, he didn't want to go back to his place alone or hang out with his friends.

    ***

Gazing down at her prime view of New York City, Aubrey sat alone in the condo, feeling sorry for herself. Last night she and Carson had spent most of their time in bed together. Today, as expected, Carson had behaved professionally at work, but now that she was home, he hadn't called. He hadn't even spoken to her when he left the office for the day.

Had she misinterpreted their time together? Maybe he'd decided that she wasn't someone he wanted to be with after all. Whatever he'd decided, he could have at least called or sent a cowardly text.

She'd faced big time rejection before, when her fiancé abandoned her because he felt she spent too much of her time and resources on her brother and mother. She loved her family and she'd loved her fiancé. The rejection had hurt, but she'd eventually come to realize that things had happened for the best. Could she continue working with Carson and reach the same conclusion?

A drop of moisture splashed down on her hand. Because of her family situation, and the fact that she'd been such a scholarly teen, she didn't have a lot of experience with men. Aubrey grabbed a tissue. Was she really crying over Carson MacDonald? *I couldn't have found a more unlikely match!* Aubrey mused as she angrily wiped away another tear. No matter how nice and accessible he seemed, Carson was a billionaire, and his ideal women were movie stars and supermodels, not nerdy black wealth management advisors!

As she stared into the neatly stocked shelves of her refrigerator, her phone rang. Relief fluttered within her when she saw Carson's name on the display and answered.

Carson sounded tentative. "Aubrey, I wanted to give you time to get home and settled and I didn't want to say anything at work. Did I mess up by not calling you sooner?"

"No," she said in a bright tone, lying to cover her hurt feelings, "What's on your mind?"

"You are."

Aubrey sighed at the bald, heartfelt statement. Another tear slid down her face. "I've been thinking about you too."

"I apologize for not calling earlier," he continued, "This is new for me. I really want to see you. Would you like to go somewhere? We could have a quiet dinner or opt for drinks and dancing. Or would you like me to pick up something and come over to your place?"

She knew that the best option was to go out, to get a feel for whether their relationship would include more than sex, but Aubrey wasn't ready to face the world on a date with Carson. She wanted to see him and be with him in her surroundings and assure herself that their coming together had not been a fluke. "Pick up something and come over," she answered.

"I'll be right there!" he promised quickly. "Do you like Italian food?"

"Yes."

"Then I'll get Italian. And Aubrey?" His tone turned husky.

Her heart beat a little faster. "Yes?"

"Can you wear something special just for me?"

Aubrey's heart melted. "I can do that."

CHAPTER ELEVEN

The doorbell rang. Aubrey's pulse sped up as she went to the keyhole to peek out at Carson. Looking more at ease than he had in the office, he stood alone in the corridor, holding a large blue and white carryout bag. She opened the door, peering around the edge to greet him. "Hi."

"Hi," he said, reaching out to touch a lock of the hair she'd washed and coaxed into soft curls around her face and shoulders. "Nice."

At his touch, tremors of awareness shot through her. Struggling to maintain some semblance of control, she thanked him for the compliment. She sensed he was not alone but didn't see anyone around him in the hall. "Where's everyone?"

Dark blue eyes full of charm, Carson's grin melted her heart. "They're close enough to make sure I get in safely, but far enough to give us a bit of privacy."

Maintaining her position behind the door, Aubrey smiled back. "Come on in."

He entered, glancing down at his bag. "Where do you want me to put this?"

"How about the kitchen? We can eat in there," she said, closing and locking the door. She followed him to the kitchen on crystal heels, aware and a little concerned that except for when he'd been standing in the hall, he hadn't really looked at her. She didn't really care about the food. She yearned for Carson, craved his attention.

Carson set the bag on the oak kitchen table and turned to look at Aubrey. Distinct appreciation gleamed in the depths of his eyes as he stared long and hard. His gaze lingered over her like a physical caress.

Aubrey's skin tingled under his perusal. She felt as if he'd stripped off every bit of the form fitting red silk gown and she was standing before him buck naked.

"All day, when I wasn't working real estate, I was thinking about you," he muttered, "and here you are, hot enough to fuel a month of fantasies! You look good enough to eat!"

Aubrey blushed. She liked sexy lingerie, but except for her former fiancé and now Carson, no man had ever seen her in it.

Before she could take another breath, she was in Carson's arms, her tongue passionately tangling with his. Leaning into him, she moaned, her fingers on the warm skin of his chest as she removed his shirt. His hands wandered over her body, caressing her feverously, pushing aside the edges of the split in the silk fabric on her thigh. His lips soon followed.

Waves of pleasure washed over Aubrey. Under Carson's passionate assault, she felt her legs begin to give way. He stood and carried her into the bedroom.

Placing her on the bed, he stripped off the rest of his clothes and followed her down. "You're driving me crazy!" he said, putting on protection.

"You!" Aubrey sighed. Her lips locked with his once more as he pushed into her, filling her until she gasped. They moved together in a wild, crazy rhythm that grew in intensity until time and space expanded and they fell back to earth. They held each other, trembling in the aftermath.

"So good," Carson murmured, brushing back her damp hair to kiss her face.

"It was," she confirmed, still floating on a cloud of satisfaction. Her ears were still ringing with the passionate moans and cries she'd uttered. There was something to be said for the soundproofing of the condo walls.

"It's not supposed to be like this," he said, his hands tracing circles on her breasts. "We've had each other...."

"Five times counting just now," Aubrey said, finishing his sentence.

"I don't seem to have any limits when it comes to you. I want to stay inside you all night," Carson said.

"That might be *hard*," Aubrey teased, her gaze locking with his.

"There's no other way," he confirmed, pushing against her to prove that he was more than halfway there.

"I want you too," she said, rubbing herself against him, egging him on.

Much later, Aubrey awakened in bed alone, her body tender and sore. The room reeked of sex. She felt wet and sticky. Her stomach growled. Again, she listened in the dark until she heard Carson moving around. Using a brush, she did what she could to tame her hair and slipped on a robe.

She found Cason in the kitchen, warming the carryout. He turned at the sound of her footsteps, his dark eyes studying her with a predatory look. Aubrey swallowed, resisting the urge to see which robe she'd thrown on in the dark. Most of them revealed more than they concealed. Having a man around to look at her in them was not her norm. She'd been enjoying Carson, but her body was starting to complain.

"Hungry?"

"Starving!" she answered, "but I need to shower first."

"I had to have one too," he said, and added, "you've got time. Should I fix your plate?"

"Please do!" Aubrey turned and hurried back to the master suite. She realized that she'd been holding her breath. If Carson had suggested that they go back to bed for another round of sex, it wouldn't have been possible. He'd said more than once that he wasn't usually so insatiable, but she wondered, what was his norm? It had been three years since her fiancé abandoned her. Afterward, she'd been shell-shocked and then too busy to date.

In the bath, hot pulsing water and scented shower gel soothed Aubrey's body. Drying off, she took care of her skin, added light makeup, and donned her natural-colored Maison slip.

"You must spend a lot of time in La Perla," Carson remarked when she returned to the kitchen. He had the table set, wine poured, and their plates fixed.

"I love it," she confided, "but the stuff is expensive! You've seen just about everything I have."

Carson's gaze lingered on her once more. "You look amazing."

Aubrey thanked him. His compliments meant a lot to her, especially since he usually spent his time with movie stars and supermodels, women who made a living off their appearances. Most of all, she liked Carson and wanted to be with him as much as possible.

They began to eat chicken and eggplant parmesan. Aubrey passed on the garlic bread, but quickly scarfed down two servings of the chicken parmesan. She put her fork down to sip her wine.

"There's a lot more food," Carson reminded her.

"I don't want to sleep on too much food," she confessed.

Carson's shoulders tensed as he checked his watch. "It is getting late." The hand massaging hers moved up to her wrist and arm. "I should go."

Aubrey nodded in agreement. "Yes, you should. I don't think either of us will get any sleep if you don't and we have a lot scheduled for tomorrow."

His hand moved further up her arm in a caressing motion. "I'd like to stay."

Aubrey nibbled on her lip. She'd discovered the hard way that she couldn't resist the lure of Carson's magic hands for long. "Why?" she asked, ignoring the little voice in her head detailing all the naughty things they'd done in bed.

"I like you, Aubrey, and I like being around you."

She smiled. "I like you too, too much to sleep with you within reach."

Carson laughed, his eyes sparkling. "I don't suppose I could sleep in the extra bedroom?"

"What would be the point?" she countered, "When you could come back tomorrow?"

He leaned across the table to cover her mouth with his in a long, lingering kiss. "I'll come back tomorrow."

"I'll be waiting for you," she whispered back.

The next few days and the weeks that followed flew by for Aubrey. She and Carson worked hard at the office each day and spent most of their nights in bed with each other. Each evening Aubrey came home to a gift from Carson. Sometimes he sent flowers or chocolates and perfume, but most often, he gave her sexy sleepwear from La Perla and Victoria's Secret that she modeled for him every evening. Then he savored the act of taking it off her body.

Life was good for Aubrey, so good it bordered on a fairytale. The client base for Crutchfield and Donner had more than doubled and they'd done well in increasing the value of their client investments. Aubrey couldn't remember being so happy. Sometimes she had to stop herself from looking over her shoulder for the thing that would happen to end it all.

CHAPTER TWELVE

Aubrey hurried down the hall to her apartment. She couldn't wait to see what Carson had gotten her. As a child, Aubrey hadn't received a lot of presents, so she really enjoyed Carson's little presents. Excitement grew as she put the key in the lock. When the door opened, Aubrey nearly dropped her purse and laptop.

With a golf shirt and jeans covering his thin frame, her brother Wyatt stood in the opening, grinning. His normally pale brown skin had begun to tan. He looked healthy. "Surprise!"

"Wyatt!" she squealed, quickly placing her laptop and purse on the table just inside and enfolding him in a tight hug, "I missed you so much!"

"Missed you too!" He hugged her back enthusiastically for several heartfelt moments, then he began to squirm. "Need air to breath!" he managed in a robot-like voice.

Laughing, Aubrey loosened her hold and glanced around suspiciously. "I know you're not here all by yourself". She followed him into her apartment. As she closed the door, she caught sight of her mother hiding behind the door.

Anitra Merrill's hair had been cut into a short, sassy style with tousled curls on top. The sleek back and sides were highlighted with a blond color. The effect was startling. In addition, she wore a short, form-fitting blue dress with gold hardware accents at the waist. She looked more like Aubrey's sister than her mother.

"Momma!" Aubrey cried, enfolding her in a big emotional hug and holding on tight. "I've been missing you!"

"Me too, sweetie." Her mother rocked back and forth with her. "Coming here was an answer to a prayer."

Aubrey gazed at her mother under the threat of tears. "I'd have come home to see you and Wyatt, but there's too much going on with the company and I made a commitment."

"I know that, Aubrey," her mother said in a gentle tone, "and I wasn't expecting to get to see you this soon. That's some boss you have."

Aubrey stiffened a little and caught herself. "What do you mean?" She glanced up to find her mother studying her intently.

"He told me to tell you that Wyatt and I are your surprise and that he wants to take us to dinner tonight."

Aubrey swallowed slowly. Was she ready to be with Carson in prime time? Would that happen if they went to dinner with her family? She blinked. "Momma, how long can you stay?"

"Just till Sunday night. Sorry, sweetie, but Wyatt has to get back to school."

"I understand." Aubrey accepted the news with a graceful nod. "How was your flight?"

Anitra grinned. "The flight was okay, and we even got to sit in first class, but you know me. Every time I take a plane, I get jet lagged."

Aubrey started thinking of carryout. Thanks to Carson, she knew several good places. "Are you and Wyatt up to going out?"

Anitra tilted her head. "I may be a bit jet lagged, but as far as being up for going out to dinner with your boss, I want to be as gracious as possible to the man who's made it possible for me to see my baby girl!"

Aubrey smiled. "Your almost thirty-year-old baby girl," she corrected.

"Don't try to cloud the issue with facts," Anitra countered in a pithy tone, "You will *always* be my daughter and if you want to get technical, *my baby girl.*"

Aubrey glanced behind her to find Wyatt on the couch, already into his tablet and tuning them out. "So, I should probably go freshen up and change for dinner?"

"That would be a good idea," Anitra said in a light teasing tone. "I'll get Wyatt to change into some regular pants and his dress shoes."

On the way to her room, Aubrey stopped and turned to face her mother with another question, "Where did you put your bags?"

"I'm in your extra bedroom and I thought Wyatt could sleep in your office or the sofa here in the great room. What do you think?"

"He can sleep in my office. The sofa there lets out into a bed." Aubrey continued to her room to freshen up and change. With the door closed, she sniffed the air. Her room smelled like Carson and sex. *Am I just imagining things?* The sheets had been changed. She couldn't even look at her room without thinking about the things they'd done together. Her gaze fell on a can of air freshener. She couldn't bring herself to use it because she liked the way Carson smelled.

Anxious to thank him and a little frustrated that she would not be able to do it in the usual way, she called his cell.

"Aubrey, hi," he answered in a warm tone.

"Hey Carson. I want to thank you for getting Momma and Wyatt here. I was truly missing my family. That was very thoughtful of you."

"You were working hard, and we needed you to stay here. I thought it would be good for everyone."

She took a breath and let it out. "Did you say anything about us?" she asked finally.

"No, I didn't know what to say, so I left it alone. Are you going to say something?"

"What would I say?" Aubrey shook her head, aware that he couldn't see her. "I think we should wait until we've had time to figure it out."

"Then we're in agreement," he said calmly, "but I'm going to miss you tonight, and every night until they go home."

"Me too," Aubrey agreed. She missed him already. "Maybe we can work something out."

"Yes, even if it's just phone sex."

"I've never tried that before," she confessed. "Does it work?"

"It's better than nothing," Carson assured her.

"Where are you taking us for dinner?"

"I've narrowed it down to two choices and both are dressy casual. That's all I going to say because it's sort of a surprise too."

"Well, Wyatt likes..."

"I've already asked Wyatt what he likes and your mother too," Carson interrupted.

Amused, Aubrey said, "It sounds like you've done your homework."

"Don't I always?" he countered before they ended the call.

Afterward, Aubrey studied the clothes in her closet. Since Wyatt would be with them, she guessed that Carson would probably pick somewhere casual. She wanted to wear something sexy for him but wasn't ready to explain their relationship or lack of one to her mother. In truth, she hadn't figured it out yet. She finally settled on a deep red short-sleeved dress that accented her curves without showing extra skin or looking too sexy. Then she headed for her bathroom to shower.

When Carson arrived to take them to dinner, Aubrey slipped into relaxed business mode. Dressed in jeans and a casual shirt, he glanced at their attire and said, "You guys didn't have to dress. We're going to a very casual place."

"Will it matter if we're a little overdressed?" Aubrey's mother asked.

"No," Carson assured her, "I'm just trying to make sure you'll be comfortable."

"Carson's wearing jeans. I'd be more comfortable in my jeans," Wyatt said.

"Wyatt," Anitra said in a patient tone, "we've got to get going."

Already halfway across the room, Wyatt shot back, "It'll only take a minute."

Aubrey decided not to change. She tried not to look in Carson's eyes for too long, because their attraction always made it hard to look away. True to his word, her brother changed quickly. They left for the restaurant with Carson and his security team.

Aubrey felt weird being with Carson and pretending that there was nothing between them. She reminded herself on several occasions to not take Carson's hand. Her mother and brother's presence helped Aubrey stay in character, but the evening out challenged her.

Carson used his limo to take them to The Smith Restaurant, which was in the Midtown neighborhood. Red letters above the door of the restaurant spelled out the name. Still fascinated with New York, its atmosphere, and its restaurants, Aubrey followed Carson and her family into the glass paneled and tiled restaurant.

Tables, wood, and more tile filled the inside, reminding Aubrey of a train station. A high-level buzz of conversation and people simply enjoying themselves assaulted her ears. The delicious scents wafting around brought her hunger back with a vengeance. The place wasn't fancy, but there was a line for seats. Somehow, Carson had gotten a reservation, so they got one of the few coveted tables.

Aubrey dined on grilled marinated shrimp and a chopped farmhouse salad, while her mother had tagliatelle, which was black pasta, sautéed shrimp, scallion, and crumbled garlic bread. Predictably, Wyatt had the prime burger and macaroni and cheese and Carson had the bone-in rib eye steak with chimichurri, field greens, and garlic smashed potatoes.

The food was amazing, but they could barely hear each other above the noise of the crowd. Afterward, Wyatt and Anitra thanked Carson profusely, but begged off his offer of taking them to a show. Ignoring the tug at her heart when Carson said his goodbyes outside the condo, Aubrey thanked him again for the surprise and for dinner.

"You're really enjoying the visit?" he asked, halfway under his breath.

Aubrey glanced to where her mother and brother were already going inside. "I am," she assured him, "but I'll be missing you."

Carson grabbed her hand, massaging it between his thumb and forefinger. "I could go in with you, come clean with them, and spend the night. . . ."

"No!" Startled, Aubrey shook her head. "It wouldn't go like that, believe me! I'm an adult, but my mother is old fashioned. And we wouldn't get any sleep, for a whole new set of reasons!"

Carson drew her close for a quick, hard kiss. "Then I guess this is good night."

Heart pumping so fast she could barely catch her breath, Aubrey added, "Call me."

"I will," he promised, then watched as Aubrey went into her building with her bodyguard.

Later that night Carson called Aubrey on her cell and introduced her to the pleasures of phone sex. Her ears burned at purely sensual and sexual things he whispered and told her to do. Aubrey found it hard to put her thoughts and requests into words, but as her imagination kicked in, she got into the experience. There was something about being with a person that could not be duplicated over the phone, but what they did was better than nothing. Afterward, she slept peacefully.

It was the weekend and Carson had more time on his hands then he could remember. He'd been seeing Aubrey for about six weeks, but because they had such a good connection, it seemed longer. He'd offered to take Aubrey and her family sightseeing in New York, but they'd declined because Wyatt's stamina was still not as good as it should be, and they simply wanted to enjoy Aubrey.

It was a cool, crisp, October Saturday, but still warm enough to golf, so Carson called a buddy and they went golfing at the Upper Montclair Country Club.

Carson hadn't played in a couple of months. He was a little rusty, but his game soon picked up.

"What have you been doing, man?" his buddy, Jay asked as they paused at one of the holes. "You haven't been available."

"I've been sort of seeing someone," Carson admitted, "It's gotten kind of heavy."

"Really? She must be something to take you away from your friends, golf, business, Scotch, and other women."

Carson grinned. "It's not like that. She's beautiful, super smart, sexy, and funny."

His buddy's look sharpened. "What's her name?"

Carson shook his head. "We're not ready for prime time."

"When will you be ready for prime time?"

Carson shrugged. "It's never been like this and it's a mutual decision, so I don't know."

"Do you love her?"

Carson hesitated. "I don't know. It's too soon to tell, but I've never let anybody get this close."

Jay chuckled. "You think I didn't know that? You and some of the other guys like those women who get with you for the money, gifts and notoriety of being on your arm."

"Don't forget the sex," Carson reminded him while quickly turning his thoughts away from Giselle, who had tried to make him think she had feelings for him. It had only been about money.

"And the sex," his buddy added. "All I'm saying is that you guys don't usually date anybody that you would consider marrying. Would you consider marrying this woman?"

Carson could almost visualize Aubrey in one of her sexy gowns, standing beneath a sign with his buddy's question in bright red letters. It bothered him. His mother had deserted his family when he was eight and his father had never recovered from the loss. Even now, his father was something of a broken man, just stumbling through the rest of his life. Carson couldn't conceive of loving anyone that much. He would never be his father, never make the same mistakes.

Carson liked being single, free, and unfettered by the chains of matrimony. The resounding no he usually uttered at the thought of marrying anyone stuck in Carson's throat. "I don't know. The thought hasn't crossed my mind."

Jay laughed. "How do you think I ended up with my wife? I thought we were simply having good times and then I got to the point where I didn't want anybody else. I don't regret it. I love my wife, but I wasn't honest with myself when it was all coming together. Are you being honest with yourself?"

"Probably not," Carson admitted as he tried to focus on the ball and his shot, "but I'm through letting you psychoanalyze me. I'll let you know if things develop further."

"I'm good with that," his buddy said, "but you should know that my wife has been anxious for one of you guys to join the ranks of the married. She's looking forward to having another wife around."

"She's probably going to have to wait a lot longer," Carson said resolutely and took his shot.

CHAPTER THIRTEEN

With Carson's agreement, Aubrey used the company limousine to take her family to the airport. The driver dropped them off at the ticketing area and waited for Aubrey in the cell lot.

Close to the security check line, fourteen-year-old Wyatt held onto Aubrey as if she were a lifeline. "I know you have to have a job and a life," he mumbled, sounding almost grown up, "but when are you coming home to visit us?"

"I'll be home for Christmas," Aubrey answered.

Wyatt's eyes were wide. "Promise?"

Aubrey promised. Then she freed herself to hug her mother.

Anitra pushed back to gaze into her daughter's eyes. "Is there something going on between you and Carson?"

Startled, Aubrey blinked and tensed. "Wh-why do you ask?"

"Because he was staring at you like you were covered in honey whenever he thought no one was looking, and you made sure you didn't look at him."

"Is that all?" Aubrey laughed.

Anitra gently shook her shoulder. "I know my daughter and I know that man spent a lot of time and money on us this weekend. He would have done more if we'd allowed it."

"He's a good man and he has a good heart," Aubrey offered in way of explanation.

Anitra narrowed her eyes. "Are you in his heart? Is he in yours?"

"I don't know," Aubrey answered honestly.

"But there is something going on?"

Aubrey nodded. "Something."

Anitra pulled her close for another embrace. "Just be careful, baby. I like your Carson. He has some of the same qualities you do, like the business intelligence and savvy, and quick wit, but it's possible that your something means something entirely different to him. Billionaires, even self-made ones, do not usually marry super smart black girls from Chicago."

"They don't usually make them CEO of their company, either," Aubrey interjected in Carson's defense.

"No," her mother agreed, "and I'm proud of you and all that you've accomplished with your brains and hard work. I just remember how hurt you were after that sorry excuse for a fiancé, Steadman . . . .."

Aubrey sucked in a breath, surprised that she didn't feel the usual burn of unshed tears at the remembered pain. In the past, she'd felt lucky if she'd been able to stop the tears. It had been a very desolate time in her life. "Momma don't destroy my dream before I can even figure out what it is," she begged.

Her mother nodded. "Just be careful."

"I will," Aubrey assured her, "and remember, I'm coming home for Christmas."

"I'm looking forward to it." Anitra grabbed her carryon and joined the security line.

Wyatt ran back for another hug. "Are you still getting me that new iPhone for Christmas?" he asked in a voice only she could hear.

"I've got you covered," she assured him. "Take care of yourself."

Satisfied, he grinned and hurried to get in line with her mother.

Aubrey watched until her family made it through the security line. Then she called the limousine and headed back out front with the bodyguard.

When Aubrey climbed back into the limousine, there was a shiny gold-foil wrapped box with a red satin bow on the seat. When she asked the driver about it, he explained that Carson had asked him to give it to her on the way back from the airport.

Excited, Aubrey sat with the package on her lap for the rest of the ride. Her fingers toyed with the silky bow. She treasured his presents and savored the mystery of the gloriously wrapped boxes, especially the glamorous, high end lingerie and sleepwear that had long been her passion. Aubrey could hardly wait to see Carson alone and now she was certain he would be coming to see her in whatever the box contained.

Carson left for Aubrey's place as soon as he got the call that the driver had dropped her off. He felt anxious and knew he wouldn't feel better until he saw Aubrey in his gift, held her, and kissed her. Tonight, there was an edge to his need for her that had never been there before.

On a whim, just as much as an effort to slow himself down, he stopped and got a carryout from their favorite Italian restaurant. The wait and the growing anxiousness within him, did not sit well with Carson. It wasn't as if Aubrey was his girlfriend. They'd made no promises to each other. So why did he feel as if he were deep enough to drown in his need to be with her?

Finally, Carson got his carryout and paid for it. He remembered nothing of the ride the rest of way to her place except everyone seemed to be driving too slowly. After parking in the space he still paid for, he hurried inside with as much dignity as he could muster. The guard on the desk nodded as Carson headed for the elevator.

Outside Aubrey's door, Carson rang the bell. The door opened. Hiding behind the door, Aubrey tilted her head to peer out at him with shining eyes. "Carson," she said softly. Her radiant smile was bright, and warm enough to melt the negative whispers at the edges of his thoughts.

Clasping his free hand, she drew him inside. He saw his gift box open on the couch, the expensive La Perla gown still inside.

"Thanks for the gift! I really like it, but I didn't have a chance to put it on," Aubrey explained. She hurriedly locked the door.

"That's alright," he mumbled, unable to take his eyes off her. A terry cloth turban covered her hair. She looked beautiful and was still damp from the shower, in the cream silk robe she'd hurriedly thrown on to answer the door. The scent of jasmine and vanilla from her shower gel filled his nostrils. His mouth watered.

"You brought dinner! Something smells good," she said as she reached for the carryout bag.

"You smell good," Carson rasped as he set the bag down on the entry table and pulled Aubrey to him. Their lips met in a deep, sensuous kiss. Carson tasted mint and Aubrey as his tongue slid against hers. Immersed in the kiss, his fingers traced her warm, soft, silk-covered curves. She flooded his senses with her scent, her taste, and her soft sighs of pleasure. The kiss went on and on until they were both gasping for breath.

Aubrey cupped his face in her hands. "I missed you," she said, gazing straight into his eyes.

"I missed you, too," he admitted, sinking his mouth back onto hers in another mesmerizing kiss. He backed her against the wall.

Aubrey pushed against his chest until he ended the kiss.

Surprised, he gazed down at her as he fought an overwhelming torrent of need.

"I want you so bad. I need you right now, Carson," she said, her brown eyes without guile. "Just take me to bed."

Without another word he lifted Aubrey into his arms and carried her into the bedroom. The covers had been pulled back on the freshly made bed. As he placed her on the bed, a trickle of moisture slid down her neck and between her breasts. Leaning forward, he caught it with his tongue, tasting her skin. He drew the robe open and lovingly laved her soft, round breasts.

She moaned his name. Her hands were in his hair, at times tugging it to urge him to stop, at other times massaging his scalp in a frenzy as he tasted nearly every beautiful inch of her skin. He immersed himself in her, barely noticing when she managed to get him out of his clothes.

Finally, they were both naked, breast to chest on the bed. He was determined to make this time the best it could be for both, but once, even twice, wasn't going to be enough.

"Protection," Aubrey whispered as she strained to get a foil wrapped packet from her nightstand. Pressing him onto his back, she put her mouth on him, tasting him. Pure, unadulterated pleasure flooded Carson. This wasn't a first for him, but everything that involved Aubrey was wonderful and beyond imagining. He held on by a thread while she opened the packet and slid on the protection.

He pulled Aubrey down onto him. Aubrey's soft cries and Carson's deep, gratified sighs filled the room as he helped her ride them both into oblivion. Afterward, they held each other on damp sheets. Carson couldn't keep his hands off Aubrey's silky brown skin. Touching her, caressing her over and over reassured him that they were both here, together in the moment. He found more of the foil wrapped packets in her nightstand. Soon, they were straining together on the bed again.

Hours later, Carson awakened alone in the bed. With all that and Aubrey had been doing with and to each other for the last couple of hours, he should have been exhausted. He felt energized. Getting up from the bed, he used the bathroom and found Aubrey in the shower. This time he grabbed more protection from the nightstand and joined her. They came together once more under the hot spray of water.

Afterward, they warmed the carryout food and ate at the kitchen table. Aubrey looked beautiful in the La Perla gown he'd given her. Carson wore nothing, but he did drape a towel over the seat of the kitchen chair. He enjoyed watching Aubrey's fascination with his naked body. She tried not to stare but failed miserably.

"This is crazy. We were only apart for a few days," Aubrey murmured at one point.

Carson grinned. "I know, but it felt like it was a lot longer. I missed you. Coming together like this has been addicting. I don't want to leave. Can I stay the night?"

Aubrey nodded. "I missed you a lot."

He pulled her onto his lap. "Me too. I'm not seeing anybody else."

"Me either." Aubrey kissed his lips, lingering. "I've never met anyone like you, didn't know it could be like this."

"That goes for both of us!" Carson chuckled. They cuddled a little longer then got up to clean up the remains of their meal.

"What do you have coming up tomorrow?" Carson asked as he wiped off the table. Aubrey had a day full of client appointments and an industry lunch. Carson told her about the auction he was attending for a mansion in upstate New York after a few morning appointments. "We are some busy folks," he remarked.

Aubrey smiled. "Yes and look what we've accomplished. The company is making lots of money right now and we have more clients than when it was under the previous owners. We brought it back from the brink of bankruptcy!"

"We're a good team in and out of bed," Carson quipped.

Aubrey covered his lips with her fingers. "Shhh, don't ruin it. Let's just see where it takes us."

"Don't you think we should talk about what each of us wants and where we want this to take us?" Carson asked.

Aubrey shook her head. "No, I want you to not worry about what you or I ultimately want. Let's not force this. I'm trying to enjoy what we have now. I'm happy now."

"And I want you to stay that way," Carson said. With that, he took her hand, and they went back to bed.

The addictive pattern of days filled with hard work and secret nights of passionate lovemaking blended into weeks and months. Except for business meetings and trips, neither Carson nor Aubrey could bring themselves to break the pattern.

Weeks later, Carson was in Aubrey's home office working on his laptop when she padded barefoot into the room. "Good morning," he greeted in his deep morning voice, lifting his head, and shifting his laptop for her lingering kiss. He drew her down into his lap.

Her full lips were soft and luscious, and the scent of her berry shower gel filled his nostrils. The kiss ended and they began another deep, drugging kiss. They broke it off, gasping for air.

"It's always good when you're around," Aubrey teased provocatively, returning his greeting.

Carson focused on her face. He knew better than to look lower.

For him, Aubrey was always distracting. On some level, he was always aware of where she was, what she looked like, and what she was doing. But here, at her condo, there was nothing to hold either of them back. His fingers at her waist, touched on bare skin.

"Getting ready for your meeting this morning?" she asked, as he nuzzled his face against her silk covered breasts.

"Yes," Carson muttered, already wondering if they had time to make love one more time. His fingers slid down her side to encounter the split in her gown and trace the curve of her thigh.

Aubrey tensed with a quick intake of breath. "We don't have time for this," Aubrey said, scooting away from him to stand.

"Tell me about it." Carson gave her retreating form a regretful look. She was wearing one of his favorite gowns.

Going to her desk, Aubrey took her seat. "I've got work to do too."

It took several minutes, but they were eventually able to focus on the work they'd planned to do and get it done. As Aubrey rose and left the room to start fixing a quick breakfast, Carson got an email. He'd forgotten to reply to his buddy's invitation to a golf weekend at a resort. It was the thing he and a few of his buddies did every year.

This year Carson wasn't sure he would go. He spent most of his free time with Aubrey. He'd considered going with Aubrey as his date, but they weren't ready for prime time as a couple, and he couldn't see Aubrey cooling her heels with the models and starlets while he played golf with his buddies.

"You're frowning," Aubrey observed as she returned with coffee. She offered Carson a cup of the fragrant liquid.

"I was going to help you with that," Carson said, accepting the cup.

"You're good. The coffee was on a timer and the oatmeal was quick and easy." Aubrey set a bowl of oatmeal topped with strawberries, blueberries, and honey on the tray in front of him and handed him a spoon.

Thanking her for taking good care of him, Carson took a few sips of his coffee and dug into his oatmeal.

She took a seat beside him on the leather sofa and placed her coffee, spoon, and oatmeal on a television tray. "You're frowning again," Aubrey remarked, "Something to do with Crutchfield and Donner?"

"It's something personal." He looked up from his food to find her watching him carefully.

"Can you talk about it?" she asked tentatively.

"Of course." Carson let his lips form a hint of a smile and felt some of Aubrey's tension dissipate. "My friends and I have a golf weekend at a resort every year," he began.

"I've never met your friends." Her tone was even, but Carson sensed her waiting for him to drop the other shoe.

"No, you haven't, because we haven't been ready to let the world know we're together as a couple."

"Are we a couple?" Aubrey asked.

Nodding, Carson leaned close to kiss her cheek. "At a minimum for sure." He felt her trembling, so he pushed the trays away and put his arms around him. "What's bothering you?" he asked.

"The same thing that's bothering you. Will they like me?"

"Of course, they will."

"Why?"

"Because you're very likeable and loveable."

"And do you?" she asked, putting him on the spot.

"Do I like you? Oh Yes! I can't think seem to stay away from you!"

"Do you love me?"

That was a heavy question and one he'd been avoiding. Mentally picking his way through the minefield of possible answers, Carson tensed. When people started talking about love, things changed, usually for the worse. "I don't know. Do you love me?"

Aubrey lay her head against his chest and locked her arms around his waist. "I don't know. Maybe...."

"Then we're even," he said quickly, relief flooding his senses. "Do you want to go to the golf weekend?"

"I—I'm not sure. What's it like? What do you guys do?"

"We have a tournament with a nice prize for the winner."

"Do the women play?"

"My buddy Jay's wife does. The other women hang out by the pool, get massages, spa treatments, and other kinds of pampering. We take all the meals together and we have a great time."

"How long have you been doing this?"

"At least seven years. I look forward to it every year."

Aubrey smiled. "Then you don't want to miss it."

"Would you like to come with me?" Carson asked.

"I think it's too soon," Aubrey confessed, looking uncomfortable.

"I could introduce you to my friends before the golf weekend," Carson offered. He was beginning to see that he should have done this already. Gauging Aubrey's expression, she'd come to the same conclusion.

"What will you tell them about me?" Aubrey asked. This tentative, unsure of herself Aubrey was one he hadn't seen. He tightened his arms around her, but she still seemed separated from him.

"That we've been seeing each other, and I really like you."

Silent for a moment, Aubrey asked, "What are the women like?"

"Movie starlets and models mostly, but Jay's wife is a news correspondent."

Carson dropped his arms as Aubrey shifted away from him to straighten her back against the sofa. She looked him straight in the eye and said, "You took Giselle."

Carson's jaw clenched at the mention of his treacherous ex-girlfriend. He nodded.

"If I go, the fact that we're seeing each other will be out. People are going to think I'm the CEO because we have a personal relationship. . . ."

Carson interrupted, "People will always have an opinion, but you can't let that control your life. Your record of success speaks for itself."

"True." Aubrey nodded, "but I want you to enjoy your time with your friends without worrying about me fitting in."

"All you need to do is be yourself," Carson insisted, trying to convince her. The truth was that he didn't really know how she would fit in with his friends. He knew that Jay's wife got along with the other men's girlfriends, but pretty much kept to herself when they weren't enjoying group activities.

"I'm being myself right now," Aubrey said raising her brows and giving him the look that said she'd made up her mind. "I want to pass on this year. If we're together next year, I'll go."

"Are you sure?" Carson asked, trying to gauge her expression. He'd asked because he didn't want to be without her, but he was also uncertain of how she'd fit in. If she didn't go to the golf weekend, when would she spend time in public with him?

"Yes, I'm sure." Aubrey met his gaze.

Carson kissed her gently. "I'm going to miss you."

"I'm going to miss you too," Aubrey said.

"If you change your mind. . . ."

"I won't," she assured him. Then she changed the subject by adding, "The food's getting cold."

Carson swallowed the other arguments that came to mind as he began to eat. The truth was that he didn't know if Aubrey would fit in with his friends or his normal lifestyle. Nothing had been what he'd call normal since they'd started seeing each other in private. He'd become accustomed to the way his life had been before he met Aubrey. He didn't know how long they could go on with the way they were.

Both retrieved their tray tables and began to eat.

Later that morning Aubrey sat at her Crutchfield and Donner desk and replayed her conversation with Carson in her mind repeatedly. It was the first time he'd invited her to appear in public as his date and she'd turned him down. She'd known what she was doing, but the feeling that she'd made a colossal mistake stayed with her.

Carson was at the top of a short list of very eligible bachelors, and she could relate to him. She liked him a lot, and they cared about each other. His relationship with her was vastly different than the one he'd had with Giselle and whomever he may have taken to the golf weekend previously.

Mentally defending herself, Aubrey knew that she would not have fit in with the other women. She wasn't a beauty queen, actress or someone who made a living with their appearance or acting skills. Her close friendship with Mira was a fluke and existed because Mira was such a wonderful person.

It would have been an unpleasant time for Aubrey to fend off the rude comments and snide remarks that would likely have dominated her golf weekend. Her job and her aspirations had forced her to toughen her skin against the people of the world who found it hard to believe that she could be who she was and successfully perform what others considered financial miracles. Being out with billionaire, Carson McDonald was a totally different game to conquer and one she only wanted to play if he loved her.

When Carson asked if she loved him, she'd choked, and said she didn't know, but in her heart, she'd wanted to say yes. It was still too soon to be certain. Aubrey wasn't naïve enough to ignore the sense of relief they'd both felt when they both admitted that they didn't know if they felt love for each other. Aubrey knew that she and Carson couldn't stay in the current holding pattern for much longer.

CHAPTER FOURTEEN

Carson went alone to the golf weekend with his buddies. Immersing himself in the intense daytime golfing activities, he enjoyed renewing and reviving his friendships. His golf game started slow, but he gradually eased into his game and warmed up enough to challenge his friends.

At the meals and the social activities in the evening he sat alone in the crowd, wishing Aubrey had decided to come along. Everyone tried to include him, but many of the women, were anxious to monopolize their dates after spending the day apart. If Aubrey had come, Carson would have felt the same. His friend Jay wandered over with a beer.

"This is the first time you've come to one of these things alone," Jay remarked. "Still seeing your secret lady?"

Carson's brows quirked upward. "Secret lady? Who are you talking about?"

Jay grinned. "The last time you and I golfed alone, you were seeing someone, and you weren't ready for primetime."

"Yeah," Carson acknowledged with a nod, "I invited her."

"And?" Jay pointedly looked around the room. Obviously, Carson's new girlfriend was not there.

"I think she choked," Carson confided, "Let's face it, us guys spend a lot of the time golfing while the women do their thing. She asked about what we would do this weekend, and how I would explain us to other people."

"Humma-humma, and you're usually so good with words," Jay said with a chuckle. "So, the secret girlfriend is still in the closet. What makes her so different, man?"

Images of Aubrey leading the Crutchfield and Donner team of advisors and continually wowing everyone with her genius ideas for moving the company and its clients ahead formed in Carson's head. He could almost hear her low pitched, often sexy voice giving him a run for his money with her sparkling wit, but an image of her in her favorite La Perla gown replaced them all. He wanted to touch her, to be with her right now. He missed Aubrey.

"You're looking kind of hungry man and I'm not talking about food," Jay cracked, with a playful fist to Carson's shoulder. "What makes this woman so different?"

"She's not the sort of woman I usually pick," Carson admitted.

"Sooner or later, she's going to have to come out of the closet," Jay rationalized.

"She'll be here next year," Carson promised, but deep inside, he wasn't certain. He couldn't put a name to what he felt for Aubrey beside admiration, desire, and need. He'd never needed anyone as much and when he paused to think about it, it scared him.

Jay's dark brown eyes seemed to see clear through to Carson's thoughts and insecurities. In a lower tone he said, "Handle your business on this one man. If she's worth the changes to your life, you don't want to let her get away."

"For sure," Carson said, ready to change the subject. "Isn't it time I kicked your ass at the pool table again?"

Jay set his empty beer bottle down on the bar. "Those are fighting words! You're on."

Although he'd enjoyed the weekend tremendously, Sunday morning came soon enough for Carson. He'd already packed his bags and arranged for early transportation back to New York. Since most of hls friends were heading home at noon, he'd said his goodbyes the night before.

Back in New York, he called Aubrey from outside her condo, and let the welcome sound of her husky, morning voice sink in. He could almost see her face when he suggested they have breakfast together. Her breathless and eager "yes' encouraged him as he got of the car and entered her building.

Excitement growing, he checked in with the front desk and headed for the elevator. On her floor, he let his security detail hang back as usual, as he approached her door. Finally, he rang her bell.

Aubrey opened the door, her warm brown eyes full of welcome and surprise. The scent of her lotion and body gel filled his nostrils, stirring his senses. "I didn't think you'd get here so soon!" she confessed, one hand going to her head full of very loose curls. Her soft, full, lips parted. "I didn't have time to put on makeup either."

"You look beautiful," Carson assured her, taking in her pretty face and slender but curvy figure in his favorite La Perla gown. "Are you going to let me in?"

"Come in!" With a quick intake of breath, she clasped his hand, stepped backward, and hauled him into the condo. Closing the door behind him with one hand, he drew her into his arms. Their lips met in a long, passion filled dance of lips and tongue.

He let himself enjoy the feel of her soft, warm, silk-clad figure in his arms. "Carson!" she moaned softly as his hands restlessly wandered her body, caressing, touching, cupping her soft breasts, and gripping her firm round butt.

Her fingers pushed his shirt up to touch the bare skin of his chest and waist. She fumbled with his belt. Carson thought he would burst.

Easing the silk gown from one shoulder, he feasted on scented brown skin, licking the brown berry of her nipple. Aubrey cried out, her fingers shaking as she finally got the belt undone and began working on opening his pants.

Impatient now, Carson picked her up and deposited her on the plush sofa.

"The bed's easier," Aubrey whispered as she landed on the sofa on her back. She reached for him.

"Can't wait," Carson growled, tugging the silk from her curvy form, and following its path fevered kisses. He paused to give devoted attention to her long, shapely legs and kiss her intimately. The sweet, spicy taste of her and her encouraging sounds of pleasure nearly finished him, but he held on as Aubrey trembled in pleasure.

With his help, she quickly dispensed with his pants and briefs. Leaning forward, she put her mouth on him, kissing, laving, suckling, until Carson could take no more. He wanted to be deep inside Aubrey and nothing else would satisfy him.

Moving away, he grabbed protection from a drawer in the coffee table and tore open the packet. Aubrey helped him slid protection on his rock-hard sex. Drawing him close, she wrapped those long legs around his waist. He was in heaven. With a groan of pleasure, Carson slid into her slick heat and they rocked together hard and fast.

His heart raced. Besides the wet, slapping sounds their bodies made, Carson heard a roaring in his ears as they frantically raced their way to the height of satisfaction. Both bodies arcing and clenching suddenly, they reached the pinnacle and tumbled over the edge together.

In the hot and sweaty aftermath, they lay together on the sofa. Bodies tangled intimately, they struggled to catch their breath and made the best of the limited room. Carson gathered Aubrey closer and kissed her lips. "Missed you."

"Missed you too," she said, rubbing her face against his. "I dreamed about you every night."

"Was it as good as this?" he asked looking straight into her eyes as he moved his sex inside her.

"No, no dream can ever replace the way it feels when you're inside me," she gasped. Her eyes widened in surprise. "You're ready for more already?"

"You always manage to inspire me," he said, squeezing the globes of her ass. "But I want you in bed this time."

"Me too," Aubrey sighed. Their lips met in a deep, sensual kiss. Moving together on the sofa, they gently disengaged their bodies and ran to the bedroom like a couple of teenagers.

After two more rounds of love making, Carson and Aubrey lay in bed spooned together. Hours has passed and it was now late afternoon. "We've only been apart only three days," Aubrey murmured.

"So why does it feel like weeks?" Carson murmured close to her ear.

"I think I'm addicted to your sex," Aubrey confessed with a soft laugh, "You really know how to keep a girl happy."

Carson snuggled closer, rubbing himself against her back and buttocks. "I know it's a typical male stereotype, but sex with you is never really far from my mind. I think about you all the time; the taste and scent of your sex, your kiss and the taste of your mouth, and your skin, the way it feels when I'm inside you. It's the best sex of my life and it means more because I care about you and I like you a lot. I admire you..."

Aubrey's stomach interrupted with a growl. They both laughed.

"I promised you breakfast," Carson said.

"Yes, you did," Aubrey confirmed, "and my stomach has spoken.

"Alright then, let's take a shower and then I'll cook breakfast."

Aubrey laughed. "Can we do that without ending up in bed again?"

Cason inclined his head. "You shower and I cook breakfast?"

While Aubrey considered his suggestion, he lifted the sheets and looked at himself. "I think he'll behave, but I still want to look at you, wash your body. What if I promise to feed you first?"

Aubrey nodded. "It sounds good to me!" She pushed the covers back and got up.

Carson grasped her hand and led her out of the bedroom. "We'll let the rest of the day take care of itself?"

Monday morning came much too soon. Carson left Aubrey's feeling relaxed, energized, and happy. Holding onto Aubrey for before he left, had felt solid and real. He'd wanted to stay but had to leave early to change clothes at his condo. He and Aubrey still needed to work out the logistics of being together, he mused.

Stopping to get his mail from the front lobby boxes at his condo, Carson found a large stack. He hadn't checked his mail in a while because he spent most of his free time with Aubrey. Scanning the pile quickly as he stepped into the elevator and let himself into his condo, he prepared to put most of it in the shred pile, but at least three of the pieces of mail were personal.

Dropping the personal mail on the coffee table, he went into his closet and used the remote. As he watched his clothes circulate around the closet and decided what to wear, his thoughts went back to Aubrey. If he and Aubrey were going to be together long term, he had the bigger condo and more of the luxuries. He wondered, *Should I ask Aubrey to move in with me?*

The question bounced around in Carson's head for several moments. Aubrey was nothing like the women he'd had in his condo and she'd claimed more of him, and of his life. When he tried to quantify that thought, he realized that Aubrey had become his anchor, his norm. If he asked her to move in with him, would she expect him to marry her?

Carson felt a tightness in his throat as he used the remote to stop the parade of clothing. Swallowing hard, he selected an outfit that had gone around at least three times. The word marriage didn't conjure up happy thoughts since his mother had abandoned them when Carson was a kid. Watching his father struggle to recover, Carson vowed that he would never let anyone get close enough to hurt him like that. He wasn't ready to marry anyone.

***

Aubrey awakened in the dark. Something was wrong. But what? She reached for Carson and found a warm, but empty place on the sheets beside her. Maybe she'd missed Carson. She lay quietly for several moments, listening in the dark. She sensed movement in the rooms on the other side of her bedroom door, but the sounds were too faint for her to define. Out of habit she glanced at the clock on the nightstand. It was four-thirty in the morning.

Throwing back the covers, she got out of bed. Snagging her robe, she put it on and left the bedroom. Except for the strategically located night lights, it was dark. She wandered about until she found Carson getting dressed in her office. A damp towel draped across the desk chair indicated that he'd already showered.

"I tried not to wake you," he whispered, "I figured you could sleep till seven."

"You're going home?" she asked in surprise. She wanted him to stay. She had been feeling as if he belonged with her for a while.

"Yes. I've got a few things I'd like to do before work, and I need to change clothes."

"Okay," she said agreeably. This was a change in the behavior he'd been exhibiting for weeks, but she could hardly fault him for going home to take care of things.

"Is everything all right with us?" she couldn't help asking.

Carson grinned. "We're good, unless something is bothering you?"

Shaking her head, Aubrey gave him a quick tentative smile. Some of the tension within her eased. "Would you like me to get you something to eat?"

He shook his head. "No. I'll grab something quick at home. Go back to bed. You could probably catch another couple of hours before you have to get up."

"I want to see you out," she said, "and you may have already ruined me for sleeping alone!" When he didn't respond, she took his discarded towel back to the steamy bathroom and placed it in the hamper. When she returned, he'd finished dressing and was gathering his things.

"I didn't think you'd mind if I left earlier," he explained, carefully scanning her face.

Stepping close, Aubrey hugged him. "I don't." She kissed his lips. "See you at work."

Returning the hug, he said that he'd see her at work then moved towards the door. Aubrey opened the door and saw Carson's bodyguards already waiting outside. They nodded.

When he had gone, she dropped down on the couch, her fingers tapping against the leather. Something was wrong. She could feel it. It had something to do with Carson leaving her place so early in the morning. But what? Things were changing between them, and she suspected that she wouldn't like the result.

***

There was only a hint of light on the horizon when Carson arrived at his condo.   His cleaning service kept it looking pristine. He hadn't spent much time at home since he'd been seeing Aubrey. He missed spending time at home planning his next moves, entertaining, and doing nothing, he mused as he glanced around the place.

Reminding himself that the clock was ticking away his day, he headed to his bedroom for a change of clothes. He'd showered and brushed his teeth at Aubrey's and while he'd enjoyed being with her and watching her, his thoughts kept straying to all the things he no longer had the time to do. He hadn't seriously golfed in months. He used to hang out with his friends one or two nights a week too and had promised his dad a dinner together at least once a month. Lately, he hadn't done much but sprint over to Aubrey's after work, eat, have lots of mind-blowing sex, and sleep. Yes, they often talked business too, but they also talked business at work.

Briefly, he tried to picture Aubrey golfing with him and his buddies or hanging out with him and his friends. He quickly discarded that idea. When he was with Aubrey, it was hard to pay attention to anyone or anything else, so what would be the point? In addition, his friends had never seen him this fascinated with anyone.

Carson wondered, how did married people and people with serious commitments to one another find time to be themselves outside of being a couple?

Carson selected a dark colored suit with a blueish sheen and a graphic print shirt and tie that picked up the blue color. Opening the bottom dresser drawer, he grabbed matching underwear and socks. As he stripped and donned fresh clothing, his thoughts came back to Aubrey.

What did he want from her anyway? Beyond the obvious, he'd been reluctant to even think about it. He wanted her in his life, but he wanted to be free to do the things he wanted to do too. *Dummy!* He thought, locking eyes with his reflection in the mirror as he fixed his tie. *You never had this problem before because the other relationships didn't mean anything! This one is getting dangerously close to the one Mom and Dad had before Mom just took off.*

Suddenly the tie felt as though it were strangling him. Carson carefully loosened it. He'd promised himself long ago that he would never let himself care enough for anyone to turn him into the broken man his father had been. After more than a decade, his old man had recovered a bit, but he was not the same carefree person he'd been. This was the first time anyone had gotten close enough to set off that internal alarm in Carson.

Carson ran a comb through his wild hair. *Aubrey is a reasonable person. I should be able to talk to her about needing more time to do other things.* Because he'd given his personal chef mornings off, Carson fixed a quick breakfast of bacon, eggs, toast, and coffee and ate at his kitchen table while perusing the morning headlines and checking his email. Heading for the door, he got his briefcase. His decision was made. He would talk to Aubrey and handle this situation before it became something neither of them wanted.

Aubrey arrived at work early. She saw that Carson was already in his office, working away. Who would even guess that he'd spent the greater part of last night in bed with her? However, he had not spent the night. Their time together had intensified over several weeks with Carson spending several nights and weekends with her.

Then Carson established a new pattern of going home in the early morning hours. This became his norm until he only stayed with Aubrey one or two nights a week. It made the other nights seem more impersonal.

Was Carson finally getting tired of her? Aubrey wondered. The prospect made her nervous. He hadn't spent a single night at her place during the last week. She needed to quit assuring him that she didn't mind if he went home instead of spending the night, but pride got in the way. During the day, they both worked hard. The business came first. But the nights belonged to them. Or at least they had.

Now Aubrey often wondered if he felt the need to get away from her. Did he feel that she was smothering him? No matter how much she agonized over it, she always came back to the conclusion that Carson was with her by choice, so she had nothing to worry about.

Pull yourself together, girl! Aubrey greeted the company staff with a smile and put her things away. Then she went to get her coffee.

Carson was alone in the coffee room waiting for the batch of gourmet coffee he'd made to finish brewing. He smiled at the sight of her. "Good morning, Aubrey. Did you sleep well?"

"Yes, I did," she answered, wanting to add that he'd certainly done his part to make sure that she did. "And you?"

"I slept well," he said, his blue eyes sparkling with unspoken satisfaction.

He'd obviously enjoyed his time with her, she reasoned, so why did it feel as if he were pushing her away? "I-I feel like there's been a change between us," she began in a low tone. "Is there something we need to discuss?" she asked. She was trying to figure him out.

"Huh? My schedule for today is in the system if that's what you mean." He studied her for a moment. "That's not what you mean."

Aubrey's mouth went dry as she gazed into blue eyes that now looked a little uncomfortable. "You come by but haven't stayed over in more than a week and you . . . just seem a little different. I was wondering why. But this is probably not the place or the time to discuss it."

"You're right about that!" he muttered, pouring a cup of coffee for each of them. "We should talk later."

"I'm looking forward to it," Aubrey said. She would have said more, but the look on his face before he turned to head back to his office made her uneasy. In her heart of hearts, she knew she wasn't going to like what Carson had to say. Stark fear ate at her stomach like acid. She was about to get dumped! Who was she kidding when she kept telling herself she wasn't falling for Carson MacDonald? She was in love with the man and had been for some time!

Aubrey tried to lose her thoughts in fixing her cup of coffee with cream and sugar. As she walked back to her office, she took a big sip and burned her mouth. Angry with herself, she set the cup down on her desk and threw herself into her work. Because she loved her job and was good at it, she didn't think about the coming talk with Carson again until she was on the way home.

After work that day, Aubrey entered her building with some trepidation. As usual, there was a gift box for her, but the size and shape were different. The small, beautifully wrapped box was more likely to hold a piece of jewelry than the expensive lingerie she liked, and Carson wanted her to wear for him.

Upstairs, inside her apartment, Aubrey unwrapped her gift. An expensive gold bracelet with diamonds was inside the box. It was beautiful and obviously valuable, but it wasn't something she wanted or expected from Carson. She stared at it, trying to determine why the fact that he'd given this gift to her added to her growing unease.

Then it came to her. She realized that the bracelet was the type of gift he usually gave to someone like his ex-girlfriend, Giselle. Somehow, Aubrey had never been in that category. In her heart of hearts, she knew that Giselle and the other girlfriends had never really known the Carson she knew and was intimate with. Why had Carson given her the bracelet instead of the usual piece of the expensive lingerie they both enjoyed? What did it mean?

By the time Carson called, Aubrey had worked herself into a state. She managed to get through their decision on a carryout without raising his suspicions. As she waited for him to arrive, she took deep breaths and talked herself into a calmer state. Why hadn't she realized how important Carson was to her before now?

The bell rang. Carson stood outside in the hallway with a carryout bag. The scent of Chinese food wafted toward her. Aubrey ushered him in. He set the bag on the entry table and they kissed for several minutes. Then Carson simply held her.

"Are you okay?" Carson asked when they finally drew apart.

"Yes, just a little nervous," she admitted.

"Why?" he asked, leading her to the couch and drawing her down beside him.

"Because you seem different, and I think I've been depending on our time together more than I should."

Carson blew out of puff of air. "So have I. This isn't something I usually do."

"I never thought we'd be together like this," she confided.

Carson grunted. "I wasn't planning on it, but I felt something from the very start. Let's face it, you're a fascinating woman. I don't usually date the women I work with or women who work for me."

Aubrey blinked in surprise. "Do you consider what we've been doing dating?"

Carson shook his head. "No, this is me, putting my foot in my mouth."

"Do you usually sleep with the women who work for you?"

"No. You're an exception." Carson squeezed her hand. "I'm trying to say that I planned to keep my distance and let things stay professional."

"Because of your rule about dating women from work? Or because I'm a nerdy black wealth management executive?"

Carson's eyes widened with disbelief. "You can ask me that after all the time I've spent with you and inside you in the last few months? I enjoyed every minute. If we weren't having this conversation, we'd be in bed right now." He tugged on her hand. "I like everything about you, Aubrey."

Grasping her arm, he drew her onto his lap and held her close. "You're not a nerd, you're a genius!" he said in a husky tone. "There is a hell of a difference." He nuzzled her neck and played with her hair. "Mmmm, you smell good..."

Aubrey touched her forehead to his. "You're trying to tell me something..."

"The truth is that you drive me crazy. I can't think straight. Every time I look at you in the office tomorrow, I'll be thinking of you in this sexy slip and thinking of how you look and the way I feel when I'm deep inside you." His fingers slid down her side.

Aubrey shivered in excitement. "You drive me crazy too," she admitted. "So?" When Carson didn't immediately answer she opened her eyes. He was watching her. She sensed that she wasn't going to like what he was about to say.

"So, I think we should take a break, have some time apart."

Startled, Aubrey felt as if he'd tossed a bucket of cold water on her. She shifted off his lap to stand in front of him. "What do you mean? Was that bracelet some sort of goodbye gift?"

Carson's head dipped. "Actually, I was going to suggest we try to fit us into the type of the arrangement I'm used to, something more casual. We've been very intense and its addictive, but I need more. Aubrey, I have friends and activities I love that I've been neglecting since we've been together. I want my personal life back."

Aubrey gasped in surprise. "Why do I get the blame for keeping you from the things you want to do, the people you want to see?"

Carson shoved a hand through his hair. "Because I haven't wanted to share you with them. Because we never figured out what this thing is between us and we never made the decision to go public with it."

Stunned, Aubrey swallowed and bit down on the inside of her lip in a bid to maintain her focus. "And it's too late?"

Carson stood. "Let's not see each other outside of work until we get a handle on this thing between us."

"How are we going to do that if we don't see each other?" she asked.

"We'll--just have to wing it." Shifting on his feet, he looked uncomfortable. "I-I don't know what I want right now but a commitment is more than I have to give."

"I haven't asked you for a commitment," Aubrey reminded him.

Carson shook his head. "I don't like my lack of control when it comes to you. It's like a commitment."

"Is this what you do when you meet someone new?" she asked.

His fingers curved around her shoulders. "No, Aubrey. I've never met anyone like you, and I've never been like this."

In a state of shock, Aubrey couldn't think of a thing to say. She fought back feelings of rejection and the urge to cry. Carson meant more to her than someone to sleep with. He let her be herself. She'd thought he understood her. She'd thought he liked her! Hell, she'd fallen for the man!

He held her gaze, still trying to explain. "I'm a jerk and I'm sorry. It's probably better that you find out now."

Aubrey nodded. She could only take so much. Grabbing the gift box with the bracelet she shoved it into his hands. "I can't accept this. I don't want it. Why don't you call the security team while I gather the rest of your things?" she suggested in a brittle tone.

Walking away, she didn't wait for a response. She wanted him gone. Focusing on growing anger instead of her hurt feelings, it didn't take long to collect his things.

Carson accepted the gym bag that she'd stuffed his things into and the uneaten carryout. "I really regret messing things up. You are perfect as CEO of the company. Please tell me that you're not going to quit," he said.

Aubrey looked him in the eye. "I'm not a quitter and I'm the best at what I do. If you want me to resign, I can get another job."

"Please stay and accept my apology for letting things go too far."

"I'll do my job," she promised, "but you're going to have to wait on my accepting your apology. Stay away from me."

The security team was on its way up in the elevator when she hustled him to the door. There, he tried to hug her, but Aubrey held him off with a stiff arm.

"You need time?" she said as she moved away. "I say we've had our time. Stay the hell away from me. There is nothing but business between us now."

When he was finally gone, Aubrey stood in the entryway taking several deep breaths and letting them out slowly. She was not going to cry over Carson MacDonald again, she promised herself.

Using the rest of her angry energy, Aubrey stripped the bed and changed the sheets. The room still smelled of sex and Carson. Aubrey grabbed her pillow and went to sleep in the guest room.

Carson went home. Despite months of little to no sleep, sleep didn't come to him. His thoughts were full of Aubrey, but unlike the many nights he'd spent in a haze of desire and possession, he was trying to forget the hurt and anger in her eyes. He'd really messed up and he was angry with himself.

He'd been mulling over making a change in his relationship with Aubrey for some time. In his heart, he knew that his deep distrust of permanent relationships was at the root of his problem. Aubrey already had more of his time and attention than he was comfortable with. He'd done the only thing he could, try to back off and when that didn't go well, cut things off.

Despite the mix of guilt and regret running through his thoughts, he felt as if a weight had been lifted off his shoulders. His fascination with Aubrey had the potential of becoming the same sort of relationship his parents had had. It had broken his father. He'd be damned if he followed in his father's footsteps.

CHAPTER FIFTEEN

Going into work the next day was the hardest thing Aubrey had done in a long time. She loved her job and the challenges it presented, but she was not ready to face Carson. Logically she knew that they'd had a fling with no strings attached, but deep inside, she was hurt that Carson's feelings for her did not stand up to the light of reality.

With Carson nowhere in sight, Aubrey stepped onto the elevator. She breathed a temporary sigh of relief as it traveled to their floor. Exiting the elevator, she entered the company offices. She could see interior light edging Carson's partially opened office door.

Carson must come to work, she acknowledged inwardly. You can do this. Stiffening, Aubrey swallowed hard. Cradling her cup of purchased gourmet coffee, she tipped into her office and carefully closed the door. Before long, she'd immersed herself in work.

By the time their ten-thirty meeting with a venture capital firm rolled around, Aubrey was well prepared with a list of questions and potential issues based on the market research report she'd ordered.

Carson was sitting at the conference table with the male and female venture company representatives when Aubrey entered the room. He paused, mid-conversation, his deep blue gaze meeting hers. Keeping herself anchored, Aubrey pinched her hand beneath the sheaf of papers she held. Even now, she felt the potent magnetic attraction they had for each other.

Lines of red marred the now slightly dingy whites of his eyes. For once, his curly hair did not look like something out of a magazine. It looked as if he'd spent a good part of the morning raking his hands through it. He looked like hell. He looked the way she felt. "Good morning."

The others echoed his greeting.

Aubrey's lips formed a friendly, unaffected smile as she returned the greetings. Carson's brows went up. Her thoughts churned as he introduced and endorsed each representative. *How dare he look surprised! I know how to act. I am a professional!*

Aubrey managed to make small talk until the meeting began. Throughout the discussions, she felt the weight of Carson's gaze whenever she wasn't looking at him. It pulled at her, making it harder to concentrate, but years in the business world had given her the skill she needed to do her job and appear unaffected.

She asked her questions, making notes on her list until she felt satisfied with the answers. In the process, she decided that a relationship with the venture capital firm would be good for their company and its clients.

The meeting ended with a joint decision to have the lawyers draft a working agreement. Everyone shook hands, happy at the prospect of a good, prosperous relationship. As Aubrey gathered her papers, the venture capitalists invited her and Carson out to a celebration dinner. She heard Carson accept.

Aubrey met their gazes and spoke honestly. "I appreciate the offer, but I'm going to have to pass this time. I've been a little under the weather and I really need to go home and get some rest."

"You're not sick?" Carson asked quietly.

Aubrey smiled sweetly. "Nothing that some good old rest and relaxation won't cure."

He nodded, his gaze hardening before he shifted his attention back to the others.

As Aubrey prepared to walk back to her office, the head of the venture capital firm moved closer so that only she could hear what he had to say. "Are you sure you won't change your mind, Aubrey?" he asked persuasively. "I am definitely one of your fans and it would be the highlight of my evening."

This was unexpected. Aubrey smiled at the compliment. She'd noticed that he'd been very intense during the meeting, but never imagined it might be personal. Still, going out with Carson and a bunch of other people was not her idea of fun, not when she was still hurt and angry about the way he'd treated her. "Sorry, maybe some other time?" she offered politely. This man was attractive, with sandy brown hair and soulful dark eyes.

"I have your card," he murmured, holding it up, "Maybe we could have lunch or dinner sometime?"

His question struck a sour note in her thoughts. Hadn't she already learned that business and pleasure did not mix? She shook her head. "I try to keep my business and personal life separate."

Pocketing the card, he nodded. "I apologize if it seemed like I was pressuring you in any way. . ."

Aubrey smiled. "No, it did not seem that way at all. Enjoy your evening out."

"Is there anything I can help you with?" Carson asked from behind the head of the venture capital firm.

"I was just thanking Aubrey for her efforts towards making the proposal work for your company," the other man said.

Carson glanced from Aubrey to the other man, clearly not believing the explanation. "We should get going if we want to get ahead of the dinner crowd," he said finally.

Aubrey said her goodbyes. As she started back to her office, she heard them settling on a restaurant.

As weeks passed, Aubrey realized that the only way she could continue working with Carson was to avoid physical contact and personal subjects. She still missed Carson and the hurt lingered, but she'd made the decision to move on. Gradually, it seemed as if they'd settled into an uneasy mode of working together.

***

Escaping the office one Wednesday, she hurried out for a long lunch with Mira and Sasha. She considered both women her best friends and she had been so miserable that she had to tell them about her relationship with Carson and its ending. They had been providing moral support and were treating her to lunch at a new restaurant that the food critics were raving about.

Aubrey exited the company limo and crossed the sidewalk to enter a dark brick building. The first-floor restaurant was a study in black and white, with white leather booths and black lacquered tables. Columns decorated with a twisting black graphic dotted the white ceramic tile floor, and the white, vaulted ceiling was accented with black art deco work.

Entering the restaurant, Aubrey found that both friends were already seated at a table near the windows. Mira looked gorgeous as usual in a yellow, off-the-shoulder sundress, her hair forming a halo around her face and shoulders. Sasha wore a knee-length wrapped, white Grecian-inspired sundress that looked both trendy and classic.

Glad that her friends had developed a friendship with each other, Aubrey greeted them warmly. They'd already ordered a glass of her favorite wine for her and the chef's surprise lunch for all of them.

"We've decided that you need to get out more," Mira announced as Aubrey sat down and took a sip of her wine.

"I get out a lot," Aubrey said. "In fact, I'm hardly ever home."

"That's business," Sasha said, "You need to get back out there and date!"

"I've had offers," Aubrey said, defending herself.

Mira cut in to say, "None of which you accepted!"

"I haven't felt like dating anyone," Aubrey confessed.

"The only way to get over the pain is to get back out there," Mira insisted.

Aubrey gave her friend a hard glance. "And how are you doing that?"

Mira wet her glossy painted lips. "I've been dating. I don't go to any events without a date."

Aubrey gasped. "You've given up on Ben?"

Mira tossed her hair back with a dramatic flair and a soft Spanish expletive. "I haven't given up on Ben. I still love him, but he doesn't want anything to do with me right now. He doesn't care what I do. I must go on with my life. You should too."

"I don't feel like seeing anyone else," Aubrey admitted. "I just want to work and live my life until it doesn't hurt, and it's all forgotten in the past."

"It'll happen faster if you go out and see people," Sasha said. "If nothing else, you could widen your circle of male friends. I could introduce you to some of my friends, who would be glad to escort you to events, be your friend. The press knows you, so you could help each other."

Mira leaned forward and lowered her voice. "I've got the perfect date for you, Aubrey. My friend Andre is very handsome, and everything Carson is not. He models for a lot of the big houses here and is on the way up to superstar status. You wouldn't be thinking of Carson if you went out with him."

Aubrey hesitated. "I—I don't know."

"You should do it!" Sasha said, her dark eyes sparkling, "I've got a bunch of new designs you could wear."

"And I have an event!" Mira said, her voice rising again with excitement. "It's a charity extravaganza and they always have reporters there. They have dinner, a fashion show, and dancing. I know that Andre is going, but he hasn't decided on a date."

"If you're talking about the Rackham Foundation Charity's Fashion Extravaganza and Dinner, it's too late for that," Sasha said, shaking her head, "they've sold out of tickets, but I have one."

"I couldn't take your ticket," Aubrey said, thanking her friend. "I'm not sure I even want to go."

"You're going," Mira insisted, "and you're going to have a good time. I promise."

"Aubrey, if you use my ticket and go in my place, wearing one of my designs, it will be good for me," Sasha said. "Besides, I didn't have a date anyway."

"You don't always need a date," Aubrey reminded her.

"But you do," Mira said, "and it's going to be Andre. Can I give him your number? So that you will at least have talked before the event?"

Aubrey sipped her wine, hesitating.

"Come on, Aubrey, you'll be glad you did," Mira urged.

"Come on, Aubrey, you should do it," Sasha added.

Aubrey looked at both her friends. She knew they had her best interests at heart. Getting out on a semi-normal date at a very public event could lift my spirits, she mused. "Okay, you can give Andre my number and I'll do the charity event!"

"I'm so glad you're going to get out!" Mira declared.

"You won't be sorry," Sasha added.

The three lifted their glasses and toasted Aubrey's decision. Then Sasha glanced up and said, "Here comes lunch."

***

At the charity event days later, Aubrey glanced across the table at her date, an-up-and-coming modeling friend of Mira's. He was gorgeous. His ruggedly handsome features were accented with blond hair and striking jade green eyes. With his coloring, he seemed the direct opposite of everything she knew and loved in Carson's appearance, even to the point that he had a big, muscular body to Carson's tall, lanky one. In the black tux, he looked like what he was, a top male model on the way up.

He caught her looking at him and flashed her a warm smile filled with perfect teeth. "Would you like to dance?" he asked.

Aubrey scanned the scattered couples already on the dance floor moving to the music coming from the band. "Not yet," she answered. "I need to get a little more comfortable."

"Whenever you're ready," he said. "I'm a really good dancer."

"And so modest!" Aubrey teased. He laughed. She sipped her glass of wine and took in the fabulous designer outfits the women were wearing.

There had been a fashion show before dinner was served, but with the mixed crowd full of well-dressed society matrons, designers, and fashion models, it might as well have continued. Aubrey didn't know the major clothing designers well enough to be able to name the designs on the attendees, but she knew quality and style when she saw it.

The Rackham Foundation Charity's Fashion Extravaganza and Dinner was one of the top fashion events of the season. Her friend Sasha would have been swooning at the moving, vibrant sea of fashion. When Aubrey studied some of the clothes for an extended period time, her date identified the designer.

In the center of the thickening crowd partying on the dance floor, she spotted Mira dancing a sexy salsa with a hot Italian movie star. Mira worried her. Her friend had been tight-lipped about her relationship with her husband for weeks, but a couple of days ago she'd told Aubrey that Ben was getting a divorce. It wasn't like Mira to give up on the man she loved, even if he was being pigheaded.

Beside Aubrey, her date got up from the table, reaching for her hand. "We can't let them have all the fun, can we?" he asked. "Let's dance. If you're shy, we can find a place in the back where we won't be seen."

Accepting his hand, Aubrey got up from the table. He was right. She liked to dance, but it had been a long time. Here she was, dressed in one of Sasha's dreamy creations, at a big event with a very handsome guy and she'd been looking at the clothes other people wore. She needed to get up and have fun, make some new memories.

Together, they made a striking couple. As they made their way to the dance floor, several heads turned. Aubrey's date held onto her, parting the crowd for her. They walked down a long aisle, past the spot where a television crew was filming. As she passed, Aubrey heard them say her name and note that she was the CEO of the company. They didn't have a name for her date, but the cameras panned them, providing Andre with plenty of free publicity. Aubrey was certain that many more people would know his name by morning.

By the time they made it to the dance floor and found a good spot, the band had switched to a slow song. She allowed her date to pull her close and lead her into a smooth, rhythmic slow dance. "You are a really good dancer!" she remarked in surprise.

He laughed and twirled her around playfully. "Just relax, I've got you!"

Aubrey did and her enjoyment of the evening amped up.

Mira danced close with the Italian actor. They'd been at the table with Aubrey earlier, but Mira loved to dance and had spent a good part of the evening out on the floor in her red designer gown. "Having a good time?" she mouthed at Aubrey.

Aubrey nodded and smiled, but she didn't really believe her friend was having as good a time as it appeared. Mira was a lively, fun-loving person and as good a natural actress as Aubrey had ever seen. With her beauty, name, and notoriety, not to mention her top name designer gown, Mira had been interviewed on camera and seen by all. Still, something was off with Mira. Studying her, Aubrey wondered, had Mira taken something?

As Aubrey watched, Mira leaned forward, as if to rest her head on her partner's shoulder for just a moment. Her eyes closed. Suddenly, she was slipping out of his arms. He leaned over, struggling to keep her from falling to the floor in a pool of red chiffon.

"Mira!" Aubrey stopped dancing to run to her friend. "Somebody get a doctor!"

Mira lay unmoving in the Italian's arms. She was out cold.

Carson sat drinking with his golf buddies at a table in his favorite sports bar. He scanned the bank of screens, passing on the football, basketball, and tennis. On one of the many screens, he caught sight of Aubrey looking beautiful in a long, form fitting gold gown. It differed little from some of the high-end lingerie he'd bought for her to wear. He stared appreciatively. She was one fine looking woman and he still wanted her. His imagination took off with vivid scenes from their past. It promptly returned when the television host started talking about Aubrey's date.

Carson gave her date a hard glance. He was one of those pretty boys, a male version of Giselle, he decided. Pretty boy was definitely not Aubrey's type. But what was Aubrey's type? Carson had made sure it wasn't him.

Carson turned away from the screen to talk as the conversation turned to his favorite team. When he glanced back, he saw the camera pan the event to focus on the people dancing. He saw pretty boy holding Aubrey close in a slow dance. She seemed to be enjoying it. Carson's jaw tightened.

"What's that?" one of his friends asked, "Is that the Charity Fashion event at the Gotham Hall?"

"Yeah." Carson turned his attention back to his drink. It felt good going down his throat.

"Hey man, I heard them call out your CEO. She's a hot one!" his friend remarked.

Carson didn't bother to respond. He didn't encourage his friends to talk about Aubrey.

"Oh-oh, something's happened."

When Carson's attention switched back to the screen, he caught a glimpse of a man holding a woman up. It wasn't pretty boy but pretty boy was close by. Some people stopped dancing and quickly hid them from view. Was the unconscious woman Aubrey? Carson's mouth went dry. In the rainbow of colors on the floor of the event being filmed, he wasn't sure.

As he stared at the screen, it showed more of a crowd gathering. They obstructed his view of the woman. He felt as if someone had grabbed his guts and twisted them. When he visually located Aubrey, kneeling close to the unconscious woman, Carson allowed himself to breathe.

Abruptly, Carson lost all thoughts of a pleasant evening with his friends. He started gathering his things to go.

"Are you going over to the hospital, man?"

"It wasn't my CEO lying on the floor. I'm going home." Carson said his goodbyes and headed out. On the way home, he thought about his actions. He wanted to go to the hospital to talk to Aubrey and Mira, show some support. But he knew he wouldn't be welcome.

***

Mira tried hard to avoid the trip to the hospital, but Aubrey and several friends insisted. Since Aubrey's date had an early assignment scheduled for the next morning, she said her goodbye before leaving for the hospital with Mira.

At the hospital, one of the doctors interviewed Mira and performed a series of tests. Then she was released. As Mira dressed, she told Aubrey why the doctor insisted that she wasn't sick before referring her to her own doctor. Then she swore Aubrey to secrecy. Mira was pregnant.

CHAPTER SIXTEEN

"Pregnant?" In the hospital room helping Mira dress, Aubrey stared at her friend.

Mira's eyes were wet. She had been crying. "It's Ben's baby. God help me, I still love that stupid son-of-a-bitch!"

Aubrey didn't bother asking how the pregnancy had happened. She knew how volatile Ben and Mira were. "You have to tell him."

"I will," Mira insisted, "eventually."

Aubrey hugged her friend. She didn't say anything more as she gathered the rest of her friend's clothing and jewelry. She didn't need to. They opened the door and headed out.

Aubrey was good at handling the conflicts that arose in business situations, but personal conflicts, especially those involving friends, tied her in knots. She felt uneasy when she spotted Ben down the hall arguing with Mira's Italian date.

Ben caught sight of Mira and Aubrey and hurried towards them. Looking worried, he greeted both women.

"Why are you here?" Mira demanded.

"I was worried about you." Ben grabbed Mira and pulled her into a tight hug. "Should you be leaving the hospital this soon? Are you okay?"

Mira struggled out of his arms. "I'm all right!"

Ben reached out to touch her face. "You've been crying."

"Don't do that!" Mira pushed his hand away. She gazed at him for several seconds, then seemed to come to a decision. "There's something you should know."

Ben's eyes narrowed as he studied his wife. His mouth opened and closed again.

"Let's go somewhere private and talk," Mira said. "It won't take long."

Ben shook his head. "Tell me you're not pregnant!" he demanded, his voice getting louder. "I didn't want to believe it. Tell me I'm wrong!"

Mira swallowed hard. "You're not wrong," Mira replied softly.

The Italian actor had followed Ben. His rapid Italian filled the following stunned silence. "Your wife is a virtuous woman. It's not mine!" he virtually shouted.

"Shut the hell up!" Ben looked as if he wanted to punch the actor. His hand formed a fist.

Mira turned to the actor. "Diego, you should leave. You're not a part of this drama."

As the Italian apologized and gratefully hurried away, Ben moved closer to his wife and lowered his voice. "Are you saying that I am the father?"

"Yes, but you don't have to be," Mira said, looking as if he'd punched her.

"Meaning that I'm simply one of the possibilities?"

"Meaning that you are the only possibility!" Mira gasped. "But I am fully prepared to raise my child on my own!"

Torment and uncertainty filled the depths of Ben's dark eyes. "Mira, just tell me that there was no one else. I need to be sure."

"You mean you don't trust me after the way you dumped me?" Mira glared at him. "Since we've been together and married, I haven't slept with anyone but you. Can you say the same? If that's not good enough for you, too bad. I won't be taking any unnecessary tests. You're just going to have to wait nine months."

Ben reached out to put his hands on her shoulders. "Sweetheart, I didn't mean that the way it sounded. I'm in shock. We weren't going to see each other anymore."

"Don't call me sweetheart," Mira snapped, "You don't remember that time. . . ?" Mira reminded him.

Ben's eyes lit up. "Yeah, how could I forget! I-I should probably stop the divorce proceedings," he amended quickly.

Mira pounded his chest with angry fists. "Don't bother! I don't need you. I still want the divorce!"

Aubrey stared at her friend in consternation. Mira had never wanted a divorce. Since she loved her husband and was going to have his baby, what sort of sense would a divorce make now?"

Obviously torn about what to do next, Ben studied his angry wife.

Aubrey chose that moment to intervene. "Mira, I have the limo. I can take you home if you like."

Mira found a tissue and dabbed at her eyes. "I'd rather stay with you and go home in the morning, if that's okay."

"You know it is," Aubrey assured her.

Mira nodded gratefully. "Thanks, you're a good friend and I appreciate you!" She stepped around Ben as Aubrey led the way to the limo.

"You're going to hear from my lawyers!" Ben called after them.

Mira didn't bother to answer as she and Aubrey ducked around the corner to avoid a group of reporters. Then they went to the limousine.

"Do you know what you're doing by pushing for the divorce now?" Aubrey asked when they were settled inside. "You could lose Ben and be stuck with having your baby raised in two households."

Mira let out a stream of rapid Spanish and she shook her head. "I couldn't help it. I refuse to lay down and let Ben walk all over me! Maybe I'll let him talk me out of it, maybe I won't. I-I just can't deal with him right now."

"Did you know you were pregnant?" Aubrey asked as the limousine left the curb.

Mira covered her flat belly with her hands. "I suspected something, but I have a stomach ailment that comes and goes. My stomach has been bothering me for weeks. That's why I haven't been eating much. I have a doctor appointment already scheduled."

Aubrey was worried about her friend but kept her thoughts to herself after that. Mira closed her eyes and relaxed against the seat. Within minutes, she appeared to be asleep.

With Mira settled in her guest bedroom, Aubrey got ready for bed. Her cell rang as she was pinning her hair up. Surprised, and then a little worried, she grabbed the phone to check the display. It was Carson. She took a deep breath, let it out, and answered.

"Carson? Is something wrong?" she began.

"Uh, no, at least not on this end," he answered, sounding tentative. I was worried about you and Mira. For a scary minute or two, I actually thought it was you lying unconscious on the dance floor."

Aubrey wasn't sure how to answer. Her heart warmed at the

thought that Carson was concerned about her, but if he didn't want anything meaningful, it made no sense to encourage him. "I-I'm fine," she managed.

"I'm glad," he said sincerely. "How's Mira?"

Aubrey sighed softly. "Angry, emotional, but otherwise alright."

"So, they didn't keep her?"

"No," Aubrey admitted. She wasn't going to tell Mira's secret. "They checked her out and let her go, but she has to see her doctor."

"Probably food poisoning or something," Carson said.

"You'd think so," Aubrey said. "Was there anything else?"

For several beats, Carson was silent. "I miss you, Aubrey. I've never been like this with anyone. I choked and made a stupid mess of things. Can we start over? I promise to make things right this time."

Aubrey's eyes stung. With all of her being, she wanted to say yes to Carson. She missed him more than she'd ever missed the man who had been her fiancé. But could she survive another breakup with Carson? If she didn't take care of herself, who would? A tear ran down her cheek. "That wouldn't be. . .smart," she said, "See you in the morning." Then she switched off the phone and turned off the lights.

In the dark, Aubrey lay in bed and tried to sleep. Every time she reached the edge of sleep, she found herself dreaming about Carson. She'd promised herself that she wouldn't shed any more tears for Carson Macdonald, but tears seemed the only way to cope with her overwhelming sadness. She patted the few that escaped with tissues from the nightstand until she drifted off to sleep.

The next morning, Aubrey spent extra time applying makeup to minimize the impact of her sleepless night. Mira was still asleep, so Aubrey ate a quick, solitary breakfast in the kitchen and arranged for the company limo to drop her off at work and return later to take Mira home.

At the office building, Aubrey and the bodyguard made it to the elevator with no sight of Carson. She knew trying to avoid him was silly, because he would be coming into work, but she still breathed a sigh of relief.

Today she would have to draw on her inner strength. She'd worn a red suit, for energy. She needed it after her late night out, the drama at the hospital with Mira, and her silly tears for Carson. She felt exhausted and hoped her love for the job would perk her up. As she exited the elevator and entered the company offices with a purchased cup of gourmet coffee, she saw the light edging Carson's partially open door. He was already in the office.

As quickly and quietly as possible, Aubrey slipped into her office and started her day.

***

Days later, Carson came in early and worked steadily for several hours. He dove into the detailed research he'd ordered for several new properties and lost himself in the process. However, Aubrey was in his thoughts as he made his way to the coffee room and poured himself a cup. He knew she was avoiding him.

As he made his way back to his desk, his phone started ringing crazily. When he answered, he heard a familiar deep but unusually breathless sounding voice he hadn't heard in ages. "I think you should meet me at the hospital. I'm not feeling too well."

The weakness in Ian MacDonald's voice fed Carson's growing

fear that he had kept his relationship with his father on the back burner for far too long. After building his business empire, Carson spent a lot less time with his dad, but he loved him. Carson's mother had abandoned them when Carson was eight, so his father was the only family he had.

"Dad?" Carson gulped down his coffee, burning his tongue and throat, and spilling some on his expensive suit. "Dad, what's wrong?"

"No energy, can't breathe. And I've got chest pains. Might be having a heart attack."

Carson drew in a breath and his words came out in a rush, "You need to call 911 right away! I could. . .."

"Already done, son. I wanted to talk to you myself and make sure you knew. It doesn't have to be a heart attack, but you never know."

"Did something happen to upset you? How long have you been feeling ill?"

His father gave an airy sigh. "Not upset son, just getting old, I guess. I went to sleep feeling bad and was worse when James woke me up."

"Is James there with you? Let me speak to him."

In the background he could hear his father talking to someone else. Then there was a new, but still familiar voice on the line. "Mr. McDonald, sir, I've already called for an ambulance. They'll be here in a minute. Called the doctor too. We're going to Northwest General, and I have his medical file and insurance information."

"How long has he been like this?" Carson asked.

"Sir, I'm not sure. He was resting and I woke him to take his meds."

"I'll meet you at the hospital. Make sure he's still breathing when he gets there," Carson ordered.

"I'll do my best, sir," the butler shot back, and ended the call.

Fear ate at Carson as he called downstairs for his limo. He knew he wouldn't be able to drive in his current condition. Standing, he gathered some of his paperwork, his coat, and his wallet and headed for the door. Outside his office he paused briefly at Aubrey's door. He sensed her solitary figure beyond the barrier, hard at work. Then he knocked quickly and opened the door.

Aubrey looked up from her keyboard and computer screen, startled. "Carson?" Her gaze sharpened. "What's wrong?"

Carson's words came out in a rush. "I've got to go. I have a family emergency. It's my dad. I-I think he's having a heart attack."

"Oh no!" Aubrey jumped up from her desk and came around quickly. Before he knew it, she was rubbing his back and hugging him hard. Steeped in her scent, the softness of her body, and her obvious sympathy and caring for him, he needed that hug, that evidence of shared humanity. "I'm so sorry!" she said sympathetically. "Do you need me to do anything?"

Briefly Carson closed his eyes. The comfort Aubrey offered was almost more than he could bear to leave. Still, it could not save him from what awaited him once he left the office. "I have to get to the hospital," he managed to say.

"Do you have any appointments scheduled for today?"

Carson's mind went blank. "I–I don't think so."

"I'll talk to your secretary. Tell me you're not driving yourself."

"I'm not," he assured her. "I called the limo."

"Do you want me to...?" She started, then gasped, as if she'd surprised herself and done something wrong. Aubrey released him suddenly, her arms dropping down to her sides as she took a small step away from him.

Carson felt the temperature in the room drop. He hadn't realized how much he'd been leaning on Aubrey's warmth.

Regrouping, she wet her lips, swallowed hard, and said, "You'd better get going. I'll take care of things here."

Carson stared at Aubrey, aware that he'd just missed something important. But what? He had to see about his dad. As he backed out of her office, need broke through his uselessly cycling thoughts. "Would you come with me?"

Aubrey's eyes widened. Her gaze locked on to his. "Are you sure you want me to?"

"Yes," he said simply.

"And it wouldn't upset your dad to see me?"

Carson threw her an incredulous look. "No!"

"Then yes, I'll come to the hospital with you," she said, running back to her desk to grab her purse and keys. "I'll tell the staff to reschedule all of the afternoon appointments."

"Fine," he muttered, his mind already working on the fastest route to Northwest General.

CHAPTER SEVENTEEN

The ride to the hospital seemed to take forever. Aubrey thought of all the times she'd rushed to the hospital, afraid that her brother wasn't going to make it and then last week with Mira. This isn't about you! Aubrey reminded herself as she held herself back from hugging Carson. Instead, she clasped his cold hand in hers. She'd never seen Carson so discombobulated. But who wouldn't be? She could still remember her father's last moments and would until the day she died.

Once they reached the hospital, Aubrey stayed close as they navigated the halls to the emergency room. She was relieved to hear that Carson's father had already been transferred to a private room in the Coronary Care Unit(CCU). As they made their way to it, Carson still held tight to her hand. Her heart ached for him. Silently, she prayed that Carson's dad would recover.

Finally, they made it through the maze of antiseptic corridors to the VIP wing of the CCU. Hospital security was strong here, but once Carson established who he was, they led him and Aubrey to the right room. The private guard outside the door explained that James, who had come in with Mr. MacDonald, had gone for coffee. He then moved aside with deference, allowing them to enter.

The door opened to reveal a slender man with curly salt and pepper hair in the bed with his eyes closed. The resemblance to Carson was unmistakable. The older man's features had more of an edge, and where Carson was lanky, the older man was too thin. Aubrey guessed his age to be late fifties, early sixties. He was on oxygen and hooked up to various machines that beeped and chimed, alerting the medical staff to his status.

A woman in scrubs stood close to the bed, making notes on his chart. "Mr. MacDonald?" she asked, her gaze going to the man in the bed and then back to Carson as if confirming the obvious.

"Yes." Carson nodded.

"I'm Dr. Baker. Your father had a heart attack. We're still assessing the damage, but he's out of the woods."

Carson's body sagged with relief. "How long will he have to stay?"

The doctor shrugged. "Depends on the damage and the full diagnosis. It could be anywhere from a couple of days to a couple of weeks." She replaced the chart and headed out. "You have ten minutes to visit with him. I'll be down the hall with another patient. The nurse is monitoring his vitals and will page me if he needs me," she said.

Dropping Aubrey's hand for the first time, Carson went to the bed. "Dad? Dad!" he called in an urgent whisper. There was no response. Leaning close to the older man, Carson put his face to his father's, cheek to cheek.

Aubrey's eyes stung with the impending threat of tears when one of the older man's pale hands lifted to gently pat Carson's back.

"I-I was afraid you wouldn't make it!" Carson confessed in a voice filled with emotion.

The older man chuckled breathily. "I'm still here! It shouldn't be this hard to get a visit from my son!"

Carson drew the bedside leather chair closer and eased into it. "I'm going to do better, I promise. You'll have to stick around to see it, though."

"I'm holding you to it!" the older man promised.

Still close to the door, Aubrey felt out of place. This was private. She had no business standing in the shadows and listening as Carson visited with his dad. She turned to quietly ease out the door.

"Stay! Please!" the older man said in a surprisingly strong voice.

Aubrey turned to find herself speared by Carson's father's sharp blue eyes.

"A-are you talking to me?"

"Yes."

Carson's color deepened. "I'm sorry, Dad, Aubrey. Dad, I should have introduced you to Aubrey Merrill. She's my new CEO at Crutchfield and Donner, and she's also my friend. Aubrey, this is my dad, Ian MacDonald."

"I'm happy to meet you, Mr. MacDonald, sir," Aubrey said, coming forward to gently take his hand.

"And I'm happy to meet you," he replied, taking a deep breath. He carefully formed his next words. "I haven't met many of Carson's lady friends."

Aubrey felt as if she were under the spotlight of the older man's gaze. She knew that Carson's lady friends were usually one type and she wasn't it. But she and Carson had been intimate. Had his father somehow picked up on that? She blushed.

"It's not like that," Carson explained quickly.

"I know," his dad assured him, "I know."

Aubrey had the uncomfortable feeling that Ian MacDonald knew quite a bit about her and Carson as she settled in the chair Carson had moved next to his. She spared a glanced for the heart monitor close to the bed. It was beeping and a red light flashed. No doubt the nurse would be in soon to kick them out so that Carson's father could rest.

Despite the older man's physical distress, he seemed determined to make the most of his son's visit. "You're good at what you do," he told Aubrey.

She nodded. "Yes, I am."

"My son is too."

Carson stared at his father. "Dad, you're looking kind of gray."

"I'm in the right place," the older man said, but his voice lacked most of the earlier strength he'd displayed.

The nurse chose that moment to enter the room. "Sir, it's been ten minutes. You're going to have to leave," she told Carson. "Mr. MacDonald is very weak and needs his rest. I'll give you a code. Family members can call the CCU to get status updates."

"Can I let him rest and come back later?" Carson asked.

"No." The nurse shook her head. "He needs his rest, and his doctor has ordered more tests. You'll have to come back tomorrow, sir."

"I love you, Dad." Carson rubbed his father's shoulder and touched his face to the older man's. "I'll be back in the morning."

Ian MacDonald's stormy blue eyes watched Aubrey. "You come too," he said.

Surprised, Aubrey glanced back at Carson. He simply shrugged. She turned back to face Ian MacDonald and said, "I will." Then she left with Carson.

Carson was still agitated as they found their way back to the limousine. "I could have lost my dad," he said, dragging his hand across his forehead for the twentieth time.

"But you didn't," she reminded him. "It looks as though he'll recover."

His head dipped in acknowledgement. "He'd better. He's all I've got."

They followed the bodyguard to a side door and exited the hospital. The limousine was outside. It was already dark when Aubrey climbed into it.

"We should get something to eat," Carson remarked as he settled beside her on the seat.

"Yes, and then I need to get home." Aubrey said, glad she hadn't voiced her thoughts of cooking something for them at her place. She still cared for Carson more than she would ever admit and wanted to support him, but this interlude was too intimate. It wouldn't take much for them to take up where they'd left off. She saw that Carson was studying her.

"I really appreciate your coming along," he said.

Aubrey grasped his cold hand in both of hers. "I wanted to. I know how it feels when there's an emergency and someone you love may not live through it. I didn't want you to face that alone."

Carson nodded. His eyes seemed to see clear through to her soul. "It meant a lot to me."

Aubrey wanted to hug him, comfort him. Carson might suck at a relationship with her, but he was basically a good guy. Holding his hand effectively kept her from administering any hugs.

In the awkward silence that followed, he gently freed his hand and drew his phone from a suit pocket. "What do you feel like eating? Italian? Chinese? Thai?"

Aubrey chose Thai food and Carson gave the address to the driver.

After dinner, the limousine pulled up to Aubrey's building. Gathering her purse and briefcase, she prepared to exit. Carson seemed a bit subdued as he watched. Seeing him all discombobulated and lost-looking had done something to her. Impulsively, Aubrey gathered him into a tight hug.

He felt warm and solid in her arms. His masculine scent filled her nostrils, and she felt his heartbeat accelerate. Hers soon followed. Holding Carson felt close to heaven. Virtually ripping herself away, she stopped short of pressing a kiss to his stubbled cheek. What is wrong with me? "Take care, Carson," she murmured, and got out.

"Good night, Aubrey," he called out as the bodyguard closed the car door.

Aubrey opened her mouth to tell him to call her if he needed her. Instead, she bit down on her tongue in consternation.

She entered her building alone, except for her bodyguard. Deep inside, she acknowledged to herself, things have got to change. I must change. I refuse to spend the rest of my year drooling over Carson MacDonald and wanting more than he's able to give. He's not the only eligible man in the city.

Inside her condo, Aubrey listened to her messages. One was from her date from the charity fashion event. Aubrey called him back and they talked for nearly an hour. Then they made plans to go to a show. Afterward, she felt as if some of the weight she'd been carrying around had lifted.

Worry for his father translated into a sleepless night for Carson. Instead of going straight to the office the next morning, he went to the hospital. Carson knew he would not be able to work if his father was still in danger. The unease that had been nagging him persisted as he wound his way through the corridors and reached his father's room.

Carson entered his father's room and released the breath he'd been holding. The older man was finishing his breakfast. He turned to look at Carson and said, "Good morning. I didn't think I'd see you this early."

Carson shrugged. "I had to make sure you were alright."

"I'm still breathing," his father said dryly. "Where's Aubrey?"

Carson hid a flash of annoyance as he made a show of checking his watch. "She's probably at the office by now."

"You mean she wasn't at your place last night?"

Shaking his head, Carson gave his father an incredulous look. "Where are you getting this stuff, Dad? Aubrey is the CEO of my new company, Crutchfield and Donner."

"So, you haven't slept with her?" His father raised his brows suggestively.

As Carson struggled with the best way to answer that question or determine if he would, his father moved on to say, "Oh, you messed up. . . ."

Closing his mouth, Carson took the leather chair by the bed. "How did you guess?" he asked finally.

"I read the papers and all those magazines that spend time making up stories about people. There've been a few about you and Aubrey, especially since you dumped that no talent actress. I've always known that if you ever found a woman as smart as you with beauty to boot, you'd be a goner. Then there's the fact that you were holding her hand just before you walked into my room yesterday. . . .."

Carson shook his head resolutely. "No, I wasn't."

"Would you like to take a bet on that?" His father carefully lifted his cup and took a sip of his coffee.

"Should you be drinking coffee?" Carson asked in concern.

"It's decaffeinated," his father assured him. "And they've decided that I'm going to make a full recovery." He set his cup down. "So how did you mess up?"

"It was going too fast and I was falling so hard that I didn't have time for anything else but her and work. I choked. . .."

"Choked and?"

"And broke things off."

Ian MacDonald sighed dramatically. "How long are you going to let what happed between me and your mother affect your relationships?"

"You're wrong about that," Carson said quickly.

"Am I? You mean you didn't for a minute see your future self as a poor lovesick slob being abandoned by his wife and never being the same? Tell me that's not the way you think of me!"

Carson's head dipped. He hadn't lied to his dad since he was eight years old, and he wasn't going to start now. "This isn't what I imagined when I rushed over here this morning."

His father quipped spiritedly, "I'm still breathing, so this is a wonderful surprise, right?"

"Right." Carson chuckled. "Dad, there's a bunch of reasons why I choked. Some even I don't know, but I wish I hadn't."

Ian MacDonald tilted his head. "She won't take you back?"

"No."

"Do you love her?"

Carson hesitated. "I think so—I'm not sure."

"Then maybe it's for the best. You can go back to the gold-digging arm candy."

"That's not what I want."

"Really?" his father asked in a provocative tone.

Carson didn't bother to answer. He'd already said more than he should have. "Have you seen your doctor this morning?" he asked, abruptly changing the subject.

"No," his father answered calmly, "but she said she'd be making rounds this morning."

Carson studied his father. Sitting in his cardiac unit bed, his father seemed more robust than he had in years. "Do you know when you're getting out of here? You seem like you've almost fully recovered."

Ian MacDonald grinned. "I didn't fake a heart attack to get myself admitted to the hospital so I could guilt my son into visiting me, but I am enjoying the attention," he said spunkily.

"I'm enjoying you too, Dad," Carson admitted, "The heart attack shook me up and it's made me reassess my priorities. I can get more money, but I can't replace you. It's going to be better between us when you get out of here. You're all I've got."

His father tilted his coffee cup in agreement. "Here's to you, son. And the doctor says I'm going to have to reassess some of the things I've been doing too. I probably should retire."

"Not unless you really want to," Carson advised him, "You're still young. You probably just need to destress."

"You'll have to help me with that one," the older man said,

"Son, shall I have them bring you some breakfast?"

"No Dad, I'm good." Carson stood. "I'm going to the nurse's station to have your doctor paged."

CHAPTER EIGHTEEN

It was close to nine-thirty when Carson arrived at the office. Aubrey was meeting with a client. Inside his office, he grinned when he saw that she'd used his information to bid on a property he wanted. The bid was almost exactly what he would have submitted. *Damn, do I like Aubrey Merrill!*

Later, he knocked on her office door. Her muffled response fell somewhere between a grunt and a grumble. He opened the door to find her elbow deep in a pile of papers. When she glanced up at him, he could see that she had been working hard and was tired. "Hi. How's your father doing?" she asked.

"Sassy, nosey, talkative, and if I didn't know better, I'd think he'd staged the whole thing for attention!"

Aubrey smiled. "I'm glad he's doing better."

"Me too," Carson said, turning serious, "and thanks again for the moral support."

"You're welcome." Aubrey's smile faded. "Was there anything else?"

Carson gazed at Aubrey, drinking in the sight of her, savoring the simple act of breathing the same air. Yesterday she'd supported him when he needed it most. Today he could almost feel an invisible barrier between them. She seemed different, but he hadn't imagined her hugging him and holding his hand as she accompanied him to the hospital. She still cared about him. "Could I take you to dinner?" he asked tentatively.

"I've got a date," she said, confounding him.

When had she found the time to get a date? Jealousy ripped his gut and his jaw tightened. Another man was already trying to claim what had been his. "Can you reschedule it?" he asked, persisting.

Aubrey's tone was even, but no hint of warmth or affection lit her eyes. "No, I can't."

Carson ignored the warning voice in his head. "How about tomorrow?"

"No." Aubrey folded her arms on the desk. "Carson, you wanted space and you've got it. Enjoy it. I didn't mean to confuse you at the hospital yesterday. With all my family has gone through because of Wyatt's bouts with cancer, I really didn't want you to face the hospital alone."

"And I appreciate that," Carson interjected calmly in his sincerest tone, "I appreciate you, Aubrey, for who you are. When I talked about my need for something more casual, something more manageable, I didn't consider all the feelings we have for each other. I was nervous and upset so I said things I didn't mean. I should have stressed the need for us to slow things down. We were very hot and heavy for a while..."

Aubrey's complexion took on a rosy hue. Was that embarrassment? he wondered. He wasn't ashamed of anything he'd done with Aubrey.

Carson studied her face, noting the stubborn set of her lips and the determination in her eyes. "You're not listening to anything I have to say on this, are you?" he accused.

Aubrey shook her head. "I can't. Carson, you hurt me and I'm not going to let you do it again."

"I've tried to apologize," he added, "I'm human. I make mistakes and I'm man enough to admit it." He studied Aubrey's frozen expression. He wasn't going down without a fight, but right now, he didn't know how to reach her without going too far. "We can't be done for good." he said, ending on a hopeful note.

"We're done," she confirmed.

"I choked and made a mistake by breaking things off. . .."

"It wasn't a mistake," Aubrey insisted. "Feeling trapped is a very valid reason for ending a relationship."

Carson drew in a quick breath. "I never said I felt trapped."

Aubrey studied him hard. "Can you honestly tell me that wasn't how you felt?"

Carson met her gaze head-on, the truth damning him. "No, I can't deny that that's how I felt."

"So, let's move on and preserve our work relationship," Aubrey urged in a reasonable tone. "I would hate for things to get to the point where I couldn't work here."

Was that a threat? Carson narrowed his eyes. He wanted and needed Aubrey, but he'd lost her due to his own issues. He couldn't lose her expertise at the company too. "It won't come to that," he assured her. "But I think you should take some time to think about giving us another chance. I think what we had is worth the effort. It could be more. . .."

Pain flashed across her face and quickly disappeared. It hurt Carson to see it. He hadn't meant to hurt her. Aubrey blinked and shook her head. "I-I can't. No."

Carson backed up. He couldn't remember the last time a woman had told him no. Aubrey seemed to find it easy. Was that why it was so hard to accept Aubrey's decision? He refused to give up. "I want you to know that I'll be here when you change your mind," he said.

Aubrey's brows went up. Her classic expression spoke volumes.

Not gonna happen! Dream on!

Carson didn't remember what he said next, but he managed to end the conversation and leave her office with some shreds of his dignity intact. Her rejection stung like a festering wound that had erupted, leaving the skin beneath raw and aching. He went back to his office and checked on his property bids.

With a list of the successful bids on his desk, Carson turned to gaze sightlessly out the twenty-fifth-floor window. His thoughts were on Aubrey. How could he have messed up so badly? The expression he'd just seen on her face would haunt him for the rest of his life.

Carson scrubbed a hand across his forehead. Trying to get back with Aubrey was discouraging. He missed the Aubrey he'd known and loved. Was it love? he asked himself. No other woman had ever completely monopolized his mind, body, and thoughts. He wanted her back. I'll get her back, he told himself.

Tilting back, he turned on his chair's massage cycle. He'd give Aubrey a chance to cool down and see what she was missing. In the meantime, he planned to work harder at enjoying his life as an unattached and very much in demand male. What woman liked seeing her man with other women? She'd come around in a couple of months. And if she didn't? Carson squashed the thought. If he had to come up with plan B, no more Mr. Nice Guy. He knew how to win.

Aubrey watched Carson go back to his office unsuccessfully hiding his dejection. She couldn't shake the conviction that her insistence on maintaining their split was a mistake. Her thoughts churned uneasily. No way could she let Carson just walk all over her. She now knew from experience that she could do just fine without a man in her life. She could also replace him. So why did she feel so sad? Why did she still have feelings for the man who'd screwed her brains out, then dumped her when he decided she was taking up too much of his time?

CHAPTER NINETEEN

As weeks passed, Carson made sure Aubrey knew he was continuing with his life of dating models, starlets, and heiresses. She didn't seem to care, a cruel fact that egged Carson on. Despite the show, none of the women made it to his bed. Carson had developed a taste for a beautiful brainy black girl with a weakness for high end lingerie.

It had been more than a month since Aubrey told Carson that they were done for good. They worked well together, as always, but lurking just beneath the surface, the issue between them still felt unresolved.

After scheduling an appointment, Aubrey arrived at his office to discuss a problem and get his cooperation.

"Long day?" Carson asked once she'd settled into his guest chair. His piercing gaze seemed to go clear through her attempt at professionalism.

"Long week," Aubrey corrected, reaching within herself for calm and control. She never quite forgot that although she was the CEO, it was Carson's company. In addition, she was still proving to herself that she could put aside her feelings for Carson and do a hell of a job as CEO. This was the time to be Aubrey the CEO, not Aubrey the woman still fighting an overwhelming attraction to Carson MacDonald. "I spent some time with the company lawyers this morning," she began.

"So, they've given up on me, huh?" Raising his brows in good natured triumph, Carson leaned back in his custom massage desk chair. He suppressed most of a grin.

Aubrey was glad that he wasn't operating the massage chair while she talked. Depending on the setting, a stimulated or more relaxed Carson would amp up the amount of distraction he naturally possessed.

"We need to discuss the way you acquire properties and conduct the real estate business end of this company," she said. Her goal was to get Carson in line with the company lawyers and policies. Although he was a genius, Carson sometimes used questionable methods that put the company at risk. The company lawyers had failed at getting him to take the company policies into account, so now Aubrey was doing her job.

Carson's gaze sharpened. "Didn't we agree that I would cover the real estate operation and handle things my way?"

"Yes." Negotiation techniques 101, find the common ground. Aubrey nodded. "And didn't we agree that we would abide by the rules and procedures needed to keep the company out of trouble?"

"You're not referring to any procedures I ever agreed to," Carson grumbled, breaking what should have been a chain of agreement. "I'm not asking permission to do what I do best!"

"No one is asking you to!" Aubrey countered. "Even out there on your own, as a real estate entrepreneur using your private funds, you listen to your lawyers, don't you?"

"I have my lawyers look over contracts. I ask then to review all my agreements and advise me," Carson said, his tone impatient. "They still do that for all my personal projects."

"And the difference is?"

Carson shot her an incredulous look. "Seriously? If I were signing the company lawyer paychecks they'd be out of a job! They insert themselves at every turn. Then they try to insist that I should not be signing any contract without their approval!"

"Without their review and concurrence or agreement," Aubrey corrected. There is a difference, you know."

Carson tilted his head. "Whose side are you on anyway?"

"Crutchfield and Donner's," she said drolly.

"Aubrey, I'm not going to be hemmed in by a bunch of green company lawyers who don't know how my deals are structured or how things are done!"

Aubrey leaned in closer. "So, show them, teach them how things are done."

Carson shook his head. "No, that's not my job. If you check your contract and the company operating agreement, training falls under the leadership of the CEO."

Aubrey bit down on the inside of her jaw. She'd had a feeling he'd say that, but she still had to find a way to get him in line. Aubrey racked her brain. *Maybe since he thinks his private lawyers are so wonderful, I could do something with that.*

"Was there anything else?" Carson studied her, ready to move on.

"Yes. We can put your private lawyers on contract with the company to review your Crutchfield and Donner contracts and agreements while considering our company rules and procedures."

Tilting back in his chair, he fiddled with his pen. "That could work. I'll present your proposal to them."

"I'd also want them to recommend changes and work arounds for our policies and spend time showing our lawyers the ins and outs of how you do business."

"That would be a way to get the company lawyers up to speed, but it'll cost you quite a bit. My lawyers are good, and they earn every penny I give them."

"We have the money for the training," Aubrey said, "but if our lawyers can't get up to speed within a reasonable amount of time, maybe we need new ones."

"Maybe." Carson took his chair out of recline mode. "Anything else, Madame CEO?"

"Yes." Aubrey leaned forward. "I want to be there when you present my proposal to them since it will involve company funds. Do you have any issues with that?"

"No," Carson's blue gaze zeroed in on her, "but I should have seen that one coming."

They gave each other hard, uncompromising stares for several moments. Then they both abruptly dissolved into laughter.

"It's a reasonable request and you know it," Aubrey said.

"True." Carson nodded in agreement. "I'd do the same."

"I guess I should be getting back to my office," Aubrey said as she began gathering her things.

"Stay a moment and talk to me," Carson urged.

Aubrey tensed. Was there an implied challenge beneath his pleasant tone? It wasn't as if she were scurrying back to her office like a scared little mouse, was it? She forced herself to relax back into her chair. "Okay. How's your dad?"

Carson cleared his throat with a sound that resembled a groan. "Feeling better and feeling more entitled to meddle. He's been asking about you."

"Really?" Aubrey smiled. "I like your dad."

"And he likes you. He's having a dinner party this weekend and he's been nagging me to invite you."

"And you haven't because?"

"Because you've been very careful to avoid anything personal with me since things fell apart."

"I want to work with you and make the company the best it can be," she explained, "but I don't want to give you the wrong idea."

"What would be the wrong idea?" Carson asked, looking as if he really didn't know.

Aubrey took a deep breath and let it out. The shaky feeling of not being in control was back. "The wrong idea is that things between us can go back to the way they were."

Carson was silent for several beats. Then in a much lower tone he said, "Because of you and what happened, I'm now a better person and I know what I want."

Holding his gaze, Aubrey could see that he believed what he was saying. But how could she even consider being so vulnerable again? She'd always known that he was like a diamond hidden among all the glass men out there pretending to be the best. Until he saw that she too was a diamond, and worth whatever it took, she could not let herself become involved with him again.

Carson's eyes heated, holding her immobile with their intensity. "What if things were better than before? Better than either of us imagined when we stepped off the cliff?"

Aubrey opened her mouth and closed it. She stood up, her legs watery, willing herself to display strength she didn't feel. "I can't imagine that," she said, gathering her iPad and papers. "Now, I really do have to get back to my office."

"Enjoy the rest of your afternoon," he called as she walked away.

Reaching the haven of her office, Aubrey gratefully closed the door and fell into her desk chair. It did not recline or massage the way Carson's did, but it felt wonderful. She still felt a bit discombobulated and couldn't explain it to herself. To get her mind back on work, she pulled a stack of letters and papers from her in box and began to go through them.

Near the middle of the pile, she found a large brown envelope. She checked for a return address and found none. Inside the envelope, she found a large smiley face magnet with sparkly eyes. On the bottom, the letters on a blue rectangle read: I hope this smile returns some of the sunshine you've brought to me and mine! Beneath the words Ian MacDonald had signed his name.

Opening the envelope and looking for more, she found a folded slip of blue paper. She read:

You're invited to a dinner party at my home this weekend. Please come! Cocktails at five-thirty. Dinner at six. Food you will love. Carson and I will be on our best behavior.

Ian

Aubrey studied the smiley face magnet. She liked Ian MacDonald. Her smile slowly faded. She wished he'd give up on her being with Carson. She deserved someone who was able to give her all the love she needed. Carson needed . . . . She didn't know what Carson needed.

Aubrey opened a desk drawer and put the invitation in a growing pile. She didn't feel right throwing Ian's hand-written invitations in the trash. Sooner or later, she was going to have to accept one of Ian's invitations.

CHAPTER TWENTY

In metallic blue Manolos, Aubrey glided into the palatial theater on the arm of her date for the evening, web company entrepreneur Zac Logan. He'd impressed her with his intelligence and wit. He'd pursued her for weeks after meeting her at a financial summit. Red-haired, green-eyed Zac wasn't bad to look at either, with his athletic build, but she was fooling herself if she really thought he could replace Carson.

Carson. She didn't know where he was in the room, but she could feel the heat of his gaze, burning her bare arms and the skin revealed by her provocatively cut gown. Was she imagining it? The source of the heat seemed to be coming from one of the tables near the center of the hall which was lined with formally set tables and antique chairs. She couldn't always dress like a nun, she reasoned, and sometimes all the resulting attention felt good.

As if he'd heard her thought, Zac flashed her a scorching smile. "Did I tell you that you look amazing?"

She returned the smile. "Yes, you did. Thank you."

"You'll probably hear it again," he declared, "because I can't take my eyes off you."

Aubrey glanced down to scan the envelope with their table number printed across the front. "We're at table six."

One of the ushers scurried forward. "Ms. Merrill, Mr. Logan, please allow me to show you to your table."

"Lead on," Zac replied gamely, holding Aubrey's hand to his arm as they followed the usher.

Maintaining her smile, Aubrey greeted some of the seated guests as they walked to their table. She stifled an inward groan at the direction they were heading. She could feel herself getting closer to

Carson. Would the event planners have placed her and Carson at the same table? It was a logical thing to do, but no way would she enjoy sitting with Carson and his date.

As Aubrey followed the usher, she felt Carson's gaze more than ever. He always attended this industry event and he'd mentioned it the other day, so she knew he was here. She glanced at the occupants at some of the tables, intent on spotting him without appearing to. And why am I looking for him anyway? she fumed, ordering herself to stop.

"Here you are, table six."

As Aubrey thanked the usher, it registered that the table was already half-filled with people.

"Let me get your chair." Aubrey's date stepped forward and drew out her chair.

"Thanks." Settling into the chair, she glanced around the table and found herself looking into Carson's blue eyes. She blinked, at a temporary loss of words.

"Good evening," he said in a pleasant voice, then greeted them both by name.

Carson knew her date by name! That made Aubrey more than a little uncomfortable. As she and Zac returned the greeting, Carson added, "Have you met my date, Ilene Harper?"

Ilene? Aubrey turned her head to get a good look. She knew and liked the CEO of Bella Foods very well. "We've met," Aubrey and Ilene exclaimed as they greeted each other warmly and spent a few minutes catching up.

Critically taking in Ilene's warm, caramel-colored skin, curvy figure, and big brown eyes, Aubrey couldn't help wondering if she was looking at her replacement. Yes, Ilene's lips and curves were fuller. Instead of Aubrey's shoulder length twists, Ilene's permed hair was cut into a short and sassy style with blond highlights. Ilene's black and gold designer dress hugged her hourglass figure and she was pretty....

Lowering her eyelids, Aubrey lifted her glass of water and took a sip. It didn't ease the sudden burning sensation in her chest. She felt sick. She didn't want to be here. Replacing the glass, she caught Carson watching her, a speculative look in his eyes. Damned if she'd let him see the jealousy ripping through her. Aubrey flashed Zac a bright smile.

Zac responded by leaning close to whisper, "This is our night."

"It is," she agreed, willing herself to believe it.

"We don't have to stay long," he continued. "I know a club we can go to after they announce the awards for company of the year, strategist of the year, and comeback of the year."

"You're expecting to win?" she asked in surprise. "How do you know?"

"Actually, all of the companies represented here are candidates for an award. I just happen to have a friend who told me that I'm high on the list for some of the awards, along with my company."

"I'm rooting for you," Aubrey said.

"I'm rooting for you too," Zac replied, giving her hand a squeeze, "You and Carson are high on the list for best return to profitability."

"We are?" The fingers on Aubrey's free hand spread out into a fan against her breastbone.

"Yes," Zac confirmed, watching her intently.

The thought of having to accept an award and make an acceptance speech on the fly occupied Aubrey's thoughts. She could do it but wasn't prepared and she had made a commitment to do her best for the company. If they won an award, should she let make Carson the speech? she wondered. The option sounded a sour note in her thoughts because Carson was not the CEO.

Zac threw her a quizzical look. "Carson didn't tell you that your company might be getting an award?"

"I hadn't really planned to attend this event," she admitted, "You're very persuasive."

Zac grinned. "Could I convince you to consider spending more time with me?"

"I'm here, aren't I?" Aubrey quipped.

"Then I'm going to have to see what else I can do," Zac shot back at her with a gleam in his eyes.

"Yes, you are." Aubrey brightened her smile.

Surreptitiously watching Carson with Ilene, was an exercise in patience, tact, and acting for Aubrey. Before her, he'd dated models and actresses. Now he'd moved on to CEOs. Ilene was intelligent, attractive, and a powerhouse in her own right. *Was Carson serious about her?* Aubrey wondered. She could tell that Ilene liked Carson very much. *But who wouldn't, when so many of the billionaires of the world were old and unattractive?* Carson was young, gorgeous, intelligent, and he had an upbeat personality.

It had been months since she and Carson went their separate ways. Aubrey wanted to be anywhere but the same table with Carson and his date. She liked Ilene, but with Carson, the woman seemed cloying and clingy. *Had Carson ever been that attentive to her?* Aubrey wondered, but then they hadn't conducted their relationship in the spotlight of the business world. Now she wondered, *had it been a real relationship outside of their mutual sexual desire?*

Aubrey's date clasped her hand, massaging it, and drawing her attention back to him. "Are you worrying about work?"

Aubrey smiled sheepishly. "A little." Carson was a big part of her work, wasn't he? she assured herself.

"This is supposed to be fun time away from the office!" Zac admonished her.

"I'll have to try harder!" Aubrey laughed.

"How about some champagne?" he asked, signaling one of the waiters.

Aubrey tilted her head to the side. "Shouldn't we wait to see who's getting the award? Then we'd know what we're celebrating.

Zac leaned in closer, lowering his tone. "I may work hard, and my business is very important, but I celebrate every time I'm with you."

Aubrey sighed and thanked him softly. He certainly knew what to say. She could almost forget that Carson was sitting close by, watching her. "Then let's celebrate being out together," she said.

Later, when Zac excused himself to accept his award, Carson moved closer to speak with her. "I'm glad to see that you were able to make it after all," he began, keeping things on a professional level.

"I wasn't going to come," she admitted, "but Zac made me realize that I needed to get out and be around other people."

"Will you be accepting the award if we win?"

"I've been considering it," Aubrey admitted, "but I don't have anything prepared."

"You could wing it," he said, encouraging her. "You know the drill, thank our wonderful staff, our clients, and the judges."

"And you," Aubrey added. No matter how she felt about Carson MacDonald as a boyfriend and lover, he had given her the chance of a lifetime and he always backed her up.

Carson's expression revealed nothing of his thoughts. "If you like."

"It's not about like, Carson," she explained, "People wait their entire lives for opportunities like you gave me and never find them. You took a chance on me and I appreciate it."

"Is that all?"

The words penetrated her mental shield and made her search harder for the emotion his question only hinted at. His expression was still noncommittal, but the look in his eyes sent a shudder of heat coursing through her. The things she'd felt for Carson weren't gone, not by a long shot. It felt so wrong to deny herself when he was obviously ready to pick up where they'd left off.

Swallowing, Aubrey tried to meet his gaze, but ultimately had to look down at the notes she'd been scribbling. "That's a conversation for another day," she managed to say.

"Let me know when you're ready," he said, heat cutting through his professional tone to give her another shiver of desire.

Aubrey nodded. "I will," she answered, still fumbling with her notes. That he could make references to their past relationship while he was out with another woman simply floored her. *Did that mean that he had nothing going with Ilene? Did it mean that he really cared about Aubrey?* He made it difficult for her to see things clearly enough to find her way through their mess of a relationship. Her cell phone buzzed faintly.

"I sent you a copy of my talking points for an acceptance speech if we do win," Carson said.

She might fail with the personal stuff, but she was going to damn well succeed at her job. Aubrey forced her head up to meet his gaze once more. "Thank you."

"You're welcome." A glint of admiration lit his eyes and quickly disappeared. Carson went back to his seat.

Pulling up Carson's email file on her cell, Aubrey stiffened, but didn't look up when she heard Ilene welcome Carson's return to her side with a girlish giggle. She was not going to engage in this situation with her thoughts, actions, or dreams.

Finishing his acceptance speech, Zac returned to his seat. "I saw you talking to Carson," he said, leaning close to speak casually. "You don't have to go, do you?"

"No." Aubrey gave him a light smile. "Carson sent me his talking points in case we win."

"All right!" Zac put her glass of champagne in her hand and lifted his. "Here's to more wins for table six!" he said, clicking his glass against hers and offering the toast to the other people at six.

"Here! Here!" Others at their table echoed his statement with the tinkling of crystal wineglasses.

Later, Carson sat lightly drumming his fingers on the table as the announcer went through the nominees for the award in his category. He had a strong feeling that he and Aubrey would be getting this one for the company since they'd accomplished more in less than a year, then anyone had thought possible.

So, how am I going to play this? he wondered. Carson knew Aubrey would like to stand in the spotlight and get the accolades for the company, but he also knew she was a little nervous and not as prepared as she'd like to be.

Mentally, he scoffed at the thought. Aubrey had a way with words, and she was quick on her feet. She'd take his notes and make them sound profound, or she'd use them as a springboard for something even better.

So, I'll go with her and stand there in case she needs help, he decided. After all, the award meant more to her than to him, didn't it? Carson checked himself. He liked to win. Period.

"And the winner of the Business Award for Best Comeback is Ilene Harper, Bella Foods!"

Carson's hand hit the table in surprise. Dammit! He made sure that his mouth was closed. Beside him, Ilene giggled nervously as she got to her feet. He patted her hand, holding her arm momentarily to steady her on her stilt-like heels.

"Congratulations!" he called out in a cheerful tone. The others echoed his words. Ilene's smile widened as she found her dignity and began the walk to the podium.

Accepting the award, Ilene began her acceptance speech with endearing enthusiasm. The audience listened raptly.

Out of the corner of one eye, Carson saw Aubrey slip her useless notes into her purse. They exchanged glances. Beneath her polite smile, she wasn't a happy camper. Neither was he, damnit! Why hadn't Crutchfield and Donner gotten the award?

Ilene slowly made her way back to the table, many people stopping her for congratulations. She looked as if she were floating on a cloud of happiness. Back at the table, she enthusiastically hugged everyone.

As people gathered their things and prepared to leave, Ilene bubbled on blissfully about her unexpected win. Carson smiled and concentrated on being a good sport. He knew he couldn't expect to win all the time.

He casually glanced a few chairs away to see Zac helping Aubrey with her evening wrap. She looked calm and seemed oblivious to Zac's intense focus on her.

"You're not upset because Crutchfield and Donner didn't win, are you?" Zac asked.

"Of course not," Aubrey assured him without a smile.

Zac let it go at that. From where Carson sat, he didn't believe her either. No doubt the loss had set a new low for Aubrey's competitive spirit.

"I want to celebrate my win." Zac put a hand on her arm. "Let's go somewhere. We could dance, listen to a little music."

Carson took in the set of Aubrey's jaw, her still unsmiling face, and a tenseness he knew well. She was about to beg off.

Ilene slipped out of her chair and sauntered over to the couple to enter her own bid for the evening. "I know a really nice little private club with a great band and wonderful drinks. Why don't we all go now? It'll be a lot of fun, I promise!"

Aubrey gave her a sharp glance. "Who all did you have in mind?"

Ilene shrugged, not appearing to notice the cool undertone in Aubrey's voce. "Just the four of us. . ." Then she glanced back at Carson. "Carson, you don't mind, do you? It could be sort of a double date and celebration for me and Zac."

Carson gave Ilene a lazy smile and confirmed that he didn't mind at all. He couldn't have planned this maneuver if he'd tried. *Your move, Aubrey. Are you going to be the first to say no?*

Zac turned to Aubrey, a tentative look on his face. "Aubrey? I'm in if you are."

"I'm tired," Aubrey began, making eye contact with each of them, "but I would like to help you celebrate for a little while. Is it worth going if only for an hour, hour and a half?"

"It is," Zac agreed quickly. "Let's go."

Surprised, Carson got up from the table, helped Ilene with her things, and followed the group out the door. Outside, Carson and Ilene climbed into the company limo. Aubrey and Zac got into his Porsche 911. With the bodyguards in separate cars, the entourage took off.

Twenty minutes later they were seated in a leather booth in a dark trendy nightclub. Although it was dark inside, candles on the tables illuminated the shadowed faces of tablemates and lighted pathways on the floor made it easier to move around. Flashing lights on the dance floor offered intriguing views of the people dancing to the live band. Carson ordered the first bottle of champagne.

Huddled together in the booth, they talked amongst themselves. When the champagne arrived, they toasted the success of Zac and Ilene. As the band began to play a fast dance, Zac maneuvered Aubrey onto the dance floor. Watching Aubrey, Carson realized that he'd never seen her dance. She had rhythm and moved gracefully as she danced with Zac, laughing, and having fun. He wondered if she would have enjoyed dancing with him as much.

Seated next to Carson, Ilene's light and witty conversation flowed like a river. Apparently, champagne loosened her tongue. He didn't have to say much. He liked Ilene and tried to listen, but Aubrey dancing with another man drew his attention.

As the song ended and the band began to play a slow dance, Carson's throat ran dry when Zac pulled Aubrey close into his arms. Carson didn't like it. Briefly, he toyed with the idea of cutting in on them.

Beside Carson, Ilene stood and grabbed his hand. "Let's dance. I just love this song!"

Getting to his feet, he followed her to the dance floor. Briefly, he wondered, *Why am I here with Ilene, when I really want to be with Aubrey?*

He realized it was time to change the game. Carson drew Ilene into his arms and moved her around the dancefloor. She snuggled up to him and dreamily closed her eyes. He concentrated on not looking at Aubrey and Zac.

Once the song ended, he and Ilene were standing next to Aubrey and Zac, waiting for the next song. Carson decided that it was time to make his move.

"Shall we switch up for a dance?" Carson suggested good naturedly. He missed the feel of Aubrey in his arms and if he had to finagle her into dancing with him to do it, so be it.

Obviously hesitating on a 'no', Zac looked at Aubrey.

Aubrey shook her head. "I'm still helping Zac celebrate!" she said. "Besides, I think Ilene would rather stick with you."

Ilene gave Carson a quick hug and smiled at him. "That's for sure. Carson is my first choice."

Dramatically twirling Ilene around with his hand held high, Carson spent the next song dancing vigorously. Afterward, he told Ilene that he felt exhausted, had a busy day tomorrow, and really needed to leave soon.

"I'm sorry you're not feeling well," Ilene said, looking as if she saw through his lie. "Do you want me to find my own way home?"

"Of course not! I brought you here and I expect to take you home unless...," he glanced around suspiciously, "unless you've met someone else?"

Ilene giggled. "I'm sorry for all the giggling," she said, apologizing, "but you are such a fun man to be around! I don't think I could find anyone better."

Carson took her hand and led her down the path to the table. "Oh, believe me, you could," he assured her.

Back at the table, they finished their champagne and prepared to leave. Ilene tilted her head as she looked at him. "I really, really like you Carson, but I can't seem to get anywhere with you. It's almost like you have a wall around you. Don't you like me at all?"

"I like you a lot," he assured her.

"But?" she asked, pressing for more.

"I was really into someone and I messed up. I've been between resolving it and trying to move on for a while." He smiled. "I'm not ready to give up."

Ilene leaned close and kissed his cheek. "The best things in life are worth fighting for. True love is worth fighting for."

Carson's head dipped. "Some of us have to learn that the hard way." Retrieving his wallet from an inside pocket, he tossed a bunch of bills on the table.

Just then Aubrey and Zac came back to the table. "My hour and a half are up and my bed is calling!" Aubrey said. "Zac's taking me home now."

"We were just leaving too," Ilene assured her. The men shook hands and the ladies hugged everyone. When it came time for Aubrey to hug Carson, she made it as quick and impersonal as possible. Still, he inhaled her scent, and relished the feel of her in his arms again, however briefly. It re-enforced what he already knew. He had it bad for Aubrey Merrill.

Carson took Ilene home in the limo. Outside her home, she kissed Carson on the cheek once more and said, "Now that I know the score, I think it's best that we don't date anymore. I hope you get what you want."

"So do I," he said, "And there's someone perfect out there for you too."

"If you see him, tell him to give me a call!" She turned and opened her door. "Good night."

Carson said his good night, got back into the limo, and headed home alone.

CHAPTER TWENTY-ONE

Christmas lights blinked and winked around the office as Aubrey gathered the items she would take home with her. In her excitement, she hummed a Christmas tune and put way too much work in her briefcase. *Better too much than not enough!* she reasoned.

Finally, with her briefcase packed and her laptop in the case, she put on her new winter coat and opened the door to her office. "Carson!" she squeaked, surprised to find him standing there.

He grinned. "Sorry to startle you. I wanted to speak to you before you left for the holiday."

Her eyes widened. "Is there something wrong?"

"Of course not." His grin widened. "I wanted to wish you a Merry Christmas."

"Merry Christmas, Carson," she said carefully.

"Can I get a hug? Some well wishes?"

She wanted to hug him. She hadn't touched him in ages, but he was still starring in her nightly dreams. Aubrey offered him her hand. "I don't think a hug is a good idea, but I wish you the best for the new year."

He stared at her for a few moments. "You can trust me," he said, taking her hand and pressing a kiss to the back of it.

Aubrey's skin tingled madly in response and she melted inside. Carson's old magic was still working. She retrieved her hand, intent on not displaying her reaction.

"I've got to get to the airport," she reminded him.

"Merry Christmas. I wish you everything you ever wanted for Christmas," he said. "Give your mother and brother my love."

"I will." Turning away from him, Aubrey shut the lights off and locked her office.

"You forgot this." Carson held out a gift-wrapped package.

Aubrey studied it suspiciously. It was big enough to hold an expensive nightgown, but Carson knew better at this stage in their relationship. "What is it?"

"Company Christmas present," Carson replied. "Why don't you open it?"

"This isn't the company Christmas present I ordered for everyone," Aubrey said.

"Each company employee also received a Christmas present from me," Carson explained.

Taking a few steps forward in the outer office, she placed her purse, briefcase, and packages on one of the assistant's desks. Then Aubrey accepted the package with trepidation. She tore it open to uncover two books: Real Estate Investing for Newbies, and Novel Techniques for Making Money in the Coming Age. Glancing back at Carson in surprise, she said, "That was very thoughtful. I'll start reading these on the plane. Thank you!"

"You're welcome. See you in January." Carson turned abruptly and strode back towards his office.

"Did you get your gift?" Aubrey asked before she realized she was talking to empty air. Intent on getting him something, she'd purchased a gift certificate for their favorite Italian restaurant and placed it in his Christmas card. *I should have hugged Carson.* Standing in the nearly empty office, she regretted her need to keep her distance from the man she loved.

She knew she would miss Carson, despite awkward moments, lingering feelings, and all. Still, she had to leave now. Checking her watch once more, Aubrey called in one of the people on the security team waiting in their office lobby and gave him her briefcase and bag. Then she headed out.

***

As in New York, fluffy white snow greeted her and the bodyguard on the ground in Chicago. Deciding not to struggle with her bags on the train, Aubrey paid for a private car to take them to her mother's new place in the Chicago suburb of Palatine.

The car pulled up to a beautiful brown brick home with burgundy accents. There were no hints of the past here. As Aubrey paid the driver, the gold-edged front door opened, and her brother Wyatt darted outside without a coat. Instead of his fifteen years, he looked more like twelve.

"Wyatt!" she exclaimed as he hugged her long and hard.

"You finally came home!" he murmured, still holding on.

"Yes, I did. I really missed you and Momma!"

While the driver retrieved Aubrey's bags from the trunk and set them in the entryway, Wyatt clung to her side and peppered the bodyguard with questions. Making the still skinny, but healthy-looking Wyatt go back inside, Aubrey dismissed her bodyguard with a promise that she would call him when and if she decided to leave her mother's house. Carson's rules about her always using the bodyguard had no weight here in Chicago.

Afterward she waited on the porch until the driver was done unloading her bags. Then she gave him a tip and went into the house full of cool colors and smart, contemporary furniture.

Inside, her mother closed the door and pulled Aubrey into a

strong, heartfelt hug. "I'm so glad to see you! Sometimes it felt as if you might never come home!"

"I'm glad to be home," Aubrey murmured against her mother's shoulder.

She pushed back to look at Aubrey. "How's Carson?"

"Fine. He sends his love," Aubrey said diplomatically.

"But you're still apart?"

"Momma, I never told you that we were together."

"But you were. I did drag that out of you. Do you think I didn't notice when you quit talking about him? You don't have to hurt in silence, honey!"

Aubrey blinked back tears. "I haven't been hurting in silence, I'm trying to get over him."

Her mother gave her a quizzical look. "Are you sure that's what you want to do? Need to do?"

"Yes. No. I don't know!" Aubrey pushed her things out of the pathway to the sofa.

Anitra Merrill studied her daughter for a few seconds more. "I'm sorry for bringing him up honey, but I worry about you, whether I say anything or not. You've had enough tragedy in your life, and I want you to be happy."

"And I want to be happy," Aubrey insisted.

Her mother sighed, then said brightly, "Let me show you to your new room! You're going to love it!"

Aubrey grabbed the handle on her big rolling suitcase and followed her mother to the east wing of the house. They stopped at a pink and grey room with familiar contemporary furnishings.

Aubrey walked the room, touching things, checking out the closet and the dresser. "I recognize this furniture," she began.

"Yes, it looks a lot like the dream bedroom you wanted years ago." Her mother said. "I hope you still like it."

"I do," Aubrey assured her, plopping down on the inviting bed. "It's perfect! So, what are we doing for dinner?"

"I cooked!" her mother said brightly. "We're going to have an old-fashioned Christmas dinner together, just the three of us. Didn't you smell the food?"

Aubrey smiled. She had smelled the savory aromas of turkey and dressing, and the buttery scent of macaroni and cheese, the moment she walked in. Her mouth watered at the memory of all the traditional Christmas foods: "Turkey and dressing, macaroni and cheese, collard greens, corn bread, candied sweet potatoes, and potato salad!"

"That's our holiday dinner!" her mother exclaimed.

"Do you need help?" Aubrey felt tired but knew cooking all that food was a lot of work.

"I can always use help," her mother said diplomatically, "but Wyatt's been helping me. You look a little jet lagged. Why don't you take a nap until dinner's ready?"

Following her mother's suggestion, Aubrey took off her shoes to lie down. With her eyes closed, she listened to the sounds of this new house, of Wyatt and her mother talking as they worked in the kitchen. She was welcome, but she really didn't belong here. Did she belong in New York?

As her body relaxed against the sheets, she thought about Carson, who would probably spend a good part of the holiday doing things with his dad. He'd probably do a few parties and hang out with his friends too.

His image formed in her mind. She hadn't handled her holiday goodbye the way she wanted to. She wished she could make up her mind and stick to it. Yes, she'd decided that things were over between her and Carson for good, but she still had feelings for him. She still wanted him. Those things affected how she interacted with him. If he only knew how close he'd come to breaking her down on more occasions than she cared to remember...

Aubrey turned over on her side. And if she'd broken down and started seeing Carson again, then what? There lay the unknown territory. She'd never gone back with anyone after the big break-up.

CHAPTER TWENTY-TWO

Later that evening, dinner with the family was new and exciting, because of the new house and Wyatt's newfound health. The familiar tasty comfort food, cooked and eaten on the Christmas and Thanksgiving holidays for many years played a starring role. For too many holidays in the past, they'd hurriedly eaten their meal, intent on keeping their thoughts of impending loss away. They'd hardly tasted their food. It felt wonderful to be in a different emotional place.

Wyatt was animated as he talked, ate, and alternately played with his new phone. His conversation covered his friends, his school, the chess club, and the overnight party one of his friends was giving. All were luxuries he'd missed in the past. Aubrey's mother smiled indulgently. Aubrey listened and asked questions. Thank God, Wyatt was living a normal life.

As Aubrey helped her mother put away the food, Wyatt's friend and his mother arrived to pick him up. She chatted briefly with Aubrey and her mother while her son helped Wyatt put his things in the car. Then Wyatt came to hug them both before setting off. Hugging Aubrey for a few extra moments, he promised to go with her to check on the things she'd put in storage when she gave up her condo in Chicago.

With Wyatt and his company gone, Aubrey and her mother continued putting the food up.

"What does the doctor say about Wyatt's health?" Aubrey asked, snapping the seal on a storage container.

"He's doing good. They're still giving him vitamin shots and he's on a new diet, but it all seems to be working."

Aubrey spooned dressing into another container. "I'm glad."

"There are no guarantees in life, so I wish you'd quit worrying," her mother said, slicing the remaining cornbread and placing it into a storage bag.

"I think it's a habit," Aubrey admitted. "It's almost as if I'm afraid to let go and just believe."

"I know what you mean," her mother put in in a frank tone, "but I have to allow Wyatt to find his new norm. It's been hard to let go, but he's so happy now! And I feel better too."

Aubrey promised to work harder at not worrying.

Aubrey enjoyed her time with the family, but as the holiday period whisked by, she saw more and more that everyone had changed and were dealing with different life issues. She dined, shopped, and visited old friends. Sometimes with the bodyguard in the background, sometimes not. She was no longer the top wealth management advisor, hidden in the back room of a Chicago firm. People asked about her work as a CEO, being in the spotlight of the gossip columns, and working for Carson.

Her mother was no longer the frantic, on edge parent of a cancer patient. She now worked for a different company as a programmer/analyst and had made several new friends. Most telling, Wyatt had lost the haunted look in his eyes and was happy and healthy with his new school, friends, and activities.

The biggest surprise of the holiday came when Aubrey's mother insisted that she accompany her and a friend to a New Year's Eve party being given by friends.

Dressed in one of the two Sasha special evening outfits she'd packed in her suitcase; Aubrey opened the door with a little gasp of surprise. Her old boss, Chase Everett, stood there, looking dapper in a black suit, his sandy hair freshly cut. "Merry Christmas!" he said in his calm familiar voice.

"Merry Christmas!" she stammered back, giving him a quick hug. "Are you taking my mother to the party?"

"I am." His gray eyes studied her, silently asking if she had a problem with that fact.

"I think that's wonderful!" she gushed with a wide smile, "I'm just surprised."

"I've always liked your mother but didn't get to see her much because of all the things she was dealing with," he explained.

Aubrey ushered him into the house. "I don't want to be the third wheel," she murmured.

Chase patted her shoulder. "It wouldn't be like that. We're friends, and we're just seeing where it goes." He glanced towards the top of the stairs.

"I'm almost ready," her mother called down, as if he'd called out her name.

"Take your time," Chase called back. "Aubrey and I are talking."

"So how is Wickerfield Associates?" she asked, taking a seat on the steel rimmed leather couch.

Chase took the steel and leather chair across from her. "It's fine. Owen has the top spot in our Wealth Management Division and we've been training some of the newer associates to find someone to take your place."

Aubrey nodded. "And business?"

"Business is good. Some of your clients did jump, but with all that happened, we ended up with more. Not everyone wants to have their affairs handled in New York and some people view Carson MacDonald as a wild card."

Aubrey grinned. "Yes, he can be," she admitted, "but most of his moves are pure genius!"

"So, you're happy with your decision?" he asked, studying her calmly.

"Oh yes! It was the opportunity of a lifetime."

"So, what's next?"

Aubrey sat on the edge of her seat. She loved talking about her company. "We've brought the company back from the brink of bankruptcy, we've got several new clients and our base is still growing. . .."

Chase interrupted, "What's MacDonald like to work with?"

Without hesitation she replied, "He's good. He does the real estate and I do everything else."

"So, you're happy?"

Was she happy? Aubrey wasn't ready to say yes or no. Her job was great, and she wasn't crying over Carson. Why didn't she have a ready answer?

"I'm ready!" Anitra Merrill chose that moment to come down the stairs. Aubrey had talked her mother into wearing the other Sasha designed evening dress she'd brought. It was a long, one-shouldered silver gown with glittering rhinestones along all the edges, including a modest split down the side.

"You look beautiful!" Chase said, echoing Aubrey's thoughts.

"You could be a movie star," Aubrey added.

Continuing down the stairs, Anitra Merrill blushed beneath the compliments and thanked them both. Outside, waiting near Chase's car, was the bodyguard Carson had insisted on since Aubrey was now CEO of a multimillion-dollar company.

"There are four of us," Chase murmured as they all got into his car.

The party was fun and pleasant. Aubrey flitted from group to group of friendly people, talking and laughing like a social butterfly. As the magic hour approached, she tried to wave off one of the determined single men who had been tracking her all evening.

"You need a partner for midnight," he insisted, refusing to be deterred. "I can kiss your cheek if you prefer, but neither of us should be standing alone at the beginning of the new year. It wouldn't bode well for the rest of the year."

Aubrey wasn't superstitious, but she allowed him to stand with her as the clock chimed to twelve. True to his word, he kissed her cheek and they wished each other the best in the new year. Aubrey saw Chase gently kiss her mother in the center of the crowd. She knew her mother deserved happiness, but it made her feel a little strange and more determined to make the life she'd claimed more of her own.

Aubrey's partner gave her his card. "Call me sometime. We could go out when you're in town."

Smiling, she slipped his card into her purse to deal with later.

CHAPTER TWENTY-THREE

Coming back to work after the holidays was a welcome treat for Aubrey. Except for her family, her life was centered in New York. She'd missed her work, the office, and her condo. The words would never pass her lips, but she'd missed Carson too. With the office closed, the work had piled up. As a result, everyone put in extra hours in hopes of catching up.

It took a couple of months for everyone to recover from the holiday backlog. Just when everyone was poised to catch a break, there was a round of capital expenditures and acquisitions that pushed the firm to its limits. Except for meetings, Aubrey barely saw Carson. When she had time to think about it and the consequences, she hoped this would help her get over her feelings for Carson.

It was almost May. Trying to maintain her composure, Aubrey sat across from Carson with her iPad and a stack of papers and files. His office was huge by New York standards and had every luxury he could think of, but it still wasn't big enough for the two of them. It felt almost as if he were breathing on her.

His dark curls were ruffled from his running his fingers through his hair while he worked on an issue with one of the new properties. He'd taken off his tie and undone a few buttons on his blue silk shirt. A hint of his toned and tan chest teased her senses. Why hadn't she arranged to meet him in the conference room? She did not need to be this close when she felt so vulnerable.

"You okay?"

Aubrey stared at him in surprise. She was usually very good at hiding her thoughts and emotions. "I'm fine," she managed in a confident tone.

Carson studied her for a few intense moments. "You always look fine, Aubrey, but you've got a few beads of moisture on your nose. Is it too hot in here? I could turn up the air conditioning."

Why can't I be less attracted to him? Aubrey wet her lips. She heard Carson's quick intake of breath. His darkening gaze sent a tremor of awareness echoing through her. "I-I need some water," she said quickly.

"Me too," he said, moving quickly to get clean glasses from a hidden cupboard behind him. He filled each with ice cold water from a dispenser near his desk. "Here you go," he said, giving her one of the glasses.

Aubrey jumped at the sensation of his warm fingers touching hers, causing some of the water to spill.

"It's all right. It's all right." Carson steadied her hands. Then he wrapped his hand around hers and lifted the glass. As she drank, his hand fell away and he used a tissue to blot the water that had splashed his desk.

As she set the glass down on his desk, she discovered that he was incredibly close. Aubrey blinked, unwilling or unable to consider that he was once again making a move on her. Heat flooded her as he scooted his chair even closer. His big hands curved around her shoulders.

His blue gaze burned clear through to her soul. "What we had was better than anything either of us had ever experienced," he acknowledged in a husky voice. "I know you think you're past it, but we're not done. We may never be done."

He pulled her into his arms and dragged his lips across hers in a masterful kiss. Moaning with pleasure, Aubrey struggled to catch her breath.

Gently cupping her face in his hands, he whispered between gentle kisses, "You know what I want. I want you, all of you."

Trembling, Aubrey leaned her cheek against his. "Not here, not now," she whispered back.

"Yes, now," Carson insisted firmly as he kissed her more insistently. His fingers caressed her shoulders and moved down to her skirt clad hips and thighs. His heat permeated her body.

Awash in a flood of sensation, Aubrey closed her eyes and allowed herself to enjoy the sensation of his hands touching her breasts and caressing her thighs. Her fingers slipped the buttons on his designer silk shirt to touch his warm skin.

"You want it just as much as I do. Admit it," Carson rasped impatiently, "Say yes."

Aubrey gulped air. It was true. His kiss, his touch, was like a homecoming. She wanted Carson like she was dying of thirst and he was that long cool glass of life saving water. She'd been fighting her feelings for Carson for so long, hoping they'd go away. This was not the ideal time or place, but why was she denying herself something she wanted so desperately?

Carson's tone grew more impatient as he stood, physically threatening to move away from her, "Aubrey?"

"Yes! I want you too," she groaned. "I tried to move on, but I can't stop thinking about you!"

She'd barely gotten the words out when he lifted her from her chair and set her on top of his desk. "Have you ever had sex on a desk?" he asked with a cocky grin.

"No," Aubrey admitted, as he gently nudged her legs open and stepped between them. "But what if one of the assistants or the secretary comes in?"

"This is my office. No one comes in here without my permission," he assured her.

Shaking her head, Aubrey still hesitated. "This isn't me. Carson, this isn't the way I do things."

Carson's blue gaze burned through to her once more. "Stay with me Aubrey. We need this," he insisted. "I'll lock the door. Please?"

Aubrey nodded, giving in because he was right. She loved and needed him. She missed the heat of his body as he quickly moved away to lock the door. Then he was back.

Sliding his hands up her skirt, he quickly dispensed with the tiny scrap of lace and pushed her skirt up and out of the way.

She gasped as he caressed her intimately, knowing exactly how to get her close to the edge. Aubrey grabbed his belt, unbuckled it, and unbuttoned his pants. He was so hard, she strained to get the zipper down. She touched the thick hard length of him, aching to have him inside her.

Carson leaned over her, his fingers in the slick moisture deep inside her. "I want to taste you, see if it's as good as I remember, and make up for some of the time we've been apart, but it's been too long. I can't wait."

"Me either." Aubrey tugged down his briefs and stared at him with wonder. Carson was beautiful. She wanted to taste him too. "Quit teasing me."

He gathered her in his arms, impaling her on his thick hard length. It was a tight fit, but they moved together in a sensual frenzy that sent them both over the edge.

Trembling in the aftermath, Aubrey held on to Carson with her arms and legs. She could feel him shaking too.

"So good, so good," he whispered.

It wasn't enough, Aubrey realized. It had been too long. She felt him lifting her and moving away from the desk edge. "What are you doing?" she asked.

"I've been having a little fantasy about you and me in that desk chair massager," Carson said.

From his arms, Aubrey studied the chair in wonder.

Then he was settling them into the massage chair, semi reclining it, and pulling her down on top of him. He set the massage cycle and Aubrey had the ride of her life.

Much later, Aubrey awakened to Carson's caresses. She'd missed that too. They were both naked and sandwiched together in the massaging desk chair. Their clothes were strewn around the office. People, cars, and trucks still bustled in the street far below, but it was getting late.

"I have a shower in my bathroom over there," he said, pointing. "We could get cleaned up and. . . ."

"Start all over?" Aubrey asked, feeling as if she were floating. She felt high on Carson.

"Yeah." Carson curved his hands over her butt and squeezed. "Or we could go back to your place or mine."

Aubrey maneuvered herself to a sitting position. This was crazy and things were happening too fast. "It-it's too soon for that." She glanced down and then back at Carson. She didn't want to go backwards in her relationship with Carson but didn't know what moving forward would mean. "I need time to figure everything out."

Carson nodded gravely. "Can I wash your body?"

Aubrey nodded. "I'll wash yours."

"Can I have you one more time?"

Aubrey nodded again and smiled. "I want that too."

"I missed you," he said as he took her hand and led her to the shower.

Outside her condo much later, Aubrey kissed Carson goodnight and prepared to get out of the limo. He held onto her for a few moments longer. She looked into his eyes. He'd already let her know in every way he could that he wanted to stay with her. *Why was I so adamant about needing more time?*

She'd already taken a big step in sleeping with him again. Letting him back into her condo was close to a total surrender. The prospect of Carson choking again and pushing her away loomed large in her thoughts. Aubrey took a deep breath and let it out slowly. Then she offered Carson her hand. "Coming?"

Aubrey awakened in her bed with Carson's body wrapped around hers. Turning in his arms, she took in the glorious sight of him, reveling in it. Then she closed her eyes and counted to ten. She'd dreamed this morning too many times to rely on her lying eyes.

Opening her eyes once more, she saw that Carson was still there. He was watching her, an amused expression on his face. "I'm still here. I'm not going anywhere until you kick me out."

Tilting her chin upward, Aubrey pressed a soft kiss to his lips. "I thought I was dreaming."

"I was beginning to wonder if you would ever take me back," he said, still rumbling in his morning voice.

It wasn't something she'd planned. His words filled her with so much emotion that she couldn't speak, so she simply snuggled closer.

Voice still rumbling, he asked, "Are you hungry?"

Aubrey looked up at him once more and smiled suggestively.

"We've got to eat," he admonished. "You're perfect but losing any more weight might jeopardize that."

She had lost weight. Aubrey shot him a warning glance. *Don't mess with the mood.*

"I'm going to take a shower, then rustle up something for us to eat," he said, resolutely pushing back the covers.

"I'm coming with you," Aubrey said, still getting used to the fact that Carson was in her here and now.

They showered together, then fixed breakfast in Aubrey's condo kitchen. It was Saturday, so there was nowhere else they had to be.

Scarfing down the omelet and coffee, Aubrey realized that she had been hungry. Carson had moved his chair so that instead of sitting across from her, he sat next to her. He looked as if he could eat her up. "I'm back, right? This isn't a temporary aberration, is it?"

"You're here," Aubrey confirmed, "and I don't want you to leave."

Carson slid his hands up and down her arms. "This time I want to do things the right way. I don't want to be without you."

"I don't want to lose you either, Carson," she said, "and I'm not pressuring you for a commitment."

"I was miserable when we were apart," he assured her.

"I hated it, but I—I couldn't be with someone who didn't want to be with me," she explained.

"I understand." Carson drew Aubrey onto his lap and into his arms and kissed her temple as he played with her hair. "I-I never felt like I didn't want to be with you. I was concerned about the way my life was changing and that I had no control. I choked. My mother left us when I was eight and it broke my father. He's never been the same. I promised myself that I would never be like my dad. What happened with my dad has affected my relationships."

"I'm so sorry she abandoned you." Aubrey put her head against Carson's chest, her fingers massaging the muscles and tendons in his neck, "For her to leave you and your father, she had to have some very strong reasons. I'm a different person, so you're going to have to learn to trust that I care enough to stay and work things out. Can you do that?"

"That kind of trust is hard for me," he said honestly, "but I need you in my life. I'll do whatever it takes to keep us together."

Aubrey and Carson slipped back into their old pattern of working hard in the office all day and spending most of their evenings together, but Carson introduced a few changes. Sometimes he took Aubrey out. Then he gifted her with golf lessons and spent time golfing with her.

Aubrey thought things were moving along until they encountered one of Carson's friend's and his wife on the golf course. His friends, especially the wife, were happy to meet Aubrey. They informed her that most of his other friends were single.

Noting that Carson seemed quiet and a bit subdued, Aubrey side stepped the other couple's offer to combine their golf outings. Instead, she suggested that they meet afterward for dinner and drinks.

When the other couple had gone, Carson said, "Please don't think I've been hiding you. I was trying to find the right time to introduce you to my friends."

Aubrey pulled him close and hugged him. "No pressure, remember? We're still finding our way."

Carson kissed her hard. "I know where I want us to go. The only problem I have is myself."

Aubrey slid her fingers through his curls, pushing them back from his face. "As long as you're not walking away, we're good."

He nuzzled his cheek against hers and kissed her neck. Then he simply held her until they heard the next group in the distance.

"We'd better get back to the game if we're going to meet Duncan and Greta for dinner," he said, releasing Aubrey and handing her the Putter.

Later, Aubrey enjoyed dinner with Carson and his friends. Duncan had known Carson since his college days, so they had a warm, easy camaraderie that included Aubrey and Greta.

When Greta and Aubrey went to the ladies' room, Greta told Aubrey that she was the only girlfriend Carson had ever introduced her to. Shocked, Aubrey tried not to make too much of the fact that Carson had not planned this time to introduce her to his friends.

Working in her office a week later, Aubrey found one of Ian MacDonald's smiley face magnets in her office mail. This one was bright yellow and had flashing gold lights in the center of its eyes. Smiling, Aubrey peered inside the envelope for more. A folded sheet of blue paper was at the bottom. Retrieving and opening the paper, Aubrey read:

Surprise! I've invited your mother and brother to my yard party this weekend and have arranged for their transportation and hotel.

You're invited too. Do come! Dress casual. Hopefully, I'll see you on Saturday, from six until. . . .

Ian

Aubrey's fingers rose to her mouth in surprise. *No, he didn't!* A smart-assed voice in the back of her thoughts noted that she now knew where Carson had gotten the manipulation gene. Would her mother plan a trip to New York without talking to her? Aubrey ran several scenarios through her head. Maybe, if Ian told her that it would be a surprise for Aubrey. Could he just be playing with her, teasing, in an unfunny way? She didn't know him well enough to say.

Aubrey's fingers shook as she lifted the desk phone and began to dial her mother's number. Had Carson's dad been talking to her mother?

CHAPTER TWENTY-FOUR

On Saturday, the limousine pulled up to a large brick brownstone belonging to Carson's father. He'd finally found a way to get Aubrey to show up at one of his events. Once the bodyguard was satisfied with the look of their surroundings, the driver helped Aubrey out of the back.

Clad in blue shorts and a matching tank with blue and white designer sandals, Aubrey stepped onto the front walk gripping her sunglasses and a small blue and white clutch. She stared at the home, which although nice, was not the display of wealth that Carson enjoyed. It was probably the house he grew up in.

Music drifted out from somewhere behind the house as well as the sounds of people talking and having a good time.

"This way, Ms. Merrill," the bodyguard urged, directing her around the side of the house to a fenced in area.

Aubrey felt nervous. Would her mother be here? She'd called her mother and tried to pick the information out of her, but her mother immediately sensed what Aubrey was trying to do. She'd acknowledged the invitation but insisted that she hadn't decided either way. What followed felt like intense grilling on what was going on with Aubrey and Carson and why Carson's father might have invited her, a stranger, to his yard party.

As they rounded the immaculately shaped greenery, Aubrey caught sight of several people dressed in white.

"Oh no!" Aubrey stopped short. "It's not a white party, is it?" The invitation had simply stated casual attire. She contemplated going back home to change.

A woman in white came out of the house and approached the gate. "Aubrey!"

Aubrey stared. "Momma?" It took effort for Aubrey to keep her mouth from falling open. Dressed in a white designer sundress, her mother looked slender, cool, and attractive. She'd even done something with her hair so that the few strands of gray sprinkling her head sparkled like auburn highlights.

"Momma, you look wonderful!" Aubrey exclaimed as she approached the gate. "Did Wyatt come too?"

Still basking in the compliment, her mother answered, "No, honey. He'd already planned to spend the weekend at a math camp. You know he's got some catching up to do." Opening the gate, she drew Aubrey in for a hug. "You all right?"

Aubrey hugged her mother tight. "I've missed you and Wyatt."

"We've missed you too." She took Aubrey's hand. "Come on in and join the party", she urged, "Ian catered the food and it's absolutely delicious!"

Ian? Since when had her mother met Wyatt's father and become comfortable enough to call him by his first name?

Dressed in white, Ian MacDonald came from the opposite end of the yard and greeted Aubrey. The paleness he'd shown in the hospital had been replaced with a healthy tan. He looked good. "You look wonderful!" he exclaimed, insisting that Aubrey hug him too.

"Did you forget to tell me this was a white party?"

Ian laughed. "What can I tell you? When some people think of a yard party, they can't wait to put on their white clothes!" On a more serious noted he added, "Everyone's not here yet, so don't worry. If necessary, I can go change."

Aubrey shook her head at the thought. "That won't be necessary."

Ian lifted his brows. "Are you sure?"

Aubrey smiled. "Yes, I am."

"Please make yourself at home," Ian urged, "The caterer forgot some of the appetizers I ordered. Give me a minute to straighten that out and I'll introduce you to everyone."

"Let me show you where the drinks are," her mother said, urging her towards the house.

The screen door opened, and Carson walked out with a gorgeous blonde. Long-legged, the blonde wore a pair of white shorts that looked more like panties and a bikini top that covered little. With pale blue eyes and a golden mane, she looked vaguely familiar.

"That's Tawna, one of Carson's old girlfriends," Aubrey's mother said. "She's a sweet girl."

Speechless, Aubrey stared back at her mother, somehow feeling betrayed. Her mother had always been staunchly on her side.

Lost in the other woman's conversation, Carson didn't seem to notice Aubrey. He didn't even flinch when the woman smiled flirtatiously and flipped a lock of hair off his forehead with a perfectly manicured finger.

Aubrey's mother drew her up the stairs, close to the couple. As they approached, Carson turned, obviously seeing Aubrey for the first time. They exchanged greetings and Aubrey's mother explained that they were getting drinks. When it appeared that Carson might join them, the blond stepped in closer and said she had something to discuss with him privately.

Carson looked surprised. "I'll catch up with you in a few

minutes," he told Aubrey and her mother.

With a nod, Aubrey held onto her temper. *If she had anything to say about it, this woman from Carson's past would remain in the past!* Inside, they found themselves in a large room decorated in a warm apricot color with several floor-to-ceiling windows. A long walnut and leather-covered bar with several stools dominated the room. There were also several matching tables and chairs.

Aubrey's gaze focused on a familiar looking guy seated on one end. She stared. Was she in a nightmare? The man turned to face them, and Aubrey was ready to leave. "Aubrey?" he called out as she turned for the exit.

Aubrey stared at her ex-fiancé. He still looked successful and attractive, but not as confident as she remembered. "What are you doing here, Steadman?" The evenness of her tone surprised her. She'd spent too much time crying over him.

He gave her that warm smile that used to make her day. It wasn't working. "Ian told me he was having a party and that you would be here. I've been thinking about you and wanting to talk."

Aubrey's brows went up. If she'd been the sort of woman to roll her eyes, she would have. "Really? What about?"

Always a man of manners, he excused himself and took a minute to speak to her mother. Aubrey watched her mother politely return his greeting, snag a cocktail from the bar, and disappear with some story about helping Ian with the caterer. It was much too convenient.

After ordering her favorite drink from the bar and presenting it to her, Steadman drew Aubrey over to a private corner of the room. "I never apologized for walking away when you really needed me," he began when they were alone.

As if an apology could wipe the slate clean! Aubrey took a deep breath and let it out. "You did what you thought was best. I got over it."

Steadman moved closer. "The truth is that I didn't get over it. It was the worst mistake I ever made. I've never gotten over you. Aubrey, you were the love of my life. . . .."

This scenario seems like something out of a soap opera, she thought. Despite the air conditioning, the room felt stuffy, too warm. Escape occupied her mind. Aubrey took a quick look around and bit the inside of her cheek. *Yes, this was really happening.*

Aubrey dropped down on one of the cushy chairs. "What is this about?" she asked, determined to get to the point.

"I was wondering if you could forgive me for not having your back, for not showing the love I still have in my heart?" He reached for Aubrey's hand, but she maneuvered it out of range.

She faced him squarely. "I have forgiven you. . . .. And aren't you married?"

"Ah, yeah," he admitted sheepishly, "but I'm planning to file for divorce."

"Well, alrighty! I wish you the best, whatever you do!" she said brightly. "I have moved on." Determined to end the torture, Aubrey stood.

Steadman closed in again. "I-I was also wondering if you could take me on as a client with your wealth management firm?"

Aubrey forced down a sip of her drink. "Our client accounts hold a minimum of ten million dollars. If you meet that requirement you can call the office for an appointment."

"Could you make an exception, for old times' sake?" he asked, looking a bit crestfallen.

Aubrey shook her head. "No, that wouldn't be a good idea. Try Marson and Anders. They'd be a better fit and they're good. Whatever you do, I wish you the best. And I'm glad we had a chance to clear the air!"

With that, Aubrey excused herself to find the ladies' room. Behind the locked door, she played with her hair and repeated the conversation with Steadman in her head. Somehow, she wasn't even thinking of crying. She wondered how and why she'd ever cried over such a sorry excuse for a fiancé!

Giving Steadman enough time to give up on any ideas he might have of pestering her further, Aubrey made sure the coast was clear before she left the bathroom.

Intent on slipping past the bar unnoticed, Aubrey nearly collided with someone. "Excuse me!" she exclaimed in unison with a casually dressed man with red hair.

"Aubrey, I've been looking for you!" he said, immediately enfolding her in a heartfelt hug.

"It's good to see you Zac!" she said, hugging him back. "How did you know I'd be here?"

"Your mother called to talk about a website issue and then she invited me."

Aubrey shook her head in disbelief. Her mother was a true techie when it came to computers and websites, so Aubrey doubted that she'd needed Zac's help for the reasons he thought. "How far will a meddling parent go?" she muttered beneath her breath. "When did you meet my mom?"

Zac grinned at her and laughed. "She's just showing how much she loves you Aubrey. Cut her a break!"

"It's going to be a little hard," she admitted as she took another look around. No signs of Steadman.

Zac hooked his arm in hers and nudged her back towards the bar. "Why? I'm always glad to get a chance to see you!"

"It's not you. I like seeing you too! You've been such a good friend and you always cheer me up!"

Zac's good humor dimmed a bit. "Did she invite other potential boyfriends?"

Aubrey nodded and patted his arm. "Uh huh."

His gaze took on a questioning look. "So, who was it you didn't want to see?"

"My ex-fiancé."

"Whoa... She didn't!"

"She did!"

Zac glanced around the room. "Well, it looks like you got rid of him."

"I did." Aubrey took a moment to order her favorite drink. "I'm just hoping that there'll be no more surprises."

Zac ordered his drink and sipped it quietly. Watching him, Aubrey gradually got the feeling that he was about to lower the boom. "I thought we were more than just friends," he said, spearing her with a hard-green glance. "I've been wanting to go for something a lot more intimate and permanent with you."

Aubrey nodded, reaching for the right words. She cared a lot for Zac and did not want to hurt him. "At times, I've felt that way too. You are just perfect and everything I want. . .."

He narrowed his eyes. "But?"

"We've never gone any further because—because although I've been fighting it, I'm in love with someone else."

"Carson?"

Aubrey's eyes widened. "How'd you know?"

"It's going to sound crazy, but I can feel the energy between the two of you. You make a good team."

"I'm sorry if I led you on." Trying to gauge his feelings, Aubrey met his gaze.

"I'm sorry that all that *fighting it* didn't work!"

He made her laugh. "Please say that you will still be my friend," she begged,

"Of course," Zac squeezed her free hand, "but you have to promise that if it doesn't work out you'll give me another chance."

"Ha!" Aubrey freed her hand in a playful gesture.

"Can't you see I'm serious?"

Aubrey searched his face, trying to understand. "I wouldn't want you to get less than you deserve," she said on a poignant note.

"If I got you, I couldn't ask for anything more." Zac's green eyes glittered.

"I'm sorry." Aubrey ran a hand over her face. Her head hurt. Her eyes stung with unshed tears. "I think you're saying we can't be friends."

"I'm saying that it will be hard." Zac drew her into another quick hug. "Now take your best shot!" he urged, whispering close to her ear. "He's right behind us."

As they broke apart, Aubrey saw Carson, standing in the doorway, watching them. He locked gazes with her, then turned and walked away.

"Carson!" she yelled after him, shaken.

CHAPTER TWENTY-FIVE

With years of unexpected experiences under his belt, Carson had arrived at his father's party early. True to his father's promise, Aubrey's mother was there, helping with the party. Carson took time to talk with her and help with some of the decorations she had an assistant setting up in various locations in the yard and the house.

He was judiciously applying tape to the sign along the side of the bar when someone hugged him from behind. A soft, curvy female form pressed close, filling his nostrils with the scent of honey and musk. Carson paused and grabbed the two pale arms and hands locked around his middle. No, it's not Aubrey, he confirmed.

"Surprise!" someone whispered close to his ear.

Gently disengaging, he turned to face his long-time college girlfriend. "Mimi!" he exclaimed. "I haven't seen you in years!"

"Too long, Studmuffin! Wanna go for a ride?" In an off the shoulder blue dress with a thigh high split, Mimi slayed with her golden-brown hair artfully tousled, and her green eyes emphasized with dramatic makeup.

Remembering some of the wildest times of his past, a half grin escaped as he shook his head. "If you'd asked me last year, I'd have been right on it. I'm into someone else right now, but you're looking good."

She tilted her curvy body in a way that confirmed his suspicion that she wore nothing underneath. "Are you sure you won't change your mind?"

"Yes," he confirmed resolutely. "So, what have you been up to?"

"I got married and divorced."

Carson nodded. "Do you have kids?"

She glanced away. "No. I should have gone with you, Carson. I don't know why doing my own thing with the performing arts theater group seemed so much more important."

"Because it was, and because I wasn't the one for you," he said, confirming what they both knew. "Who did you marry?"

"Guy Slater."

"The movie director?"

"Yeah, I was in one of his movies."

"Good for you!" Carson clasped her hand and pumped. "I'm going to have to get a copy of your movie."

"Don't bother. It flopped."

"I'd still like to see your work."

She leaned close to kiss his cheek. "You were always such a great guy, Carson. Are you sure you don't want to see if we can get the fire back?"

He nodded. "I'm sure. I'll introduce you to my girlfriend when she arrives."

"I guess I should go," she murmured.

"No, stay and have some fun. My father always invites a lot of singles. He's still single. If you're wondering about any of the guys, just come and ask me."

"I will. Thanks, Carson." With that Mimi headed for the yard, where a band was starting to play.

Carson decided to go check out the yard too. He was almost to the door when it opened and another vision of loveliness from his past filled the opening. He moved his wandering gaze away from the long shapely legs in butt hugging booty shorts and the matching bra top that covered little. *Damn, what had his father said to these women from his past to make them pull out all the stops?*

"Hello Carson." The sexy voice had never failed to get him going in the past. Now it sounded. . .phony.

Golden blonde hair framed a heart-shaped face, pale blue eyes, and a full pink mouth.

"Tawna," he acknowledged, dropping his hands to his sides in the interest of staying out of trouble. "Good to see you."

"You're not acting like it," she said with a challenging look. "You know what I want. . .."

Carson just looked at her. Tawna had always been wild, in and out of bed. It was in his best interests not to encourage her. "What do you want?" he asked finally.

"You." She gave him a catlike smile.

"Is that why you walked away?" The words came out so fast they surprised Carson.

Tawna's eyes widened. "Carson, you walked away from me."

"You gave me an ultimatum and I passed on it," he reminded her. "Then you started dating other guys."

Tawna sighed and carefully wet her lips. "You let me know that I was wasting my time."

What had he ever seen in this superficial woman? Carson narrowed his gaze. "And what makes you think you're not wasting your time now?"

"Your dad thinks you might finally be ready to settle down. . .."

"With you?" Carson was incredulous.

Tawna moved closer. "Why not? You could never get enough!"

"I need more than sex in a real relationship, let alone a marriage," Carson said.

"Whatever you need, I've got it and you know it," Tawna insisted angrily.

Carson's temper flared. "We haven't seen each other in at least four years. What makes you think you can step back in the limelight and continue where we left off?"

Tawna gasped. "All those messages on my phone and the texts you sent, you're not over me!"

Carson gave her a hard look. "Guess again. It's been years. I'm over you. Go home Tawna!" With that he stepped around her and opened the screen door.

As he stepped out on the porch, she maneuvered herself in front of him. The screen door closed. "Is there something else?" he asked, trying his best to be civil in front of the guests near them.

"I will not be treated this way!" she said, smiling flirtatiously as she reached up to flip a lock of his hair out of his face.

"So, what are you going to do about it?" he asked, already at his limit.

"You'll see. I promise you won't like it," she said.

Carson's jaw tightened. "Go home, Tawna," he repeated. Counting to five, he walked away, intent on finding his father. He was at the end of his patience for surprises. What the hell was his father expecting to accomplish by bringing all the women from his past to this party? This surpassed anything else the old man had ever done.

It took several minutes, but he eventually found his father and Aubrey's mother in a semi-private corner of the yard, sipping Long Island iced teas with a stranger they introduced as Chase Everett.

"You look upset," his father observed when he pulled him aside. "Is everything okay?"

"You know it isn't," Carson fumed. "Just what did you hope to accomplish by ambushing me with my exes?"

Ian Macdonald set his drink down. "I was hoping you'd think about how far you've come and where you're going. I was hoping you'd figure out what you really want."

"I've seen Mimi and Tawna and I've had it!" Carson all but grunted.

"Son, you don't have forever and you're not getting any younger," Ian said.

"I know what I want," Carson insisted. "And having the wild women from my past try to tempt me back isn't it. I'm too old for this! Stop interfering! If you've got any more surprises like that in store for me, I'm leaving right now!"

Ian nodded reasonably. "That's all and you got the message. I didn't want to invite your corporate spy arm candy and the one before her I couldn't stand either. Have you seen Aubrey?"

"Not too long ago," Carson said quickly. "I was supposed to find her. Aubrey is still here?"

"She's been circulating, but I've seen her hanging close to the bar area within the last hour," Anitra Merrill informed him.

"I've been meaning to talk to her," Carson said.

"You've been busy," Anitra said with emphasis.

"Damnit!" Carson exclaimed. He'd been too busy fending off his exes to spend time with Aubrey. "I'm going to find her and straighten this out," he said.

Carson retraced his steps, checking all the groups of people laughing, talking, drinking, swimming, enjoying the band, and playing games. As he'd thought, she wasn't there. He tried to remember what she might have seen when he was with Mimi and Tawna and drew a blank. He'd been surprised and angry. Finally, he mounted the back steps and opened the door.

Framed in the area near the bar, was Aubrey in Zac Logan's arms and it looked like a tender embrace. Carson knew Zac had fallen hard for Aubrey, so he kept an eye on him. Zac's gaze swung towards him, his green eyes zeroing in on Carson watching them. He whispered something close to Aubrey's ear. The couple broke apart. Carson didn't stay long enough to see more. He heard Aubrey call his name.

Carson walked back into the noise of the party. What had he just seen? It could have been an innocent hug, but it didn't look like it. Had Aubrey seen something, and Zac comforted her? Or had Zac found a new way to put the moves on Aubrey? Carson knew that Zac had been working on Aubrey for months.

Carson found an empty chair and sat down. What was he going to do? With all he'd done to avoid a commitment to Aubrey, he couldn't stand on the high moral ground and confront them. Right now, he was too angry to talk. He wanted to pummel Zac.

Someone settled onto his lap. Aubrey? For the second time, tonight he found himself looking at Tawna. This time the strap on her bikini top was broken and one ample breast was spilling out. "Carson," she cooed, "There's no need to be so rough!"

Is she crazy? he wondered. Dumb question. He'd always known Tawna was a little crazy. "Get your ass off me!" he ordered, making sure his hands did not touch her. As he tried to think of the best way to get her off his lap, Aubrey hurried over. A camera flashed.

"Carson?" Aubrey's voice quivered with shock and emotion. Her mouth opened and closed. "I've had enough of this-this social experiment. You. . .call me when you're ready to talk!"

"I said you wouldn't like it!" Tawna laughed as Aubrey turned and hurried off. "Was that your girlfriend?"

Carson stood, throwing Tawna off balance. She fell on her butt. His security team and a couple of guests rushed forward to help.

"Find the person who took that picture!" he ordered his security team. "And delete it!"

Still laughing, Tawna seemed drunk. Done with her antics, Carson charged one of his female assistants with driving Tawna back to her hotel and instructed security for the party that she was no longer welcome.

By the time Carson extricated himself from the situation to follow Aubrey, she'd taken the limousine and left.

CHAPTER TWENTY-SIX

Glad he'd driven himself in the Maserati, Carson climbed in minutes after Aubrey bolted from the party at his father's house. He started the engine and took off in a roar of power. What was the use of having all that power if you couldn't use it? His security team leader had insisted on riding with him, so the others followed in another car.

With all the shortcuts he knew, Carson arrived at the condo as Aubrey stepped onto the sidewalk. Hopping from the car, he left it running as he hurried to her with his bodyguard close on his heels.

Jaw tightening, Aubrey straightened and squared her shoulders as she turned to face him head-on. She looked shell-shocked and her lashes were wet, he noted as he approached, his thoughts on explaining the things she'd seen. Her eyes glittered. Had she been crying?

Guilt and corresponding pain washed over Carson. It was his fault that she'd been hurt. He needed to fix the problems threatening to keep them apart.

"Who was that on your lap?" she asked when he finally reached her.

"Tawna, my old girlfriend from my college days," he said, shuffling his feet uneasily. "I haven't seen her in years!"

"But she was invited to your father's party?"

Carson shook his head. "Not by me. You got waylaid by some of your old boyfriends too. I figured by now you'd guessed that the party and its special guest list was something our parents cooked up in a bout of misplaced meddling!"

"So, what was she doing on your lap?" Aubrey asked, eyes

narrowing.

An attack of nerves hit Carson like a wave of doubt. He knew what had happened, but the visual was too strong to discount. People he'd known for years had been staring at him in amazement. "I-I was upset. . .. And she jumped into my lap and... was making a scene! She wanted to make it look like I was still so into her I ripped her top. Can you believe that?"

Aubrey was silent for several scary seconds. Then she surprised him with a reluctant grin. "Actually, no. Not even you can work that fast! You were in the doorway a short time before that. It took me a few of minutes to find you, but. . .no. I don't believe what it looked like. I don't think you wanted her so badly you ripped her top in the middle of a party. How could you be with someone like that?"

Carson shook his head and shrugged. "At the time she was hot, she was beautiful, and I was lost, looking for thrills, hot sex, and good times. I was going to school, making a name for myself in real estate, and partying hard. It's what a lot of people do when they're young and in school and trying to figure out who they are." He stopped explaining to throw Aubrey an I-can't- believe-you're-making-me-do-this look. "Hey, I haven't seen her in four years!"

"It looked like you were making up for lost time!" Aubrey looked straight into his eyes. Carson knew that the future he'd began envisioning for them was truly at stake, balancing on the knife edge of his response.

"So, did you figure out who you were?" she asked.

Carson held her gaze. "No, not really, not then. We need to talk. Alone."

Aubrey pointedly glanced at the chauffeur, her bodyguard and Carson's team. The bodyguards from the car that had been following him had parked and joined them. "You mean as alone as we can get?"

"Come with me." Carson extended his hand, breathing a sigh of relief when Aubrey took it. He could feel her trembling as she followed him to the car and got in. "It's going to be all right," he promised as he shut her door on the two-seater.

"Is it?" she didn't look convinced.

"Yes," he confirmed as he got in on his side.

"You know, that really was some sort of intervention our parents dreamed up," he said, starting the engine and taking off."

"I figured it out," she said, "especially when my ex-fiancé found me and tried to work the old magic."

Carson threw her a sharp glance. He had a file on Aubrey's ex and the guy was a sleaze. Carson didn't like the pictures forming in his thoughts of the guy trying to 'recreate' the old magic with Aubrey. "Did it work?"

Aubrey shook her head. "No. That magic died a long time ago. He was never the person I thought he was. He even thought he could charm me into handling his money."

"So, what did you say?"

Aubrey smiled. "I did get some pleasure out of telling him I had moved on! Then I told him to try Marson and Anders since their account requirements are lower."

"Would you have handled his money if he had met our requirements?"

"Hell no!" Aubrey declared. "Nobody wants to see their biggest mistakes on a regular basis."

Carson turned the car into Central Park. "Let's get out and walk," he suggested. Her shoulders were stiff, and her hands were clenched together in her lap.

They walked awhile, with some of the security detail in front and some behind them. Used to them, Carson viewed them as a necessary evil, but knowing Aubrey felt differently, he signaled them to give him and Aubrey more space.

The physical exertion seemed to ease Aubrey's tension. Some of the stiffness in her shoulders disappeared. They stopped to sit at some empty benches near the Bow Bridge.

"I want to know what happened with Zac," he said. "Was it because of what you saw between me and my exes?"

"It had nothing to do with you," Aubrey explained, leaning close to lay her head on his shoulder for a few moments. "I really like Zac. He's perfect for me. . .."

Growing concerned, Carson wrinkled his brow. "But?"

Aubrey sighed. "I know we've never said it and I've been fighting it..."

"Fighting what?" Carson interrupted.

"I've been fighting my feelings for you, trying to ignore the fact that I—love you."

Staring at her, hearing the words, Carson felt immense relief. This was where he usually cut his losses and ran, but he wanted to keep Aubrey with him forever, whatever it meant. "Can you repeat that?" he said. "I think there's something wrong with my ears."

Aubrey looked at him, her big brown eyes clear and shiny with emotion. "I said I love you, Carson. That's why even though Zac is perfect for me, he's never been anything more than my best friend."

"I'm glad about that!" Unable to hold back any longer, Carson grabbed Aubrey and held her tight. He could feel her trembling as he kissed her berry-colored lips and her cheeks reverently. "I love you too, Aubrey."

Grabbing his shoulders, she pushed back to study his face. "Are you sure?"

"Yes, I am. I've never felt this way about any other woman. I've never said this to another woman."

Aubrey started trembling again. "Then how do you know?"

Carson smiled. "I know because I don't want to leave you. Ever. I can't imagine my world without you in it."

Still studying him, Aubrey moaned. A tear slid unchecked out the corner of one eye and down her cheek. Carson wiped it away with the tip of his finger.

Aubrey closed her eyes for a moment, then focused on Carson again. "I couldn't take it if you changed your mind. I realized today that I got over my ex quickly because I really didn't love him. I didn't know him. He wasn't the person I thought he was."

"You know who I am, warts, fears, and all," he assured her gently. "Let's walk a little more," Carson urged, grasping her hand, and drawing her up from the bench. He walked briskly, urging Aubrey to the bridge and then towards its center. "I know this bridge has a beautiful view and I want you to see it," he said.

"I'm trying to understand you and put things in prospective. I don't care about the view," Aubrey complained.

"You will," he promised.

At the center of the bridge, they looked out at what was left of the setting sun.

"It is beautiful," Aubrey agreed after several moments. "It's just that you've got me so. . .."

"So, what?" Carson drew a box from his pants pocket.

"Confused! I never know where I stand, what's next. . .." Aubrey exclaimed as he dropped down on one knee, "Are you all right?"

"I will be." Carson opened the box. A large, three carat crown of light solitaire diamond centered in a row of several others sparkled in the waning light.

"Carson!" Aubrey's high-pitched cry was filled with emotion.

"Will you marry me, Aubrey?"

"Yes, yes, yes!" They were both shaking so much it was difficult to slide the ring onto her finger. It had taken every bit of his diminishing control for Carson to keep from dropping it when he lifted it out of the box.

Having accomplished his goal, Carson struggled back to a standing position with Aubrey hugging him tight and crying.

"Are you sure?" she asked when she could talk.

"I asked you," he reminded her, "and I love you. You don't doubt that do you?"

Aubrey shook her head. "No, but your friends, your life, and the things you want to do. . .."

"Are all second to you," he explained. "Aubrey, I want to be with you more than anything else in the world."

"Me too." She kissed him. "But we're going to have a long engagement just to be sure you're ready."

"Whatever you want," he said agreeably.

Lifting her hand in the waning light, Aubrey admired the sparkling diamonds on her finger. "I love it! It's perfect! How did you know what I would like?"

"I had a little help from Sasha and Mira," Carson admitted.

Aubrey gasped. "No wonder they've been acting a little strange lately! How long have they known?"

Carson drew her closer. "Does it matter? This is what we both want."

Aubrey murmured in agreement and sealed the promise with a tender kiss. "Aubrey Merrill MacDonald." She sighed and laid her head on his shoulder. "I wish we'd gotten pictures of this moment."

"Pictures? I had the whole thing videotaped. Why do you think it had to be this beautiful spot?" He pointed to the man who had been discreetly videotaping them all along.

Aubrey hugged him enthusiastically. "I love you, Carson."

"I love you too, Aubrey. You're going to have to move over to my place. It's bigger."

"All our memories of being together are at my place," she reminded him.

"We'll figure it out," he promised, "just as long as we're together.

The End

ABOUT THE AUTHOR

Escape to Natalie Dunbar's world for an enjoyable and satisfying read. She writes smart, strong women and loving, irresistible men. There is always a happy ending. Her books run the gambit from contemporary romance to paranormal romance, science fiction romance and romantic suspense. An engineer living in the Detroit area, she has been a longtime member of RWA. She has written for Genesis Press, BET Books, Harlequin and Silhouette Bombshell, Harlequin Intrigue, and Silhouette Romantic Suspense, Parker Publishing, and Dana Lorayne Publishing. Her books have been featured on Romance in Color, Black Expressions Book Club, and Romantic Times. Her first novel, Best of Friends, was a Black Expressions Book Club pick. Her books have also been featured in articles for Detroit Free Press, Detroit News, The Oakland Press, The Warren Weekly, and The Eastsider newspapers. Visit her website at nataliedunbar.com. Follow her on Twitter:@nataliedunbar16

FB: https://www.facebook.com/natalie.dunbar.779

Look for Book 2 in the Love and Money Series, **The Billionaire's Ex**, available at Amazon in November 2021

Made in United States
North Haven, CT
16 October 2024